d'Ispere

Benedict Beaumont

Beautiful Mountain Press
Brighton, UK

Copyright © 2014 by Benedict Beaumont.

All rights reserved. No part of this publication may be reproduced, distributed or transmitted in any form or by any means, including photocopying, recording, or other electronic or mechanical methods, without the prior written permission of the publisher, except in the case of brief quotations embodied in critical reviews and certain other noncommercial uses permitted by copyright law. For permission requests, write to the publisher, addressed "Attention: Permissions Coordinator," at the address below.

Info@BenedictBeaumont.Com

Publisher's Note: This is a work of fiction. Names, characters, places, and incidents are a product of the author's imagination. Locales and public names are sometimes used for atmospheric purposes. Any resemblance to actual people, living or dead, or to businesses, companies, events, institutions, or locales is completely coincidental.

Book Layout & Design ©2013 - BookDesignTemplates.com

d'Ispere/ Benedict Beaumont. -- 1st ed.
ISBN 978-1499119367

'The road of excess leads to the palace of Wisdom'

William Blake, Proverbs of Hell

Part One

The First Days

1

WE WERE DRIVING along the shores of Lake Annecy, an hour out of Geneva airport, before Andy finally spoke. "So what brings you to despair?" he asked, his sharp voice cutting through the silence.

I was watching the rain patter down on the lake, absorbed in my own thoughts. Normally Annecy was pretty as a picture, but today it was cold and lifeless. The grey mist obscured the mountains on the far side of the water and the clouds above looked black and threatening. It matched exactly the atmosphere in the small van.

I looked nervously over at Andy, unsure what he meant. He was a large man with strong, handsome features, on the cusp of middle age, but with an expression as dark and as forbidding as the weather outside. Since meeting me in the arrivals hall, he had spoken exactly twice. "James?" he had asked in a gruff voice as I approached, and then:

"This way," before leading me to the car park. All my attempts at conversation after that were either ignored or answered with grunts.

"I'm sorry?" I said hesitatingly.

"It's what us locals call Val. Despair, d'Ispere, d'Isere, Val d'Isere. Our little joke if you like," he smiled to himself. "What brings you to Despair?"

"Oh, I see," I replied. "I've, er, got a job for the season there."

"Yeah, well I figured that one out. Slasher wouldn't get *me* to pick up a punter." He emphasised the word *me*, with an almost bitter tone in his voice.

"Slasher?" I asked.

He looked at me for a moment, before turning his attention back to the road. "Slasher is what we call Jen, Jen Heppell. I presume that you have heard of her?"

"Yes of course," I replied quickly. "Jen interviewed me on Skype last week and offered me the job here."

"Ah, so you haven't met her face-to-face. Well, she got the nickname 'Slasher' because she's got a sharp tongue and likes firing staff. Jen's the toughest girl in Val and everyone is afraid of her."

"She seemed lovely when we spoke," I said surprised. Jen had a soft midlands accent and although she had been thorough in her questions, she had seemed quite gentle. I couldn't imagine her as a 'Slasher'.

"Appearances are deceptive. You won't want to cross her, believe me." Andy ran his fingers through his hair and paused for a second before continuing. "So, anyway, what are you doing in Val?"

"Ski guide," I replied promptly. "I'll be taking groups of guests out round the slopes each day and ..."

"Yes, yes, I know what a ski guide does," he interrupted me impatiently. "How come you are coming out now, a month into the season?"

"I sent my CV into ValSki a few months ago, but they didn't have any jobs then. Anyway, the current ski guide broke her ankle last week and I got a call. I suppose her misfortune is my luck."

"Luck?" Andy snorted. "I'm not sure about that. Maybe she's the lucky one. She got out of Val. Maybe you won't."

"What do you mean?" I asked.

"Despair," he said slowly. "Val gets its name for a reason. It breaks you."

"I still don't understand." I said. I had felt confident on the plane about coming to Val d'Isere for my first ski season, but now Andy was making me feel stupid and nervous.

"Everyone thinks that Val d'Isere is a magical Shangri-La, a frozen winter wonderland high up in the Alps, but it is far from that. Val is a poison; it gets into your blood, gets into your brain, gets into your heart and breaks you, destroys you, in one way or another. For some people it's their wallets, some people their bodies, some people their spirit, and everyone in one way or another gets their head done in. Val is beautiful, oh yes, it's beautiful alright, but deadly too."

As the van drew up to a junction at the end of the lake, the rain started falling more heavily. There was a deep thrumming sound as the water bounced off the windscreen and the wipers struggled to clear it quickly enough to see. Andy peered out, rubbing at the glass impatiently, vainly trying to see what was coming. After a few fruitless minutes he pulled out but it was just as a red sports car was rounding the bend at speed. I jerked back in my seat instinctively, feeling a crash was inevitable, but Andy swerved, slammed on the brakes and bought the van to a halt only inches from the now motionless car. He swore as it pulled away and honked its horn at us. Andy waited a couple of heartbeats, then turned the wheel and bought the van out onto the road without mishap.

"For a start, it's damn expensive," he carried on as if there had been no interruption to our conversation and we had not almost died. "Lift pass and ski hire are free, and you get discounts on other things, but prices are still way higher than anywhere else in Europe. You might get tips, but you only get paid a pittance. Don't expect to save any money, most people leave with massive debts."

"What do they spend their money on?" I asked, my heart still hammering in my chest from the near miss.

"Booze!" Andy laughed humourlessly. "Some of it's free, and you get a small discount in the bars, but when you're a functioning alcoholic, and everyone is in Val, it's damn expensive."

"Do people really drink that much?" I asked. I knew that everyone drank a lot in the mountains, but would not have called them alcoholic.

"You would not believe," Andy replied. "Most guides have a couple after the slopes with the guests, drink during evening service and then go out at night and drink until they can't remember getting home, if they get home at all. Chalet staff are even worse; if they are not still drunk when they get up, they are usually so hung over that a breakfast drink is the only thing that will get them through morning service."

"Yeah, I don't really drink a lot..." I started but Andy interrupted me, shaking his head and carried on.

"You will drink; you won't be able to help yourself. No one does. Everyone has good intentions when they arrive, but most leave with their livers fucked by the various shooters and slammers they guzzle. Duvel and Jaeger bombs were last year's drinks of choice, but it will be different this year."

I nodded as if I understood what he was talking about.

"But it's not just the drink that fucks you," he continued. "Full English breakfasts, three or four course meals every night, afternoon cake and as much pate and blue cheese as you can stuff yourself with means that unless you are out on the slopes every day you will become a fat bastard. And most seasonnaires are too lazy or hung over to do that, so at least half will get a chalet girl's arse. Or gout," he added.

I nodded, but again I didn't think that would affect me. I didn't have a huge appetite and as I was going to be skiing almost every day, I was pretty sure I would burn off whatever I ate.

"Other people go mad chasing sex," Andy was continuing. "Everyone is shagging everyone and that creates all sorts of problems; arguments, feuds, fights are the least of it. The girls get fucking bitchy and the boys turn into cavemen. You know there is more chlamydia in Val than anywhere in Europe? Brothels are cleaner; they make you bag up there."

"I'm not much of a ladies man," I said and meant it. I knew that I was not ugly, but I never had the confidence of some of my other friends and was generally terrible with girls.

"Oh, don't worry, you'll get plenty up there. Unless you are looking for love. Are you?"

"Well, no, I er, I mean that I wouldn't mind..." I trailed off embarrassed.

"Well don't expect to find any up in the mountains. If you do, by some mad chance, find a girl you really like, expect to have your heart broken. People turn as cold as the weather up there."

He paused, brooding for a moment before continuing. "But you know what the worse thing is? Worse than falling in love or having your heart broken? What sends more people crazy than anything?"

"No, go on," I asked both appalled and fascinated. I had never heard anyone say anything bad about Val d'Isere; everyone I had spoken to who had been there loved the place. I wondered idly what had happened to Andy to make him so vitriolic about it.

"It's the snow that sends most people loopy. People fall in love with the slopes and damage themselves doing tricks in the park or going off in the back country. Half a dozen people get swept away in avalanches every year, and scores more seriously injure themselves attempting crazy stunts. More than most of the other resorts put together."

"Why here? What is it about Val that makes everyone so crazy?" I asked.

"I don't know. Maybe it's the altitude; the resort is at least two hundred metres higher than most other resorts. Maybe it's because it is so remote and takes so long to get to. Maybe because it's at the end of the valley, right at the edge, there is nowhere else left to go..." he paused again, thinking. "Maybe it's the mountains themselves," he added slowly. "Solaise, the Sun Mountain, Pers and Rousse. There are legends about them being haunted..." he trailed off.

"Right," I said, unsure what to make of this, but he wasn't finished yet.

"But you know," he said suddenly breaking his reverie, "it's not the ones who break themselves that are the unlucky ones. At least they get out. It's the ones that stay for years and do season after season that you have to watch out for. They are the really fucked up ones. And you know, they don't even realise how mad they really are."

There was an uncomfortable and brooding silence when he finished. It took me a couple of roundabouts as we went through a small village before I plucked up courage to speak.

"So how many seasons have you done then?" I asked.

"This is my thirteenth."

"And are you fucked up?"

Andy looked at me angrily and then suddenly laughed, finally lightening the atmosphere. "Very good. But you see I don't live in Val, I live down the mountain. I get your point though; I could be fucked up as well." He paused, again thinking for a couple of moments before carrying on.

"Look Jimmy, can I call you Jimmy?" I nodded. My name was James, but I wasn't about to argue with him.

"You seem like a nice kid and clever too. What are you twenty one, twenty two?" I nodded again, "Twenty two," I confirmed.

"Well you're certainly a looker, and if you are guiding for Jen, then you are obviously no mug and probably a shit-hot skier to boot. Anyway, as well as picking up the fresh meat from Geneva, I have to take them down when they break themselves, and I hate doing that. As I said, you seem like a nice kid, but you look young and inexperienced. I would hate to see you done in. So, just look after yourself up there. Don't trust anyone. Don't go crazy. Come back down in one piece and don't come back again."

I looked out of the window and caught my rain distorted reflection in the wing mirror. Despite cropping my hair very short and trying to grow stubble to look older, I still looked young. Andy was right about being inexperienced too, I was pretty much fresh out of university and had done little with my life so far.

We had left the villages behind and were now driving along a flat valley towards a huge range of white mountains. Snow had settled on either side of us, and I could feel the temperature dropping. It had stopped raining but the sky was darker and more forbidding than ever.

At that moment though the sun appeared, low and red, dipping below the layer of cloud. It was only a few minutes before sunset, and it ignited the bottom layer of the cloud into glorious reds and pinks, turning the threatening sky into something beautiful.

Andy looked up at the sky and sniffed, apparently unmoved by the spectacle. "There is another snowstorm coming," He said darkly. "We'll be lucky to make it before it starts shitting it down and getting dangerous."

And with that it appeared our conversation was over because he stared straight ahead at the road and ignored all further attempts at conversation.

2

ANDY WAS RIGHT about the weather; half an hour later, as the last of the light died away, the snow started coming down. It was gentle at first, just a light dusting on the windscreen, but the darker it got, the heavier the snow fell. By the time we reached Bourg-St-Maurice, the wipers were struggling to keep the snow off the windscreen and driving was beginning to get hazardous.

"The Police Municipale might not let us through," Andy grunted as we stopped at some lights. "That'll be a fuck up."

Sure enough, at a roundabout at end of the town we were flagged down by a Police Officer, a ghostly figure picked out in silhouette by the van's headlights.

"*Où allez-vous?*" he asked as Andy rolled down the window. My French was limited but I could understand a little.

"Val d'Isere," Andy replied hunching his shoulders and staring straight ahead.

"*La route est très dangereuse,*" the policeman said gesturing at the road. "*Avez-vous d'aller ce soir?*"

"Oui, j'habite à Val d'Isère." Andy said, still not looking at the policeman.

"*Avez-vous des chaînes à neige?*" he asked.

"Bien sûr," Andy nodded his head.

The policeman grimaced, and shook his head, debating whether to let us through. Eventually though he said "*Okay. Bonne chance, bon nuit,*" and waved us past.

"Thank fucking Christ," Andy muttered, and drove on. I looked back in the mirror, but within seconds, the policeman was lost in the swirling snow.

Andy was a good driver and took no chances; for the next hour we drove slowly but steadily through the storm, the road winding through a series of switchbacks, ascending steeply all the time. It was completely black outside and I could only see what the headlights picked out. A tree bent double and grotesquely out of shape, a ruined farmhouse and the occasional signpost.

The road went through several tunnels which caused a brief respite from the storm, but the sodium lights casting shadows on the roughly hewn walls and refracting through the ice stalactites hanging from the ceiling made it just as eerie. Andy did not turn the wipers off and they dragged across the windscreen, making a spine-chilling noise. The real world began to feel a long way off.

When we exited the third tunnel, the snow stopped falling and I realised I could see further than just a few yards ahead of me. Off to my right there was a large lake, and as we rounded a small turn, through two huge rocks standing like sentinels at either side of the road, there was a blaze of light.

"Welcome to Val d'Isere kid," Andy said with a genuine smile on his face. "We're here."

The snow was piled deep on either side of the road into Val, but I could still make out some fabulous looking chalets just behind them. I had forgotten what an exclusive resort Val was reputed to be.

At the bus station, Andy pulled over, retrieved a phone from his pocket and dialled a number. "We're here," he said curtly and hung up. "Come on, let's get your stuff," he said turning to me. "Giles will be along in a minute to pick you up."

"Who's Giles?" I asked as we got out.

"The Resort Manager for ValSki. He'll take you up to the staff accommodation."

It was strangely quiet as we walked through the snow to the back of the van; there was no traffic and only a couple of people walking by. "Where is everyone?" I asked.

"Dinner," Andy grunted as he lifted my ski bag out of the back of the van. "It'll start to get lively again in an hour or so. If it stops snowing that is." Thick flakes had started to fall again, and already our tyre tracks in the road were beginning to get swallowed.

"Are you staying here tonight?" I asked, trying to make conversation before Giles arrived, but he just shrugged and turned back to the van. It looked like he was not going to wait with me.

"Well thanks for the lift anyway," I said holding out my hand. He looked back at me, paused for a moment and replied "Good luck kid. Remember what I told you, don't get broken," and then he walked back to the car without shaking my hand. I watched him drive off, not sure what to make of him or his warnings.

Then I was alone, stamping my feet in the snow. I looked around, all the shops, bars and restaurants seemed closed and the few people had gone. It seemed as though I was in a ghost town. What would happen if no one came I wondered?

But I need not have worried; a few minutes later a battered white van pulled up. The window rolled down and a plummy voice called out: "Are you James?"

I nodded and called out "Yeah."

"Good show!" The door opened and a figure in a light blue ski jacket with the logo for ValSki emblazoned on it, came bundling over.

"Hi, I'm Giles, I'm the RM for ValSki. I'll be your boss," he said brightly. He was slightly podgy, with chubby red features and masses of blond curly hair poking out from under a red woollen bobble hat. With his rich tones and boyish features he looked like he was straight out of public school.

"Pleased to meet you," I said holding out my hand. This time there was no hesitation; Giles grabbed it tightly and began pumping it up and down.

"Great to have you on board. I'm really looking forward to having you in my team," he said with gusto. He emphasised the word 'my' as if he was all at once trying to assert his own authority and wanting to be my best friend at the same time.

"I thought Jen was my boss?" I asked as he opened the back of the van and I bought my gear over.

"Technically yes," he said slowly, "but she is away a lot and she trusts me to fill in for her when she is not here. Right," he said slamming the doors and turning to me. "Let's get you back to staff accom' and get you settled. Are you hungry?"

"No, not really," I called out over the van as we opened the doors and got in. "I ate on the plane."

"Oh that's a shame," he said crestfallen once we were both seated. "I got one of the hosts to plate up some dinner for us. Never mind," he said again brightening up. "I'll just have to eat it myself. Anyway, home James and don't spare the horses." He gunned the engine and started off through the snow.

"So have you been to Val before?" he asked a moment later.

"A long time ago when I was just learning to ski. I came with school," I replied.

"Ah, practically a virgin then," he beamed at me. "That means I can fill you in on all the important bits out here. Firstly, the bars!"

"What about the skiing?" I asked.

"Ah, yes, that too, that's important alright. It's why we are here of course," he winked at me conspiratorially. "Well that's what we tell everyone back home, eh!" he laughed out loud. "So back to the booze. Tonight is a big night actually. We have a day off tomorrow so we always like to have a few little cheeky ones so we can have a hangover in peace. There are all sorts of places we will go to tonight; Blue Note, Saloon, Danois, Dicks....

"What, all of them!" Perhaps Andy was right about the drinking after all.

Giles grinned at me inanely. "Yes, as I said we all like a little drinky here in Val," he winked at me again. "Gets the girls in the mood!"

"Right," I said slowly. The idea of Giles getting girls in the mood was slightly creepy. "So tell me about Val then?" I asked as we pulled off the main road, over a bridge onto a smaller narrower road.

"Well that's the Isere River beneath us," Giles began in a lecturing tone. "It starts from way up the valley near the Italian border. You can drive over it in summer, but now we are cut off, the end of the valley. The ski area, or Espace Killy as they call it, starts from there all the way down through Val to Tignes Les Brévières, past the lake."

"So, who else is on the team?" I asked quickly to change the subject again. I didn't want a geography lecture.

"Well," Giles said, "there are about a dozen or so hosts who cook and clean in the guest chalets. They're alright as a bunch, but their job is pretty simple. Then we have the guides, that is you and Heather, Danny the hot tub supervisor and Gwat the maintenance man."

"Gwat?" I asked. "Is that a real name?"

"It's more of a description than a name. You'll understand when you meet him. Right, hold on, this bit is steep." Giles pulled off onto a road that was little more than a track. The snow was deep and the engine began to whine.

"We've got snow tyres on," he said loudly over the racing engine, "but I should have put chains on in this weather. I just didn't fancy doing it in the snow and Gwat wasn't around. Never mind, he can put them on tomorrow." He spun the wheel and the car rounded a sharp corner. "There, that's the worse bit over now."

We passed a few chalets nestled amongst the trees, and then the buildings vanished behind us as we went deeper into the woods. "Not far now," Giles said trying to be jolly. "It's quite a long way back. Here we are," he said and pulled over.

Through the falling snow flakes, I could just about make out a rambling wooden building picked out in the van's headlights. It was nothing like the expensive looking buildings on the road, in fact it looked as if it was on its last legs. In several places planks were coming away from the walls leaving concrete exposed, and many of the balustrades were broken.

"Welcome to Chalet Chamois," he said as he turned the engine off. "It's a bit far out, a bit basic on the inside, and as you can see, a bit rough on the outside."

"It looks interesting," I said slowly, wondering how long it took to walk up the slope carrying skis and gear.

"It's a traditional valley build, one of the oldest in Val actually." Giles carried on as if he was conducting a history lecture. "You don't see many like this, more's the pity. These days it's all faux Savoyard kitsch, stone cladding and decorative timber. This is much more authentic."

"You're not kidding!" I replied. "It looks like a set for a horror film."

"Ha," Giles forced a laugh. "How did you know?! It's a great location too; fantastic views of the valley and the river too. Anyway, it's home for ValSki." He paused surveying the building a moment, lost in thought. "Right, let's go on and get in then. Supper and then some drinks await!" he said with a flourish and opened the car door into the snow.

3

THE SNOW WAS coming down thicker than ever and by the time that we had lugged my suitcase and ski bag round the building and up some steps to the front door, we were covered in heavy wet flakes. The porch inside was crammed with skis, boards, boots, shoes and coats and it was tricky to walk through, let alone carry two big bags.

"There is never enough space," Giles shrugged apologetically, as I knocked a pole over and a whole pile of skis came down like dominoes. "Never mind, not to worry, we can pick it all up in the morning."

Once through the inner door, Giles bustled on ahead down a short corridor and through another door. "Ahoy there, it's...." he called out, but before he could carry on a male voice shouted angrily back, "Giles, shut the fuck up will you. Kenny's reading the weather report."

I followed Giles into the brightly lit room. There were a couple of old, beaten up sofas around a coffee table, a small kitchenette area and a table with two benches. Against one wall was a huge fireplace that sat empty and cold. The other walls had a couple of old posters, the most impressive being a large framed bas relief map of the mountains. Three people, two guys and a girl, were sat at the table listening intently to a rich and rolling American voice coming out of a radio.

'...expecting over two metres in resort by morning and more at altitude making this the heaviest snowstorm for some time. The gendarmes have informed us that a curfew is in operation; so do not leave your accommodation unless strictly necessary, I repeat do not leave your accommodation unless necessary...'

One of the guys at the table switched the radio off and shook his head in disgust. "That's fucked it then," he said, a slight northern drawl to his voice. He was dressed in jeans, t-shirt and check overshirt with a beanie hat pulled almost to his eyebrows. I could make out dark eyes and a big jaw but that was about all.

"Why, what does it mean?" the girl asked. She was slim and petite, with delicate almost pixyish features offset by short dark spiky hair and several piercings on her ears. She was dressed in blue jeans and an olive vest top which showed off a number of swirling tattoos on her arms.

"Over two metres of snow at resort and more higher up," the first guy answered. "With these winds and temperatures, the lifts will be too dangerous to open tomorrow. I think they will shut the slopes."

"Shit," the girl banged her fist on the table. "All that pow and we can't get to it."

"Eeee," the second man, also dressed in check and with a beanie pulled down low, emitted a strange kind of half-whistle, half-grunt. "Have to get drunk then, eee!"

"Ahem," Giles cleared his throat, announcing his presence. "This is James the new Ski Guide." The three figures at the table looked over. "This is Danny, Heather and Gwat," Giles continued.

"Hi mate," the first guy stood and extended his hand. "I'm Danny," he said. "James," I replied as he took my hand. He was just above average height with a strong lean physique. Now I was a bit closer I could also see that he had handsome features underneath the hat.

The girl nodded a welcome too. "Heather," she smiled as she looked up at me. I couldn't help but notice her intensely green eyes.

"Gwat," the second guy grunted at me, "eee!" He rolled up his nose and tilted his head back as he emitted the 'eee', a strange, high-pitched whining, almost animal like noise. I blinked, unsure what to make of him, so held out my hand. He peered at it suspiciously from under his beanie for a second or too, as if he was unsure what to do with it, before taking it briefly into his own. Unlike Danny, his hat seemed to be more of a disguise; he had a long pointy nose, dark stubble and squinty eyes. There was something almost feral about the way he hunched over the table. "Skier or boarder?" he lifted his head in question to me.

"Skier you fucking retard," Heather snapped quickly at him. "He's a Ski Guide remember!"

"Oh yeah," he said looking a bit sheepish. "Anyway, the resort is closed so let's get drunk. Find gwat, bring it back, eee." The last phrase was almost a kind of chant.

Danny looked at him indulgently, as if he was a kind of ugly but beloved pet, before turning to me. "You any good then Jimmy?"

"What at? Skiing?" I asked. Danny nodded, looking me up and down, sizing me up.

Giles jumped in for me. "Oh yes, he is very good he..."

"I didn't ask you Giles," Danny said without taking his eyes off me. "Are you any good?" he asked again, quietly this time. I could feel the challenge in his voice.

I'm not a particularly confident person, preferring always to back down and avoid confrontation, but one thing I knew was that I was good at skiing. I had been skiing every year since I was five, and had made my university team the year before. Plenty of instructors had commented on my technique and encouraged me to take my interest further. One had even said that if I worked hard enough, I might even have a chance of making the England team. Anyway, I was pretty sure that I would be able to beat anyone here in a flat-out race. A sudden silence seemed to descend on the room.

"Yeah," I nodded slowly, "actually I am."

"Really," Danny raised his eyebrows and stared at me intently for a second as if he were sizing me up for a fight. Then his face cracked into a grin. "Good. I could do with some competition!"

"You're a fucking boarder," Heather snorted. "You can't compete with a skier, Danny. And stop being so fucking macho and give it a rest with all the alpha male shit. James has just got here."

"Yes, he has!" Giles interrupted brightly, "and I expect you'll be wanting to settle in and unpack. Come on," he said turning to me, "I'll show you to your room."

"Yes of course," Danny sat down and leaned back against the wall. "Unless you would like a drink with us? A toast to your new arrival? As

Gwat says, there is not a lot else we will be able to do tonight." I could feel another type of challenge being set, but this time I didn't take him up on it.

"In a bit maybe," I said. "I think I really should get a shower and change first."

Danny nodded. "Well, we're not going anywhere, at least for a bit. Come and have some drinks when you are ready."

"Okay then!" Giles said chirpily. "This way to your palace," and he led me out through another door on the far side of the room. As I left I could see Gwat pouring out something into glasses and music start up as the radio was turned on again.

The wooden floor was uneven and some of the walls seemed to be at funny angles. "This is all original," Giles commented as he led me down the corridor. "Solid wood," he said thumping at the walls, and then coughed as dust came down in small cloud. "Well it was when it was built. I don't know how much longer it will be here."

"Well as long as it lasts the season," I said, ducking to avoid a low beam.

"I mean it's a complete fire risk," he carried on, "that's why we can't light the fire in the lounge. We only got it as staff accom as they can't get the insurance to let it out as a guest chalet any more.

We don't matter as much as paying holiday makers it seems."

We ascended a rickety set of stairs and onto another landing with three or four doors leading off it. "Right, this is your room," Giles said opening a creaky door on the right.

It opened into a small, oddly uneven room, tucked under the eaves. There was no proper bed, just a ladder to a sleeping platform, right underneath a skylight. Some shelves and a hanging rail made up the rest of the furniture. "Sorry it's so basic," Giles said apologetically, "but at least you won't have to share with anyone else. The bathroom and toilet are just opposite."

"No, this is just fine," I said, and I meant it. I liked old buildings and I immediately felt at home in this quirky, odd and uneven chalet.

"Great!" Giles relieved. "People can get so funny about bedrooms, you would not believe how much some of the hosts complained when we arrived. Anyway, I'll leave you to get settled," he said, squeezing himself up against the wall as I wheeled my big bag into the room. It took up almost all of the floor space. "I'm going to have a bite of dinner, and then I'll see you back in the lounge for a bit of a drinky."

"Cool," I said without looking round. "I'll see you then," and closed the door behind him.

4

FORTY MINUTES LATER I had unpacked, showered, changed and was beginning to get bored. I lay on my bed, looking out through the skylight listening to the noises coming up from the lounge below. It sounded fun; I could hear the thump of music, the clink of bottles, and voices raised in laughter.

But I had had a long journey and had my first day of work tomorrow. It would be better if I stayed in bed and had a quiet night, I told myself, so I would be fresh in the morning. Besides, Andy's warning about alcohol was fresh in my mind. 'You will drink, you won't be able to help yourself. No one does.' "We'll see about that," I said out loud.

The music seemed to get louder and I heard another round of laughter.

"Fuck it," I said and swung off the sleeping platform onto the floor. "One drink, I'll have one drink with them then come back for an early night."

Downstairs, the lounge was livelier than when I had arrived. Giles was not there but a couple more people had joined Danny, Heather and Gwat round the table. A 'dubby' dance track was blaring out of the radio and more bottles were lined up.

"Jimmy," Danny called over from the table. "Come for that drink then?"

"Yeah mate," I said, squeezing in beside him. "Line me one up?"

"That's the spirit!" he nodded approvingly and Gwat gave another of his eee sounds. "Okay," he added, pouring out a clear liquid into a glass and handing it to me. "This one's for you, a special welcome to ValSki."

I eyed the drink in front of me; there was no label on the bottle and it smelt dangerous. It felt like he was laying me down another challenge, one that I could not back down from. I closed my eyes and tossed the contents back. I heard a cheer as the liquid hit the back of my throat and then felt a terrible burning sensation all the way down to my stomach.

"Jesus!" I choked out. "What in God's name is that?"

Danny had a big grin on his face and everyone else was laughing. "Génépi, home brewed by a mate of mine. Pretty good stuff eh?"

"Hell yeah!" I said my eyes still watering. "Give me another!" Everyone laughed again.

"Gently, gently," Danny said. "This is powerful medicine. Now, let me introduce you to the others. This is Dylan," he indicated towards one of the new faces, a tall thin lad with a goatee and long hair tied back in a ponytail. "He is one of the better of our chefs...."

"Pleased to meet you, bro," He spoke as if he was stoned, but he had a friendly face and held out his hand. He was dressed in a black t-shirt with a design of two crossed skis on the front, and he too wore a check shirt over the top. I realised that it must be some kind of informal uniform here, and made a note to myself that I should get one to try and fit in.

"And this is Joe," Danny carried on with the introductions. A smaller, younger, fine-featured guy wearing a flat cap instead of a beany, and waist coat instead of a check shirt, tipped a salute to me. "Alright mate," he said in a thick London accent. I shook his hand as well. "Do you cook too?" I asked him.

"Nah mate, just host," he grinned. "Shit job being a chef if you ask me, besides, any monkey can do it. I deal with the punters, and that takes a lot more skill."

"Shut up!" Dylan's eyes widened in anger and everyone sniggered.

"Just joking big man," Joe clapped his hand on Dylan's shoulder. "Chefs aren't really monkeys. That would be really insulting," he paused, "to monkeys!" And everyone laughed again.

"Boys, boys, behave in front of our guest." Heather tried to soothe things over.

"Not guest," Gwat commented. "Ski Guide."

"Yeah," I nodded. "Just one of the gang now."

Danny nodded approvingly and then said: "Okay, we're just waiting for Johnners and the girls then we can go."

"Go?" I asked surprised. "Go where?"

"Out, of course!" Danny said grinning. "It's day off tomorrow, so as Gwat said, we go out tonight and get drunk."

"I thought it said on the radio that there was a curfew and we should not leave our accommodation." I replied.

"Yeah, that's just for punters. A couple of the bars will be open for seasonnaires," he said. "Come on, time for another drink." This time he lined up five shots of génépi. "To our new Ski Guide!" he announced as he raised his glass. "Let's hope he lasts longer than the last one."

"Cheers," everyone called out and clinked glasses, and then suddenly the burning sensation was back in my throat and my eyes were watering again. "Jesus," Joe croaked, "what's in that shit!?"

The conversation around the table began breaking down into smaller discussions. I found myself asking Heather what happened to the last ski guide.

"She broke her ankle." Heather said. "Got drunk and fell down in Dicks Tea Bar, the local night club."

"What, not even on the slopes? Christ, that's bad luck." I said.

"Yeah, she didn't really fit in anyway," Heather added pulling a face.

"What was wrong with her?"

"Oh you know, just got off on the wrong foot with everyone. Didn't really fit in. Was never really part of the gang."

"Smashed her back doors in, eee," Gwat butted in a smug grin on his face.

"Yeah, you still owe me a euro for that," Danny also joined the conversation. "I got there first remember."

Heather rolled her eyes. "Jesus you're like fucking animals sometimes," she said.

"You love it!" Danny said tousling her hair, "dontcha?" and true enough her glare quickly faded. She obviously had a soft spot for Danny.

Just then the door opened and a tall well-built man in his early twenties came in, brushing snow from his hair. "Feckin' 'ell, it's chucking it down out there," he said in a strong Yorkshire accent. He too was wearing check, but his face was open and friendly. "You must be the new Ski Guide," he said holding out his hand. "My name's Clive, but everyone calls me Johnners."

"Pleased to meet you," I said warming to him immediately. "James."

"Have you got the girls with you?" Danny asked him.

"They're just getting changed Danny, they'll be down in a minute" he answered. "Are we going out? I heard there was a curfew on."

"Fuck yes!" Danny answered a big grin on his face.

"Well then, I better have a drink then!" Johnners smiled. "Pour me a gen'."

A couple of shots later, I was beginning to really relax and enjoy myself. Dylan was describing to Heather some amazing sounding dish of slow cooked and rolled lamb he had served that evening, Gwat was telling Joe about a girl that he pulled a couple of nights before and Danny had his arm round Johnners and they were deep in conversation. I had only known the people around me a short time, but they were welcoming, friendly and laid back. Already I felt part of the group. The staff accommodation was good, I had my own room and I was in the best resort in the Alps. I didn't think that life could get a lot better.

The door banged open again. "Hold the party, we're here!" a sing-song voice called out, and in danced a girl wearing a soft white woollen dress. She had hair the colour of honey, tied up in a white bandanna, blue eyes, flawless skin and a face fit to grace a magazine.

"Oh God, someone get me a drink," she said looking at me. "I'm desperate."

I watched with my heart in my mouth. She looked like an angel.

5

"WHO ARE YOU?" she asked me curiously, coming over.

I felt my mouth go dry and my stomach start to churn. There was something captivating about her that just froze me. "I'm James..." I began to say, but Danny jumped in. "This is Jimmy," he said. "He's the new Charlie."

"No," she shook her head. "He's definitely better looking than Charlie. Hi, I'm Faye."

"James," I said rising from the table and holding out my hand, feeling like everyone was watching me.

"We kiss in greeting over here," she said smiling in amusement. The next thing I knew her body was pressed against mine and I felt her lips on my cheek. "There," she said disengaging, "now we are friends."

"Put him down," Johnners called out. "He has only just got here. You can't destroy him just yet!"

"Tsk," she hissed at him. "Just being friendly. Anyway," she added with fire, "you can talk! I seem to remember you smashed Claire's back doors in the first day she arrived!"

There was a round of laughter at the banter between them and Johnners started to go red. "Yeah, but that..." he started to say but Danny interrupted him smoothly. "Face it mate, she's got a point. Where is the lovely Claire anyway?"

"Here darling, have I missed anything?" Another girl, dressed in a clingy cream jumper/dress with horizontal navy blue bands, walked in. She was pretty too, with long dark hair framing a winsome face. "You must be the new Ski Guide, James. Jen showed you us on Facebook."

"Eee," Gwat called out. "StalkBook, FaceRape!"

"Oh, erm..." I was still flustered from being so close to Faye.

"Don't worry," she said laughing, seeing my discomfort. "We're just very nosey here. We didn't find anything bad out about you."

"Okay boys and girls, drink up," Danny called out loudly. "This is your five-minute warning!"

"Are we really going out?" I asked. "Won't it be dangerous?"

"Of course," Danny winked at me. "We're going out drinking. That's always dangerous; you never know what will happen."

"No I meant with the weather..."

"Oh, we'll be fine," Faye put her arm round me, "don't worry. Danny will look after us."

"Resort closed tomorrow, go out, get drunk, eee!" Gwat said.

"No, you can't go out," a voice called out. Giles had come into the living room dressed in pyjamas, slippers and a dressing gown. "Didn't you hear the radio? There is a curfew on," he said flatly.

"Look Giles, you stay in if you want to. We're going out." Danny said without looking at him.

"No, it's dangerous, I can't let you go out," he said a little louder.

Danny raised his head and shrugged. "We're going out Giles," he repeated. "Sorry, but that's the way it is." A hush seemed to descend on the room as everyone turned to watch what would happen next.

"As a manager I can't let you endanger everyone's safety by giving you permission to go out," Giles tried a different tack.

"You don't have to give us permission. You're only a fucking manager Giles, don't be a bigger twat than you are."

Giles flinched at the insult. "I'm not going to let you go out, and that's that," he said with as much authority as he could manage.

"What?" Danny said quietly as he stood up and turned to face Giles. "Are you going to try and stop me?" There was an atmosphere of impending violence, as if before a fight in a playground. Danny looked ready to smack Giles and I realised how muscular he was; Giles would not stand a chance if it came to blows. A rush of adrenalin swept through my body as I realised we might have to separate them.

"Are you threatening me?" Giles looked suddenly flustered and nervous as Danny moved a step closer to him. It was so tense I thought I was going to throw up. I hated physical violence, it bought back too many memories of the school yard.

"Oh come on Giles..." Faye interjected, stepping close to him and taking his hand and breaking the tension. "We are only going out for a quiet little drink. We have to show James the town."

"If we stick together, we'll be perfectly safe," Claire wheedled as she took his other hand.

Danny still looked like a bull about to charge, but the atmosphere had changed.

"Look, I really don't think it's a good idea," Giles said stubbornly, but he did not remove the girls' hands and I could tell he was weakening.

"We'll only be gone an hour," Faye said.

"And you don't have to tell Jen," Claire added, "You could just pretend you went to bed and we snuck out."

"Well, I er..."

"Oh thank you Giles! You're the best manager ever!" Faye stood on tip toes and pecked him on the cheek.

"Well, perhaps we never had this conversation," Giles shook his head. "Now listen James," he said turning to me. "You don't have tomorrow completely off. Jen wants to see you and Heather at eleven."

"Fucking great." Heather exhaled loudly.

I nodded. "No problem," I said looking at Heather. "We'll be there."

"Right then, well, er, I'm going to stay in anyway," he said. "If anyone wants to join me in a game of cribbage then I'll be upstairs." He looked round the room hopefully, but everyone looked away or at the floor. "Right then, have a good night everyone, and be careful," he said after an uncomfortable pause and shuffled towards the door. There was a collective sigh of relief when he finally left the room.

"Fucking prick!" Danny exploded as soon as he was out of earshot. His jaw was clenched and he was actually shaking with rage. "Jumped up fucking prick. Fucking how dare he tell me what to do..."

"Shhh," Faye went up to him and held him. "It's alright, he's not worth it," she whispered gently to him as if to a child.

Gradually in her arms he calmed down and eventually got himself under control. "Alright, I'm alright now," he said and shook himself free of her. "He's just such an arrogant prick, I can't stand him."

"I know," she said, "but you can't do anything about it."

"We'll see about that," he said darkly, "we'll see." There was an uncomfortable pause, with no one really knowing what to say.

Johnners broke the awkward moment by pulling a funny face at Claire, who started giggling, and then Faye and Heather started too.

"Ready for a drink, bro?" Dylan came over and put his hand on Danny's shoulder.

"Come on mate," Joe added. "Let's go and get battered."

Danny shook Dylan's hand away before answering. "Yeah, let's go and get battered," he said. He was smiling but there was a cold and distant look in his eyes.

6

"JAMES!" SOMEONE WAS shaking me. I was not aware of much but I knew that there would be a world of pain if I opened my eyes. It would be far easier to just keep them closed and drift off back into sleep...

"James!" the voice called again, louder and more insistent and the rocking grew more intense. Could I ignore it I wondered, would it go away?

"JAMES, WAKE UP!" a voice bellowed in my ear accompanied by a violent shake.

"What," I sat bolt upright in shock. "Where am I? Ah, Christ, my head!" I said as a violent pain exploded behind my eyes.

"James!" Heather, the Ski Guide with the green eyes and short spiky hair was in front of me. "It's ten-thirty. We've got less than half an hour to get to Jen and it'll take twenty minutes to walk there."

"What?" I said uncomprehendingly.

"We have to see Jen," she said impatiently. "Come on!"

I was on my sleeping platform, still fully dressed in the clothes I had put on last night. What the fuck had happened?

"Right," I said slowly taking a deep breath and trying to pull myself together. "Okay, umm, right..." I didn't seem capable of rational thought.

"Look," Heather said, this time slowly as if talking to a child. "I'll wait downstairs. You get up, put some different clothes on, hell maybe even have a shower, and then we leave. It's not fucking rocket science."

"Okay," I said taking another deep breath.

"You've got nine minutes," Heather said looking at her watch as she walked out the door. "Jen doesn't like to be kept waiting."

It took me eleven minutes to get showered and changed into fresh jeans and a clean top. 'Pretty quick,' I thought to myself smiling as I tumbled into the lounge. There were some benefits to being a boy.

Heather was waiting for me dressed in dark green ski trousers and black jacket. "You look like shit," she snorted. "Come on, we'd better get a move on."

"Are we skiing?" I said confused, looking at her outfit.

"No," she said, "but there was an awful lot of snow last night. If you go out in jeans, you will get wet."

"Ah, shall I get my ski gear on then?" I asked as she walked out into the hall.

"No time," she said looking at the clock. "You'll just have to get wet."

Outside, the sky was a leaden white, but it wasn't snowing. There was plenty on the ground though; once we had left the chalet and started the walk out to the road, it was almost up to my thighs. "Shit," Heather muttered, "It's deep." She was a lot shorter than me, and kept losing her footing.

"Here, I'll go first," I offered, and ploughed ahead making a path but getting myself soaked into the bargain.

"Thanks," she said gratefully. "It should get easier once we get over the bridge. The bashers will have cleared the road from there by now."

As we tramped through the trees, I started to have some flashbacks to the night before. I remembered a chain of about ten of us pushing though the snow, just like we were doing now, with flakes still coming down heavily around us. I remembered more vaguely drinking shots and somewhere a large jug of something sweet. But where it all happened and what order I had no idea. The memories were as faint as the tracks that we had made the night before.

By the time we made the steep slip road, my jeans were soaked. The going was easier, but the piste basher had not been up here yet. Heather looked ahead in dismay and sighed. "Oh well, guess we might be a little late after all."

In the end, we arrived at our appointment only a few minutes after eleven. It took about twenty minutes to reach the main road, but once we were there, it was easy. The path was clear and it was only a short walk to the ValSki chalets and office.

"These are nice," I said appreciatively, looking up at the six stone and timber chalets around me as we walked across a courtyard set just off the road. They looked like they were out of designer magazine.

"Yeah," Heather said walking quickly, eager not to be late. "They're not bad, only a few years old. They're even nicer on the inside."

The office was tucked around a corner near some garages. Heather knocked on the door, and then entered without waiting for a reply.

Inside it was much plainer and more ordinary than the outside hinted at. There was a large window with a nice view but the walls were just painted breeze blocks and there was no carpet on the floor. There were some desks against the wall, covered with masses of paperwork. I could see the back of a blonde head seated at one of them, Jen I guessed, engrossed in a phone call. Heather sat down in one of the chairs, but I stood in the doorway, unsure where to put myself.

"Tell him he's got to go in," she was saying. "There's no ifs and buts about it. He left the chalet in a mess, he has to clear up. Hang on," she said suddenly, and then turning to us, "CLOSE THE DOOR!" she yelled. I realised I had left the door open and a cold breeze was blowing in.

"Where was I," she turned her attention back to her phone conversation. "Yes, he has to go in and do his job properly. And tell him he can come and see me tomorrow and explain himself as well. Right, gotta go. Byeee!" and put the phone down then picked up a diary and made a couple of notes in it. She then swung round to look at us.

Jen must have been in her early thirties, quite short, with fair hair and freckles. She was dressed in the same outfit of jeans and check shirt that everyone seemed to wear, but with her quaint accent, she seemed more like someone who worked in a bakery or tea shop in a picturesque village than someone who managed a ski company. There was a firm, no nonsense edge to her voice however, that made me realise that she was no fool. Andy had called her 'Slasher', I was beginning to see why.

"So, James, you made no hesitation in getting acquainted with Val last night did you? You made quite an impression," she said primly.

"What do you mean?" I asked, trying to sound innocent, but a feeling of dread slowly materializing in my stomach.

"Broke the curfew, had Jaeger bombs in the Fall Line, drank a cocktail in the Lodge Bar and then dancing on the table at the Danois," she counted off on her fingers. "Oh I think you made yourself known to the resort last night."

"Umm, really, did I?" Vague memories of different bars and drinks had started to come back but it was still hazy.

"Oh yes," Jen said smiling coldly. "There was probably more too, but I haven't heard from everyone yet."

I hung my head, feeling guilty and stupid and wondering if this to be the shortest job I had ever had.

"Not to worry love," she said almost kindly. "Not a bad first night, no different to anyone else after all, and you are here, almost on time. It's not really your fault; Danny and Anthony are to blame. They are the naughty ones."

"Umm, I don't think I met anyone called Anthony last night," I said.

"Gwat," she said dismissively, "is what everyone calls him, don't ask why. Anyway, I haven't called you in to tell you off, I'm your boss not your mother. If you want to go out and get wrecked, that is absolutely your business, frankly I do not care. But," she added fixing me with a steely eye, "do not ever be late or drunk at work. Is that understood?"

"Yes," I nodded vigorously.

"Well then, let's talk about the next few days. Obviously today is day off so you don't have to do anything, but tomorrow you'll be out with Heather and the guests. Danny is going to guide, so you will just be shadowing him until you learn the ropes. Are you happy with that?"

"Yes, that's fine," I said just relieved that I was not about to be 'slashed'.

"Good," she said. "Is that alright with you too?" she said turning to Heather who was still sat on a chair watching quietly.

"All good," Heather answered. "I presume we are still meeting the guests at the normal place and time?"

Jen nodded. "There may be a few more of them than yesterday. We had another group sign up for guiding last night."

"Cool." Heather added.

"Okay then," Jen said finally. "That is all I wanted to say. I really wanted to meet you face to face,"

"Well, thanks for giving me the job. I promise that I will do it really well," I said desperate to make a good impression.

"Yes, I am sure you will!" she said. "Now, go and enjoy your day off. I've just heard that the pisteurs want to check the lifts for storm damage, so they will not open them for a few hours yet. You can go and get some rest. Thanks for bringing him in," she said turning to Heather as we both rose to go.

"No worries, see you tomorrow," Heather said and we trooped out of the door.

"Well," she said a few moments later once we were out on the road. "I think she likes you; you had a pretty easy time in there, it could have been a lot worse. I've seen her tear people apart."

"How did she know what happened last night when I barely remember?" I asked.

"Jen has been here over a dozen years. She knows every barman from here to Bourg, and they all spy for her."

"Oh," I said. "So we can never really be bad?"

"Don't worry," Heather said a broad smile on her face. "She has a soft spot for naughty boys. It's why Danny and Gwat are still here. I think you will fit right in."

"I'm not naughty!" I protested.

"Yeah, not much," she laughed. "Do you remember last night? Do you remember what happened with Faye?"

Another wave of dread hit my stomach. "Oh God, what happened?" I groaned.

"Oh don't worry," she laughed again. "Nothing bad. Well not too bad. Come on, let's go to the Danois. Everyone else should be arriving there soon for breakfast," and she walked off down the hill, leaving me standing with my jaw open wondering what I had done to Faye and what else might have happened the night before.

7

ON THE WAY to the Danois, Heather refused to answer any of my questions about what happened. "Stop digging!" she warned me as we walked down the hill to the main road. "I'm not going to tell you. It's in the past, everyone will have forgotten about it by the time we get to the bar. Besides, I suspect there will more bad behaviour later anyway."

"Well can you tell me a bit about everyone instead then?" I asked. "It feels like everyone knows everything about everyone and I know nothing about anything or anyone!"

"Yeah, I can see that is must feel like that," she nodded, "but it's not really true. You live and work together here, which is pretty intense, but it means you get to know people very quickly. The reality is though that most of us are new and have only been here a few weeks."

"Who is new then?" I asked. "Are you?"

"New to Val and ValSki, but I did a season in La Rosiere last year so I kind of know the ropes. Dylan and Joe are fresh meat; I don't think they had even been in the mountains before, but they have taken it like ducks to water."

"The others are all old hands then?"

"Well some and some. Faye was hosting for ValSki last year, but this is Claire's first season. She's friends with Faye from back home and came out to visit a couple of times last year and had so much of a good time she decided to come back and work. Johnners might have had something to do with that! He is on season number three, Gwat four or five, and Danny, God knows how many. Maybe as many as Jen."

"Really," I said. "He doesn't look that old."

"You'd be surprised," Heather said. "He's well over thirty now."

"Jesus," I answered. "I thought he was only a couple of years older than me, twenty six, max."

"As I said, appearances can be deceptive." We turned onto the main road and started walking into town, past all the nice chalets. The piste bashers had done a good job clearing the snow and the road and path were pretty much clear. Traffic and pedestrians moved freely.

"And how long has he been with Faye?" I asked nervously, trying to sound natural.

Heather glanced sideways at me. "They're not together."

"Oh, I thought..." I said confused. The way Faye had comforted Danny after the confrontation with Giles was as tender and intimate as a lover.

"They were together all last year, but Danny dumped her on the last day of the season."

"Really!" I couldn't believe that anyone would want to get rid of someone like Faye. "Why did he do that?"

"Who knows?" Heather sniffed. "Danny's a bit of a free spirit; he doesn't like to be tied down. It gets in between him and the mountain. He could do better anyway."

A sudden flash of intuition told me that Heather desperately liked Danny, but he was not interested in her. "What exactly is his job anyway?"

"Not much really," Heather said. "He is supposed to look after the hot tub, do a bit of driving and delivering, but generally he does as little as possible. I think Jen just likes having him around."

"If he's done so many seasons, then why isn't he...?"

"Manager?" she finished my sentence. "Oh, he was for a couple of years. He did Giles's job, but just decided that it was too much hassle. He didn't like the responsibility, it was getting between him and the mountain, and Danny lives for the snow."

"Ah, that would explain why he didn't like Giles telling him what to do."

"Oh, it's not that," she said. "Danny is usually pretty helpful, it's that Giles is a fuckwit and lords it around. No one likes him."

"Ah, okay," I said. "I had been beginning to get that feeling."

"He means well. It's just..." she left it hanging. We turned off the main road by a roundabout and walked up a short hill. It was a bit more slippery than the main road and we had to tread carefully to avoid falling over.

"What about Gwat?" I asked. "What's his story? What does he do?"

"He is supposed to do maintenance, but he is fucking lazy."

"Why is he called Gwat?"

"Don't ask," she rolled her eyes. "It's disgusting, he's disgusting. All he does is get drunk and chase girls. And that noise he makes..." she shivered. "Why anyone gets with him is beyond me." She paused and again I felt that there was something that she was not telling me. "Look, I don't like him at all. I have to work with him, but trust me he is not a good person."

"What about Johnners and the girls, Faye and Claire?" I prompted when she had been silent for a few moments.

"I'm fed up of talking," Heather said suddenly. "You're turn. You tell me something."

"What would you like to know? Where I'm from, what I did at home, what I studied at university?"

Heather laughed. "No, none of that. It's a kind of taboo subject really. Once you are in Val, the outside world doesn't matter anymore. No one is interested in what you did, who you were or where you came from. Some people that you meet are obviously spoilt little southern rich kids and others are poor northern monkeys, but it's considered rude to pry on people's background. Once you get to the Alps, you are all in the same boat and everyone gets a chance to be who they want to be. We are all in the most beautiful place in the world; we all have to work, so we are all equal. So, a piece of advice for you, don't go round asking people where they are from or what university they went to. They don't want to know."

"But how do people get to know each other then?" I asked as we turned off the main road and started walking up a pedestrian street.

She shrugged. "Oh trust me; you get to know people pretty quickly. Life is extreme up here, and it brings people together. It's not just the altitude, the temperature and the weather; it's the lifestyle too. You work together maybe ten hours a day, you ski together for about four or five, then you drink together for another four or five after that. If you are lucky, you may even sleep together. And you know it's not just other people you get to know in that kind of environment, you get to know yourself too. You get to find out what kind of person you really are."

We were just coming up to a bar I vaguely recognised from the night before. 'Le Petit Danois' was written in red paint on a wooden board and adorned with a horned helmet.

"And what kind of person are you?" I asked, intrigued. The more time I spent with Heather, the more interesting I realised she was. She was intelligent, articulate and mysterious too. I suddenly felt very good about working with her for the rest of the season.

"A thirsty one!" she said as she swung the cowboy style doors to the bar open.

8

INSIDE THE PETIT Danois it was already starting to get busy. There were more than a dozen people at the bar, and even more around the tables down one side. Waitresses were bringing plates of fried food out, TVs were showing the news, music was coming over the speakers and people were playing pool at the far end of the bar. It wasn't even mid-day but it felt like it was a busy evening.

"It always gets like this when the lifts are closed," Heather shouted at me as we entered. "There's not much else to do here really. Look," she pointed, "our lot are over in the corner. Why don't you join them and I'll go and get some drinks. Are you hungry?" I nodded, realising my stomach was rumbling. "I'll order breakfast for us both then. Eight Euros for a Full Monty. Is that okay?"

"Sure," I nodded and she headed off to the bar whilst I made my way to the corner and the ValSki staff. Danny, Johnners, Dylan and Joe were there, along with a few other people I didn't recognise.

"Hey there hero!" Danny called out in greeting. "You didn't get slashed then?"

"No, not yet," I said grinning. His enthusiasm was infectious.

"Ha, well you've passed the first test anyway, getting up and going to work after a night out! This is Toby and Calli," a couple in their twenties who looked oddly similar to each other, both dressed in hoodies and beanies, looked up at me and nodded.

"And this is Ash, the little baby of ValSki," Danny introduced the person sitting next to him. A tall, gangly lad with a already thinning curly hair smiled shyly at me. "Allreeeeet mate!" he said in a thick West Country accent.

"Good to meet you," I shook hands with them all. "Are you drinking already?" I noticed everyone had a beer in front of them.

"Fuck yes!" Joe said. "What kills you cures you."

"So are you!" Heather came up behind me with a pint.

"Oh, right. I'm not sure..." I trailed off, suddenly feeling queasy. After the excess of the night before, I was not sure if I could handle alcohol so early.

My face must have betrayed how I felt because Heather laughed and said "Of course you can, it will make you feel better!"

"Oh, go on then," I said and took a big gulp. This got a small round of applause from round the table, but then everyone drifted back to their own conversations.

"So lad, did you enjoy yourself last night then?" Johnners asked as I squeezed in next to him.

"Yes, I think so," I grimaced. "I can't remember much to be honest."

"No, well that's the jugs for you," he said. "That's why we drink 'em."

"Can I ask you a question?" He nodded. "Last night, did I do or say anything stupid?"

"What, you mean apart from telling Faye that you wanted to marry her and take her away from all this?"

"Oh God!" I said appalled, "did I really?" I could feel myself going red with embarrassment.

"Oh yes," Johnners smiled. "Don't fret though lad; she thought it was really sweet. Although she didn't let you kiss her, despite a lot of trying."

"Shit. Christ." I could feel the panic rising in me. How could I try and kiss Danny's ex-girlfriend on my first night.

Johnners smile broadened. "Oh, it's alright. You're not the first to try it on with her. Dylan had a go at the beginning of the season, but she blew him right off. She is not the kind to put out. You were not the worst behaved anyway, everyone was pretty outrageous."

"What did they do?" I asked, hoping that their bad behaviour might eclipse my own.

"Well Dylan got thrown out of the here for mine sweeping drinks. I had to stop Danny battering some posh twat and Gwat was getting pretty rapey with a Mark Warner girl. She was well out of it."

At that moment, as if on cue, Gwat came lurching in through the door, still wearing his clothes from the night before. His cap was pulled down low over his face but it could not hide how rough he was looking; his face was red and blotchy but there was a look of triumph in his eyes. "Eee, eee, eee," he called out in time with his steps.

"Where the fuck have you been?!" Danny asked when he was close.

"Eee! Nanny Gwat! Smashed a Mark Warner bird last night," he replied grinning.

"Ah, I was beginning to worry," Danny said wryly. "I thought you were losing your touch. It's been what, three days since you last pulled?"

"You didn't end up in a ditch then? We were hoping you might have passed out in a snow drift," Heather said. Although she spoke with a smile on his face there was a touch of iron in her voice that hinted that the words were not entirely in jest. There were obviously currents and tensions going on beneath the surface that I didn't know about.

Gwat pulled a face at her and then wandered off to get a beer.

"So is it like this all the time?" I asked Johnners quietly. Andy's warning about the excess to be found in Val suddenly came back to me.

"No, not every week," Johnners replied. "Usually it's much worse."

I shook my head, determined not to get so drunk again. Despite the promises I had made to Andy, I had got wasted on my first night and tried it on with a girl. I had no intention of behaving like that again.

"Look, will Danny mind about me saying that to Faye?" I asked, still feeling guilty. "I can't help but feel there is unfinished business between the two of them." I looked over at Danny. He seemed to be the life and soul of the party; he was locked into a deep discussion with Joe and they were moving sauce bottles around to demonstrate something.

Johnners shrugged. "Nah, I don't think so. She was the only girl he has been with for more than a week, and although he really fell for her, he's the one who finished it. He's been with plenty of girls since her too. Anyway," he clapped me on the shoulder, "we're in Val mate, doing a season. Even if he does, he'll just have to man up and take it."

I nodded, still unsure, but then sighed. There was nothing I could do about it now. Anyway, if Danny was pissed off, he didn't look it.

"Jaeger bombs!" Gwat was back from the bar with a tray full of drinks. "Stefan owes me a favour and I called it in in alcohol form."

"Nah, seriously, it's not like this all the time," Johnners said to me, passing me a tumbler full of a golden liquid with a shot glass of black tar floating round in it. "I mean, we all work damn hard and go up the mountain every day as well. You need to unwind every so often and this is how we do it. Cheers!" He downed his drink and then turned as Dylan called to him across the table.

"I don't think I can..." I began, but Danny interrupted me.

"That's twice now Jimmy," he said, a steely edge to his voice. "Twice someone has bought you a drink and you've tried to avoid drinking it. You're new so maybe you don't realise, but up here, if someone buys you a drink, you drink it, no questions. Anything else is rude."

He stared at me, and I suddenly felt that perhaps he did mind about me making a pass at Faye after all. I felt a cold shiver go up my spine. "I, er, didn't mean, I..." I tried to answer nervously.

"What?" he asked forcefully, adding to my discomfort.

"I just know that I have to work tomorrow, and I don't want to let anyone down," I finished lamely.

Danny suddenly grinned. "That's tomorrow," he said. "That's a long way away. Right now, it's day off, the lifts are closed, so we drink. Cheers!" He tipped his own glass back, swallowed and bought the glass crashing down on the table.

"Yeah, don't worry about tomorrow, that's tomorrow," Heather squashed in next to me, holding her own glass. She had watched the exchange between me and Danny with interest. "If the lifts are closed, you gotta drink." She too downed her Jaeger bomb.

My face must have looked a picture, because she suddenly softened. "Look, it's just a kind of unwritten rule, even if you don't like the person who got you one," I saw her glancing over at Gwat, before turning back to me. "Don't worry though, it's not going to be suicidal drinking like last night. I'll look after you and make sure you get your beauty sleep."

"Really?" I asked dubiously and looked at the drink in front of me. But despite my misgivings, and my promise earlier, I still gulped down the liquid. Fortunately it was not as foul or as strong as I feared.

"I don't suppose the lifts will be closed tomorrow as well," I asked when I put the glass down.

"No chance," Danny answered. "They cannot afford to close them for more than a day, they lose too much money. It will be open tomorrow without doubt."

"So, two Full Montys?" a pretty waitress with a lovely Scandinavian accent came over.

"Yes please," Heather called out and took the plates. "See, I told you it won't be suicidal drinking. We're eating, that will keep us sober. Now, can you pass the sauce please?"

After breakfast, I let Heather persuade me to have another beer, but I drank it slowly. She was right, by drinking and eating I didn't feel drunk in the slightest. When Faye and Claire turned up a bit later, I felt confident enough to have another shot. This one must have had some effect though, as I then felt brave enough to apologise to Faye.

"Darling," she said after I fumbled my way through an explanation. "I thought you really meant it. You've really hurt me..." she paused and for a moment I felt myself choke with embarrassment before I realised she was joking.

"Bloody drama queen you are!" Johnners commented from the other side of the bar, and I realised that everything was alright.

We had another beer at the Danois and then, when a couple more ValSki staff joined us, we moved to a bar over the road and up some stairs where we played a pool competition. It was a relaxed atmosphere, and by the end of a few frames I had talked to everyone; Ash was a sweet kid, Toby and Cali were polite but reserved, Dylan and Joe bickered like a married couple and Faye and Claire were very tactile, and hugged or held everyone they talked too. Johnners was like a northern comedian making everyone laugh with his quick responses to Gwat's usually filthy comments. Out of everyone though, Danny was the life and soul of the party. Wherever he was, there was laughter, shouts and cheers. It was obvious that, whatever Giles thought, he was the real leader of ValSki.

Heather, true to her word, stayed with me all evening, making sure that I was not left alone.

When there was no one else around, she carried on where she had left off on our way to the Danois and filled me in on all the gossip of the staff. Whilst she was in the toilet, after a couple of more beers, and I had a moment to myself, I began to realise that not only was she one of the shrewdest judges of characters, but she was also extremely intelligent and kind too. I was lucky that I was going to be working with her over the coming months.

"Eh lad, what are you grinning at?" Johnners called out to me interrupting my thoughts.

"Think I've landed on my feet here!" I answered smiling.

Heather was also right about the alcohol. Unlike the night before, however much we drank, no one seemed to get too drunk. I felt clear headed and in control.

We finished the pool competition and then headed back over to the Danois to watch a band play rock covers and all ended up moshing round to the heavy tunes. Afterwards, someone suggested a calm-down drink somewhere, so we headed to a small place called the Blue Note.

As it started to get dark though, everyone's energy started failing and people started drifting off home. Heather, Johnners and I picked up a take-away pizza on our way back to the Chamois and when we got there devoured it in seconds.

"Time for bed," Heather yawned. "You ready for tomorrow?"

"Yeah, I think so," my eyes were getting heavy and I had started to nod off. "I'm going to get some air before I go though."

"Cool," Heather said. "But don't be late tomorrow."

I stood outside for a few moments and looked up through the trees to a sky that was free of clouds and blazing with stars. Val town, a hundred metres or so below, was lit up like it was Christmas. It was the kind of view that people paid thousands of pounds for on a week's holiday, and we got it for free, all season. Only forty eight hours earlier, I had been staring up at a leaden British sky, with no idea what my future held, and now this. My smile was so wide that my cheeks started to hurt.

The door opened and Heather came out onto the balcony. She stood silent for a while, then slipped her hand into mine. "You know, Faye isn't the only girl here," she said and moved in closer to me. It seemed the most natural thing to bend my head down to kiss her.

9

I AWOKE WITH a start, the alarm ringing in my ear and sun streaming through the skylight. I was alone; Heather must have gone in the night. Or had I just imagined the whole episode? No, I was pretty sure I had not spent the night alone. 'Shit' I said to myself wondering what I had done. Sleeping with a work colleague, especially when she knew I was infatuated with someone else, was probably not the ideal start to a new job.

It only took me a few minutes to shower and get into my ski gear. Downstairs, Danny, Gwat and Heather were at the table drinking tea and eating cereal. They all looked fresh and well rested. I would never have guessed that they had been on a twenty-four hour bender.

"Eee," Gwat said in greeting, rolling his nose and tilting his head back briefly.

"Eee," I said back to him, strangely comforted by the animal sound. He smiled, pleased that I had used his greeting, and went back to his cornflakes.

"You want any breakfast?" Heather asked neutrally as I sat down. She gave no hint that only a few hours earlier we had been thrashing around in bed together.

"Umm, no thanks, just some coffee please." She poured a mugful from a jug on the table and passed it over to me.

"So you ready for a day up the mountain?" Danny asked sipping his tea.

"Yes," I said and I meant it. Drinking was all very well but I had come here for the snow.

"Good," he said approvingly. "So normally Giles would give you a talk, about what it's all about, what to do and what not to do. Blah, blah, boring, obvious shite. He has had to go in for a meeting with Jen though so it's me. Which is good for you, because I know what I am talking about whilst Giles is a dick. But it is not good for me, because I," he paused and then said carefully enunciating each word, "fucking hate guiding. So listen carefully, I don't want to have to repeat myself. Now, what do you think your job is?"

"Ski guide? Umm, to show people round the mountain?" I asked, unsure of what he meant.

"Well, yes, but it's not really about that," he said patiently. "Why do ValSki offer guiding?"

"Because people are nervous about skiing? Because they want help on the slopes?" I hazarded a couple of guesses.

"No," Danny said shortly. He picked an orange from the bowl on the table and began inspecting it. "We are not allowed to teach on the slopes. If the lifties or the French Ski Schools even suspect that we are helping people ski then we get taken off the mountain immediately."

"I didn't know that," I admitted.

"Well don't even give any hints away. Even if they are snow-ploughing down La Face, it's just not worth it, you will get pulled off and your lift pass taken away, and that's you fucked for the season. Anyway, we ask that people can ski red runs with confidence, so everyone who comes guiding can ski already. So it's not that."

"Are we there to show them where to go?" I asked, still not sure what he was driving at.

"Most of the guests have been coming to Val for years and will know the resort much better than you. They will have skied top to bottom hundreds of times. So it's not that." He started to peel the orange.

I shrugged my shoulders. "I give up, I don't know," I said. "Tell me."

"People come here on holiday to relax," Danny began. He finished peeling the orange, and discarded the skin, all in one long coil. "They don't want to think or have to make decisions about where to go and what to do, that's what they do at home. Ski guiding is about telling people what to do; where to go, what to look at, where to eat, what to drink and what is going on. That, believe it or not, is relaxing for people."

"Really?" I said. "The guests really want to be told what to do? Are you sure?"

"You'd be surprised." Danny grimaced. He detached an orange segment and started pulling the stringy bits of pith off it. "Look, people, and punters especially, are like pack animals. They like to know someone is in charge, they feel comfortable when there are rules to follow. Whilst they are on the mountain, you are the Alpha Male, the Pack Leader, the Daddy. If you make and enforce the rules, then everyone will not only follow you but they will be happy about it too. So remember, it's important. You are the boss. Do you think you are up to it?" He looked at me intently, his blue eyes boring into mine. I found that I could not hold his gaze for long.

"Yes, I think so," looking at the table.

"Good man," Danny said, inspecting his segment. "I reckon you can too, I think you've got it in you." He popped the orange piece in his mouth.

Heather was looking at Danny shaking her head. "You're so full of shit Danny. Don't listen to him," she said to me. "It really is just about showing people round the fucking mountain."

"That's the trouble with you H," Danny said, taking another segment. "You've got your eyes closed. You just do not realise what's really going on."

Gwat drove us down in his car to the meeting point near the slopes a few minutes later. "Sebastian Gwattel, Gwat Alonso, eee!" he squeaked as he did a handbrake turn round a hairpin bend. I tried not to feel sick.

Danny had given me his light blue ValSki jacket to wear. "We look a right pair in these," I muttered to Heather.

"Most fashionable colours in resort," she said sarcastically at me.

"Get used to it!" Danny grinned at us. He was dressed in his own gold parka style jacket and looked a lot better than we did.

We pulled up outside a restaurant not far from the lifts. Danny quickly got out, picked up his snowboard and strode confidently towards a group of about a dozen people waiting on the terrace. Heather and I picked up our more cumbersome skis and trailed behind him.

"Hi, good to see you all," Danny called out as he approached and then passed through the group. "Brian, glad that you could make it," he said shaking a hand. "Sheila, it's been a couple of years hasn't it?" He gave a kiss on both cheeks to a middle-aged lady. "Matt, welcome back. Hi, I'm Danny, your ski guide today. You must be Abi," he said to a girl in her thirties with curly brown hair sticking out of her hat. "You're in charge when I break my leg! Martin, Adam," he nodded at two men in their twenties, "good to see you again." He had a word or gesture for everyone, just like a TV game show host. I felt in awe of his confidence and ease with everyone.

"I thought you were hot tub boy these days?" one of the guests called out, which caused a ripple of laughter around the group.

"Yeah, I've been 'promoted' for a day," Danny smiled. "We have a new Gki Guide too, Jimmy, who flew in yesterday. Come over here fella," he gestured me over from where I was hovering nervously at the edge of the group. "I am just showing him the ropes today, but he will be your guide as of tomorrow. Jimmy, I'd like you to meet some of ValSki's best guests. This is Brian and Sheila, they have been coming for years now. Abi is a Doctor, and Martin and Adam are terrific skiers. This is

Valerie, and this is Terry..." he reeled off the names of all the people there, even the ones he had not met before. It was pretty impressive, and the guests loved it. "And of course you all know Heather," she smiled and waved at them all.

"Now," he carried on. "Where are we going today?" he looked around. "Anyone got any preferences?" The guests shrugged and shook their heads. "Well in that case..." Danny turned to look at the mountains and appeared lost in thought for a second. "We will go up to the glacier at Le Fornet. The piste bashers clear there last so the slopes will have untracked powder on. Most people will head straight over to Tignes, which means we will have it to ourselves. It's going to be a good day!" he beamed at everyone.

Clipping into my ski boots, I felt a huge rush of excitement. I had not been skiing for almost nine months and I ached to feel the snow beneath my skis again. This was what I lived for, what got me up in the morning, and had got me through some dark times in the last year. Skiing was what I had come here for, not the parties or the bars, the drink or the girls. Finally I was about to hit the slopes again.

Danny noticed me grinning inanely. "What's got you so excited?" he asked as we waited for a ski lift.

"Just pleased to be back skiing again." I said simply.

He nodded. "Ah, so you are one of those. Good, makes a change from most of the staff at ValSki. But don't expect too much today. We are with punters so the skiing will be très dull, just blues and greens with a lot of stops. No off-piste, no park, no kickers or tricks or anything exciting at all." He scuffed his boot against the snow as the lift swept us up and stared moodily out at the slopes. "The others will all be heading out in an hour or so for some of the pow. Damn guiding."

Whatever Danny said about it being boring guiding, I didn't care, I was just happy to be in the mountains again. It was stunningly beautiful, a frozen wonderland, hidden away, high up on the roof of the world. The sky was deep azure blue, the peaks towered above us and the snow stretched ahead, clean and white, soft and inviting. It was all I could do not to break down in tears as we got off the lift and the first run a few minutes later made me the happiest I had been in months. I sped down in one big arc, laughing ecstatically, all the way to the lifts.

At the bottom, Danny pulled up next to me a few seconds later, pirouetting elegantly on his board. "You enjoyed that then?" he said wryly, taking off his goggles and noticing my grin. I nodded, unable to speak.

He smiled too, my enthusiasm infecting him too. "It's magical isn't it, like nothing else, and this is just a blue run. But," he raised a finger. "Don't forget we are with guests. You can't run off like that, you have to look after them. You are not here for your enjoyment, for that you will have to wait. Fortunately, this is something that they can handle."

The guests pulled up one by one, smiles etched on their faces too, with Heather bringing up the rear. "That was amazing!" said one, "Brilliant," said another. "Oh my God, the snow is fabulous," a third called out. Danny smiled at them all. "I knew Fornet would be good," he said. "Now, who wants more?!" Everyone cheered.

The day panned out pretty much as Danny described. We cruised around green and blue runs at the top of the Fornet ski area, whilst Heather took three or four guests on slightly harder runs. After an hour, we had a hot chocolate at the highest restaurant in the Alps and then another one an hour later at a place lower down. At twelve, we headed to another ski area called the Solaise, and after a couple of runs had lunch at a restaurant there with a panoramic view down the valley. The afternoon followed pretty much the same pattern; gentle skiing, a few rest stops, and lots of refreshment breaks.

I started to get to know some of the guests; Brian and Sheila were a retired couple from Berkshire who had been coming to Val since their children had left University. Matt was Sheila's older brother and been on every holiday with them since his wife had died. Abi was a doctor from Manchester who was travelling by herself, whilst Martin and Adam were trainee lawyers for a City firm. They were all interesting people who loved skiing and I enjoyed talking to them.

Without exception the guests all seemed to love Danny. Many of them knew him from previous holidays, but even the ones who were new could not stop talking about what a good boarder he was or how well he knew the mountain, or how he always managed to find the quietest runs and the best snow. A few of the guests told anecdotes about his legendary drinking or exploits around town and a couple wanted to know about one or more of his ex-girlfriends. He seemed to be so popular that I could not but help feel a little disheartened.

At about four thirty, he stopped us halfway down a green run and took his helmet off. "Shh," he called out, as the guests gathered round. "Can you hear it?"

"Hear what?" one of the younger guests, Adam asked. I could hear nothing but the sound of skiers slicing past us in the crisp snow.

"The drums," he replied mysteriously.

I strained my hearing, and sure enough, I could hear a faint sound of music coming from somewhere.

"What's that?" Adam's friend Martin asked.

"That," Danny said smiling and pulling his hat and goggles back on, "is the Folie Douce. Probably the most incredible bar you will ever see. "

The older guests were smiling as well. They had obviously been there before.

"Ready? We'll meet there." Danny said, and without bothering to wait, sped off down the slope.

We were all only moments behind him. The run bottomed out after a hundred yards, and we sped along as a group along the flat, the dance music getting louder and louder. I stopped on a small hill as everyone else carried on, and looked out.

Danny was right; it was probably one of the most extraordinary sights I had ever seen.

At the bottom of the next decline, nestled in a little bowl, was a large rambling farmhouse that had been converted into a bar. The distant mountains spread out on either side, giving it almost perfect panoramic views down the valley, but this was not what made it special. After all, many bars and restaurants had equally magnificent views.

What made this place different was that there were hundreds of people dancing round outside in full ski gear to the high-powered techno music that was blasting out of the huge speakers on the roof. People were climbing up on chairs and tables and waving their hands around as if they were at a full-on rave.

The music suddenly cut out, and a lone voice started singing. I noticed a stick-thin figure on the roof, dressed in an outrageous fur parka, clutching a microphone and cavorting about in time to the music. I realised that he was leading the ensemble below like a conductor in front of an orchestra.

"Is he singing live?" I asked as Heather pulled up beside me.

"Yes," she answered smiling. "And it's not just him. Look, can you see the others?"

I looked down and slowly started to see other musicians join in one by one. There was a drummer at one end of the decking, a saxophonist jumping up and down on a table and a guitarist striking a Jimi Hendrix pose in the middle of the dance floor.

"Incredible," I said.

"That's Kelly Starlight and his crew. They are a bit of a local legend around here."

"I can see that," I said nodding. "Look there's Danny!" He was leading the group of guests out to the middle of the dance floor, young and old, and encouraging them to dance. Within moments, they were all jigging about clumsily in their ski boots.

"How does he do it?" I asked. "He really is amazing too."

"Hmm," she said in a non-committal way.

We paused for a second, surveying the scene below us. "Look, about last night," I said wanting to clear the air. Neither of us had acknowledged what had happened, and it seemed childish to pretend that we had not slept to together.

"It didn't happen!" she hissed at me suddenly, changing the mood completely. "It was a mistake. Let's just pretend it didn't happen, alright?"

"Alright," I said surprised. "I was just going to say..."

"I don't want to know," she said almost angrily. "Look, it happens here sometimes, we go to bed with the wrong people. It doesn't mean I don't like you or I didn't enjoy myself, but we have to work together every day. Sleeping together is a shit idea."

"Okay," I said, a little bit stung. I was going to say something similar, but her bluntness was surprising.

"So we won't mention it again alright?" she asked.

"No, not if you don't want to." I said lamely.

"Good," she said finally. "Right, I'm going back home. You can go and hang out with wonder boy and the guests." I watched her turn her skis down the hill and race off in elegant turns. Shrugging, I turned my own skis down the mountain to the bar.

One of the guests bought me a pint, and tried to get me up on one of the tables. I just shook my head and watched them all from the side lines. The exchange with Heather had put me in a bad mood. There was no reason for her to be such a bitch. I sipped my pint, and wondered what her problem was.

After about fifteen minutes, Danny led the guests, red-faced and happy over from the dance floor. "That's enough of that!" he said when they had all gathered round him. "Don't want to tire you out for tomorrow."

"Amazing!"

"Ridiculous!"

"Crazy!"

"Let's go again!"

"Sorry guys," he said in smiling. "We have to get back to the office. Jimmy will be with you for the rest of the week, but I will try and stop by your chalets before you go." A chorus of thanks rang out from the happy guests, as we walked away.

"You are fucking amazing with the guests," I said.

Danny just smiled at me tiredly. "So did you enjoy that?" he asked as we strapped into our gear outside the bar.

"Yes, I did." I replied and I meant it.

"It was fucking shit." Danny said shaking his head and moving towards the slope. "Fucking punters pootling about on green runs. I thought I would die of boredom."

"Really," I said surprised by his change of attitude. "I thought you..."

"No, you don't get it." He jumped his board and moved a few feet away before stopping, his eyes strangely distant. "I hated every minute. It kills my soul just doing that boring shit on the mountain. There is so much more up there that people like that will never realise."

"Like what?" I said intrigued. For the first time I had seen real fire in Danny's eyes rather than the smooth talking salesman patter that he did with the guests.

"Wait until next day off," he said. "I will show you what the mountain is really about," and he turned his board down the mountain.

10

WE DIDN'T DO much that evening. Gwat had made a chicken curry for us back at the staff accommodation and we all sat down together to eat. Giles joined us but fortunately there seemed to be no trace of any tension between him and Danny. Perhaps they had buried the hatchet when I wasn't there.

Giles asked me a couple of perfunctory questions about the day but as I seemed to be coping, he didn't push too hard. "So you are okay to do it by yourself tomorrow?" he asked.

"Yes, I think so. Heather has given me the route, and quite a few points to meet up. I have your number if there are any problems."

"Good show," he said stroking his chin, but he seemed distracted by something. "Right, then, I'm off to beddy-byes. Goodnight," and he shuffled off.

"Right, me too," Heather said standing.

"Watch shit TV, knock one out, fall asleep, eee," Gwat added and stood to go too. Danny remained seated with me and watched them both go.

"So," he said after a few moments quiet. "Faye?"

"Yes, er, right," I stammered, butterflies suddenly loose in my stomach. I had been dreading this conversation. I knew that they were no longer together but still I knew it would not be nice for him to see other guys chasing after her.

"You like her, don't you?" he said softly. Was it my imagination or was there a threatening edge to his voice. My knees started to go weak.

"Er, I hardly know her," I prevaricated, stalling for time.

He shook his head, his dark hair loose and curling round his face. "You can be honest with me Jimmy, I'm not going to bite." He stared at me intently and looked exactly like he would. I felt like a mouse frozen in fear in front of a cat, knowing whatever he did or whichever way he ran he would get pounced on.

I gulped. "Yes, I think she is really attractive, but I had no idea that she is, sorry, was your girlfriend. I don't want to tread on any one's toes. I would never go after her..."

Danny paused, still eyeing me up, and then suddenly banged the table, sat back and laughed. "Damn! I thought you were going to shit yourself! Don't sweat, it's cool, bro. We're history, a long way past. She is her own woman now."

"Oh, right, okay," I said relieved, but not sure that the danger was completely past.

"Now she is a special kind of girl, a complete wild card. But I think she likes you too..." he looked at me smiling.

"Umm," I was lost for words, completely wrong-footed by the turn in the conversation.

"But then, there is something else, isn't there? Someone else?" His voice dropped and slowed again, and I felt the fear that had momentarily abated return.

"Umm, I'm not sure what you mean..." I began, but he interrupted.

"Heather."

"Oh right, yes, last night, we, er..." I stumbled over my words again.

"Oh I know all about that," he said smiling. "But how is that going to affect things with Faye, what will she think of that?" he sat back again making a motion like weighing scales. I could make no reply, just look at him, like a rabbit in the headlights of a car.

"And what about Heather? How do you think she feels right now?" he sat up leaning in closer to me. "Shall I tell you what I think?" he said, his voice almost a whisper now. "Shall I tell you what I think you should do?"

I nodded silently, terrified of him.

"Whatever the fuck you want to, do whoever you want to. They are both big girls, they can make up their own minds. Don't forget, you're in Val now, you can do anything you fucking want."

I was mesmerised by him, not sure what to say or do.

"But," he said suddenly leaning back again. "What do you want Jimmy? Why are you here? I'm still not sure. Most people I can get pretty quickly, but you I still don't know.

"You're not here for the drink, I can see that. Oh you got pretty drunk, but I can see that that is not it for you. Nor is it the girls, although you have started pretty well with Faye and Heather," he smiled. "I don't think you are either running away from something or killing time before you do something else. I can't work it out. Why are you here?"

I sat at a loss. Heather had asked me something else the morning before but I had avoided her question. I didn't think that Danny would let me go quite so easily. Why was I here? I knew as well that it wasn't for the drink or girls or the laughs or just for something to do.

"It's the snow," I said eventually. "I am here for the mountains, here for the powder. That's what I came here for, nothing else."

Danny nodded approvingly. "I thought so. Not like most of the people here, they just don't get it." He stared away unfocused for a moment. "When you climb off into the back country and you feel the powder beneath your board and there is no one else in sight and you are miles from anywhere and anyone... well that is about as close to God as you can get."

He stood up suddenly, almost embarrassed, and began to clear the plates. "Sermon over. Don't worry, kiddo, we're gonna get on great. And don't listen to what I said about guiding either. You're gonna be on the mountain a lot, and that is never a bad thing. Punters are pains, but they are nowhere near as bad as chalet hosts. You should hear them complain. We are going to have a great season."

Despite being scared of Danny I was also in awe of him as well. He was strong, good looking, confident, funny and clever. I felt like I had been accepted by him and was now part of his gang, and it felt good.

"Yes, I think we are." I said, nodding slowly.

11

IN MANY RESPECTS, the next day was very like the last. I got up and had breakfast with Heather, Gwat and Danny, then went off to go guiding with Heather. We took the guests out on the gentle blues and greens of the Bellevarde area in the morning, and then down the slightly harder red run to Val Claret in the afternoon. We stopped several times for hot chocolates, coffees and a leisurely lunch. I had interesting conversations with lots of people on the lifts and during the breaks, and even had a pint with them afterwards in the bar.

But something was different, something was missing. Although the weather had not really changed from the blue skies of the day before, it was as if the sun had gone in and it was dull and grey. I realised in the afternoon that the difference was Danny. He made everyone feel comfortable, everyone laugh, and everyone feel like they were skiing the best runs in the best resort in the world. He had some kind of magic to make it feel special. Without him there it felt like just another day on the mountain.

I thought about what he had said about the guests wanting someone in charge. Was this what was missing? I obviously was not the leader that Danny was now, but would I ever be? In my heart, I knew that the answer was no, and that was a sobering and depressing thought.

"What's the matter soldier? Why the glum face? Not having second thoughts about the job?" Heather asked as we walked back home. The spikiness of the day before had vanished and had been replaced by an unexpected warmth. This was confusing, but I was not going to complain.

"No, it's just that, it's just that..." I paused struggling to find the words. "I was feeling a bit crap compared to Danny. He was amazing with the guests yesterday."

"Ah, I see," she nodded. "Well don't sweat it, everyone gets an inferiority complex when they measure themselves against Danny. He is the best looking guy, the best boarder, the best chalet host, the best ski guide, the best lalalala... God it would be boring to be him!"

"You like him, don't you?" I asked quietly.

Heather bristled a moment and seemed on the edge of saying something harsh, then seemed to change her mind. "Oh, I don't know," she sighed. "I did. I mean, who wouldn't. But now... the more

I see of him, to be honest, the more I feel sorry for him. He hasn't really changed in ten years; he's still doing the same kind of job, drinking in the same bars, doing the same ski runs in the same resort, just the people are slightly different each year. It must get fucking tedious. He hasn't grown, or done anything with his life; it is just like he is trying to be a Peter Pan, living in Never Never Land forever. How long can he keep it up for? Another season? Two, perhaps? He should be fucking good at guiding, he has had enough practice!"

The more she spoke, the angrier she seemed to get, until at the end I thought she was going to spit with fury.

"Bet you'd still sleep with him though?" I joked, trying to diffuse the moment.

She looked at me for a moment with pure loathing, and then laughed. "Sorry, did I get a bit worked up there? Yeah, fuck yeah, I'd sleep with him."

"I'm sure it will happen," I said consolingly as we turned up the steep hill to get back to our staff accommodation. "He can't resist you forever."

"Oh, I don't know," she sighed. "Gwat got me first. I think Danny has a rule about going with someone after someone else has been there."

"Really," I said shocked. "I thought you couldn't stand Gwat?"

"I can't," she said flatly. "I didn't like him even then. I just don't know how it happened; I mean really I don't know, not like with you. I was drunk in the Saloon, and the next thing I remember was him on top of me back in his room, grunting and squealing away," she shuddered at the memory. "I have no idea how I got there or what happened." She slowed down, and then stopped walking altogether. "I tried to get him off me, but it was too late, he wouldn't stop." She spoke quite calmly, almost without any emotion in her voice at all.

"Christ, isn't that...?" I started.

"Rape?" she finished my sentence. "I don't think so. It's not like he dragged me back and forced me, but it's not something I would ever do sober."

"I'm sorry," I said and went to put my hand on her shoulder.

"Don't!" she said. "Don't touch me, please." She paused, and took a deep breath. "And now I have to live with him and work with him and get on with him."

"Shit," I said, not sure what to say.

"Oh, it's alright," she shook her head and then carried on walking. "I mean, fortunately I didn't get pregnant or catch a disease. And I'm not going to let that fucker spoil my season, I'm made of tough stuff."

"Thanks for being so honest with me. I appreciate it." I said as we rounded the corner on the way up to the Chamois.

"Well I wouldn't normally be quite so open with someone I have just met, but, hey, we kind of got to know each other pretty well the other night."

"I thought we weren't going to mention that again?" I said.

"I know. Look, I'm sorry if I was a bitch yesterday. I was just thinking about Gwat and Danny, and how much I hated men, and it all came out wrong. I know that you're not like them."

"It's alright kid," I said. "I think I understand a bit better now."

"Thanks," she said simply.

"It was good though wasn't it?!"

She grinned at me. "Yeah, it was. Thank you for that, kind of reminded me that sex can be enjoyable." She stopped. "I still don't think that we should sleep together again, mind you."

"You are probably right," I smiled too. "I'm glad we got to talk though."

"Yeah, me too." Heather said and then laughed. "We're a right pair aren't we? You and Faye and me and Danny. Perhaps we should double date?"

"Yeah, like that's ever gonna happen!" I snorted.

"I bet you get Faye before I get Danny," she said with a twinkle in her eye.

"Fat chance, she's well out of my league."

"We'll see," she said grinning and linked her arms through mine. "Now you know it's staff meeting tonight don't you, and then transfer day tomorrow?"

"No, shit! What happens then?"

"Hasn't anyone gone through the routine with you yet? Jesus, Giles is fucking incompetent." She sighed and shook her head. "Alright, well the meeting is pretty self-explanatory, but I'll go through transfer day with you tonight."

"Thanks," I said. "I owe you one."

"I know!" she laughed. "Don't worry, you'll pay it back."

12

THE STAFF MEETING later that evening was in the office where I had met Jen a couple of days earlier. With all the ValSki staff, close on twenty people, it was crammed full. When the inevitable banter died down, Jen started the meeting.

I was officially introduced to everyone. Although I had met most of the staff, there were a few people that I had not come across yet; an older couple called Pete and Caroline who lived in and ran an old-fashioned farmhouse chalet at the other end of town and two girls, Alice and Harri, who ran a chalet together. They were straight out of university, fresh-faced and timid.

Jen had quite a lot to say to the chalet hosts; some positive comments that she had received from guests, but also a few moans about cleaning and food stocks. "I don't expect to find anything out of place that shouldn't be there when I come round and do cleaning checks next week. I will call people back from the mountain if things are not satisfactory," she warned. "Okay, that's it from me. Giles, have you got anything to say?"

"Erm, yes, right," he cleared his throat. He was sitting down, lolling back on a swivel chair. "I just want to say that some people broke a curfew a few days ago when it was snowing and went out when it wasn't safe. I won't name names, but that can't happen again. If it does then it will be an immediate disciplinary and a verbal warning. Isn't that right Jen?"

"Erm, yes," Jen looked surprised at Giles's declaration and not particularly impressed. "Umm, we probably shouldn't go out when the guests are not allowed to."

I looked around; there was a mixture of surprise and contempt on most people's faces, Giles really was not popular. "Yeah, snow's right dangerous," Johnners said innocently after a second, and there were a few chuckles.

"Yeah," Dylan added. "You could catch a chill in it!" Another ripple of laughter went round the room.

"Or have fun in it!" Joe muttered and there was a snigger somewhere.

"Does that mean we shouldn't go to work when it's snowing?" Danny asked Giles directly and the laughter was open now.

"You know what I mean," Giles spluttered, a red flush spreading up his neck.

"Boys," Jen interrupted. "That's enough. Now Giles," she added smoothly, "what's happening with the departures tomorrow?"

"Right, yes, well," he was still flustered. "Right, the coaches leave at seven-thirty. We were a few minutes late last week, so I would like all the non-chalet staff here at six-thirty to make sure we are not late again."

Danny and Gwat exchanged looks and rolled their eyes. "Really?" Danny asked. "Do we have to? What's the point? It wasn't our fault that the coaches were late last week; we got all the bags in on time. They made it to the airport early anyway."

"Nevertheless," Giles said primly, "I would like you to be here at six-thirty. I want ValSki to be seen as prompt and punctual."

"But getting here early won't make any difference!" Danny protested. "We will just be standing around in the cold."

"Still, six-thirty please, Danny." Giles said smugly pleased with his exercise of power. I could see Danny was going red and struggling to keep quiet.

"I think that's about it," Jen said smartly. She had also noticed Danny getting worked up, and moved to diffuse the situation. "Has anybody got anything else that they would like to add? No? Then I think we are about done. Thank you everybody," she said decisively. "Meeting is over. Off you go," she motioned for everyone to leave. "You too Giles," she added as he made no effort to get up as everybody filed out. "I want to speak to James in private a moment."

"Oh, yes, of course," Giles blustered and got up to go with the others.

When everyone had gone, I sat down next to Jen, my heart beating quickly. Had I done something wrong? Was I about to get 'Slashed? "So," she asked after a moment. "Is everything alright? Are you enjoying it so far?" she asked.

"Yes," I answered truthfully. "I am. I think I can do the job, I like the guests, the accommodation is great, and everybody seems friendly."

"Good," her eyes narrowed. "I just wanted to check. Everyone has taken to you too, so it seems from my point of view, that everything is alright. Both Danny and Heather think that you will cope on the mountain."

I smiled, relieved. "Just one thing," she paused. "Don't get too swept with everything here. The drinking, the girls and the snow are all pretty overwhelming at first and I wouldn't want you to get lost." She paused as if remembering something or perhaps someone. I might have imagined it, but

I could almost see a tear in her eye. "Remember why you are here."

"Funny," I said. "Andy said something similar on the drive up here."

Jen narrowed her eyes and pursed her lips. "He's a fine one to talk. Right, you can go. If you see Giles out there, can you send him in?"

I left thinking about what Jen had said. Who had she been thinking of? Was it Andy? Had something happened between them?

Giles was hanging about outside looking nervous. "Jen wants to see you," I said, preoccupied.

"Right, er, thanks. I'll see you later or tomorrow morning."

Back at the Chamois Heather was chopping some vegetables. "Do you want some soup?" she asked.

"Yes please."

"What did Jen want?" she asked curiously.

"It was a bit strange actually," I replied. "She told me not to get lost."

Heather snorted. "Yeah, right. Like that's not going to happen. Right, shall we go through tomorrow and what you have to do?" she said as she put the vegetables into a pan of simmering liquid.

For the next half an hour, we went through the schedule for the next day. We would load bags into the little van, and then take them down to the coaches waiting at the bottom of the hill. When the guests arrived just before seven-thirty, we would count them in and check them off and then go down to the airport with them on the coaches. Once they had checked in, we would then wait around to pick up the next set of guests, get them on the coaches with their luggage, and then come back up with them to Val, answering any questions on the way. It seemed straightforward enough.

"So we are basically like sheep dogs, making sure no one wanders off and gets lost?" I asked.

"Exactly," Heather said. "Just like guiding."

"And we start at six-thirty?" I asked.

"Yeah, that's a shit. Normally it's seven, but the coaches were late last week. There really is no need for us to get there so early, but Giles was showing off to Jen and trying to put Danny in his place. He is such a cock." Heather said contemptuously.

"Danny didn't seem too impressed." I said. "I thought he was properly going to kick off."

"Oh he will," Heather said thoughtfully. "At some point he will. I wouldn't want to be Giles then, it won't be pretty."

13

IT WAS DARK and bitterly cold at the chalets the next morning when we arrived to load the luggage. Giles watched from the office, sipping tea, as Danny, Gwat and I humped bags into the little Transit van. We barely spoke except to offer terse instructions or comments to each other.

Just as Danny had predicted, we finished well before the chalet hosts arrived with the guests, and we were forced to stand around, stamping our feet and blowing into our gloves to try and keep warm. Once they did start to arrive, at least Heather and I could stand in the coaches, counting people off and chatting to the guests about their holiday. Danny and Gwat had to wait outside just in case of problems with the luggage.

Just before seven-thirty, Giles climbed onto the coach to give a goodbye speech to the guests. It could have been just a simple 'Good bye and thanks, hope you had a good holiday', but Giles, in love with his own voice, managed to string it out for about ten minutes with cringe-worthy anecdotes and smarmy comments. I could see the guests were bored and wanted to be on their way, but he just droned on and on. When he finally finished, I watched him shuffle off to Heather's coach to repeat the process there. I shuddered as the coach pulled away, just before seven-forty. Heather was right, he really was a cock.

The rest of the day was almost exactly as Heather had described. We pulled up at the airport on time, helped the guests with their bags, made sure they checked in, and then had a coffee whilst we waited for the next set of guests to arrive. When they did, we made ourselves visible, holding up signs, and then directing people to the right coaches. On the drive back up, I read a pre-prepared script about ValSki, the resort, the weather conditions and what would happen throughout the week and then answered individual queries from the guests. A couple I couldn't answer so I had to ring Heather on the other coach and check with her, but most were about the mountains, ski hire or passes which I knew.

We arrived back in Val about three. Danny, Gwat and the chalet hosts were waiting for us, and we helped load the luggage from the coach into the smaller van to be taken to the chalets whilst Giles gave another pompous welcome speech on the coach. The guests then were taken off by the hosts to their chalets, and we drove the luggage round to deliver to each chalet. It was straightforward if tiring work, but we were done by four.

"That's it," Danny said as we took the last suitcase of the van and put it in the boot room of the last chalet. "Another transfer day, done."

"Eee, no luggage lost. Hundred percent record, eee," Gwat grunted, smiling.

"So what do we do now?" I asked.

"We're done mate, finished." Danny answered.

"Really, but it's only four!"

"Yeah, hosts will be working 'til about ten, but we are done. Go home, get some rest. It's a big night tonight, everyone will be out."

He wasn't lying. At nine, when the four of us started drinking in the Blue Note, it was dead, but by ten the place was rammed; four deep at the bar, and more people were arriving every minute. Danny had anticipated this and he bought a double round in whilst Heather came back with a tray of shots.

"Up fucking yours, Giles!" Danny shouted as we smashed the glasses together and then downed them. "Six-thirty start my arse!" he said and downed his second almost before I had finished my first.

Everyone around me was drinking very quickly. Everywhere I looked shots, shorts and pints were being knocked back. There was a mad, almost suicidal frenzy in the rate that everyone was drinking. Of course, Danny was at the centre of a lot of it, wherever he went, he was offered shots, most of which he took.

"Christ, what's wrong with everyone tonight?!" I asked Heather.

"Do you mean what's right with everyone?" she looked at me, and I could see already her eyes were already beginning to glaze over. "It's transfer day. Time to get fucked up!"

"Eee!" Gwat muttered. "Scandi gwat over there," he nodded over to a corner where a group of gorgeous blonde-haired girls were sipping drinks. "Gwat hunting!" he winked at me, and swaggered off to talk to them.

"What does Gwat mean?" I asked Heather. Now she had had a few drinks, I figured she might tell me.

"Gash With A Twat!" she shouted over the music. "His word for a girl he would like to shag. Gwat's real name is Anthony, but he said that word so much that it kind of stuck with him. Look at those poor girls, they are only about sixteen. It's fucking disgusting," she thought for a second. "I'm going to have a word with them; I'm not going to let Gwat get his paws on them."

A few more of the ValSki staff drifted in, in various states of sobriety depending on how much chalet wine they had drunk at dinner. Johnners, Dylan and Joe looked sober, but were chatting away ten to the dozen. Toby and Ash, however, were already starting to slur their speech and lose focus. Faye waltzed in looking hot and sexy with Claire trailing faithfully behind her. Drinks were immediately put in their hands.

"Jimmy!" Faye called out to me, and came over for a hug, sending my heart rate rocketing. "Where have you been? I've missed you!"

"SHOT!" Danny was back with a tray of shooters, and Faye stopped her conversation with me and almost leapt into his arms. "Danny!" she squealed. Despite not being together, she obviously still adored him. My heart sank as I realised that there was no way she would ever feel that way about me.

"Whoa!" he said and danced round her with the tray of drinks. "Careful, we want to drink, not wear these little babies!"

Faye just pouted at him. "Where's my wine?"

Danny stared at her a second then winked at her. "Come on then, we'll do one at the bar," he said and waltzed her away leaving me awkwardly with Claire.

"So, how long have you and Johnners been...?" I turned to her.

"Smashing each other's back doors in?" she grinned at me.

"Erm, yes, I suppose you could put it like that!"

"Since I got here. I met him last year when I came over on holiday and really fancied him. He was one of the reasons I came out to work here truth be told. Look, James," she said suddenly seriously. "You hear a lot about how much people shag around out here, but not everyone is like that. You can find the right person up here if you look hard enough. Or maybe not..."

She looked over my shoulder, and I turned to follow her gaze just as Heather and Gwat came back to the table shouting at each other. "Whatyoudothatfor?" Gwat raged. He was so angry his words flowed into one another. "I was fucking well in there."

"Don't you fucking DARE go anywhere near them," Heather shouted back at him.

"Fucking bitch told them I had chlamydia!" he said turning to me and Claire, still spitting with rage.

"You're a fucking animal." Heather said back to him, an icy coolness entering her voice. "You can't go round spreading diseases. It's fucking irresponsible."

"I've taken tablets," he retorted defensively. "I'm clear!"

"Have you been to the doctors, have you taken a test? No, I didn't think so." Heather turned to me as well as if I was some kind of referee. "He orders antibiotics over the web from India. Problem is he never knows if they work. Fucking dickhead."

"Fucking cock-blocking bitch!" Gwat looked about ready to punch her, but before she could reply Danny arrived back with Faye.

"Jimmy," he said smoothly, noticing the tension. "Why don't you take Gwat outside for a fag?"

Outside, the air was so cold that it hurt to breathe in too deeply.

"Little bitch has had it in for me all season," Gwat said as he fumbled at a packet of cigarettes. "Any chance she gets she puts the knife in."

"Is that because you..."

"Oh, I don't know. That was just a bit of fun," he said bitterly as he picked out a fag. "It didn't mean nothing. I mean she's got a great body on her. I'd love to have another go..." he drifted off replaying the event in his mind. I stayed silent, hoping that he didn't know about Heather spending the night with me.

"I'm fucking clear before you ask," he added as he sparked up.

"I'm not making any judgements!" I said holding my hands up.

"I mean I did, a few weeks ago," he said almost without listening to me. "Some dirty little tramp from Crystal gave me the cockrot, but I've taken the medicine now and I'm all clear."

"But you didn't go to the doctor's?" I asked.

Gwat snorted. "Eighty fucking Euros a test and then another thirty for the medicine; no fucking way. It's easy to diagnose and you can get the right antibiotic over the net easily enough."

"Really?"

"Yeah, Erythromycin, shipped in all the way from India. I bought a load before I came out. I had a feeling I might get riddled." He took a drag of his fag, his bad mood disappearing. "I've got the drugs for pretty much any infection," he winked at me. "If you need anything, just let me know. I can get all sorts, not just medicine."

"Like what?" I said intrigued.

"Viagra," he said promptly. "If you have any problems down there..." He trailed off.

"Nah, mate, I'm good."

"Well tell me if you change your mind. Right, time to move on. Saloon I think for a jug. You been there before?"

I shook my head. "Shouldn't we wait for the others?" I asked.

"Nah," he said stubbing out his cigarette. "Fuck 'em. They can catch us up. Time to go Gwat-hunting. Eeeeee!"

The Saloon was a large, old fashioned alpine bar with low ceilings just around the corner from the Blue Note. It was quiet when we arrived, but very quickly it started filling up. By the time we had drunk a beer, all the ValSki staff had joined us, and it seemed half of Val too. We moved over to a space by the dance floor, where we could dump our coats.

I quickly noticed that everyone was behaving very differently here. There was no real attempt at any conversation; everyone was drunk and acting outrageously. Pete and Caroline, the oldest and supposedly most mature of all the hosts, were there swinging round each other trying to dance to the music pumping out, Faye was leapfrogging over Claire on the small dance floor, Johnners had picked up young Alice and was spinning her round whilst Joe and Dylan were standing with their trousers down gyrating. I shook my head, it seemed insanity had engulfed everyone. Only Giles, sensible and boring as ever, looked sober, sipping a beer at the bar, taking it all in.

Heather was suddenly there at my side with a jug of colourful orange liquid. "How you doing?" she shouted at me.

"Yeah good, taking it all in." I shouted back to her. "Are you okay? Is everything alright with Gwat?"

"Yeah," she laughed. "It felt good to fuck him over for a change."

I suddenly noticed that her pupils were as large as plates and she was swaying on her feet.

"What are you drinking? It looks strong?"

"Long Island. You gotta get yourself one."

"I'm not sure," I answered. "It's been a long day, maybe..."

"Come on James, let yourself go. It's transfer day, end of the week, we have to let off some steam. Trust me, if you don't get fucked, you generally get fucked up."

"I don't know if I can," I said sadly. "I just don't think that I can be that wild."

"Yeah, sure you can. Try some of this," she said holding up the jug.

I hesitated, unsure. "Come on," she whispered, leaning in close.

"Fuck it," I said, slightly intoxicated by her proximity. I grabbed the jug and took a big gulp.

Heather took a step back and smiled at me. "Now, go and do something unexpected, something out of your comfort zone."

"Like what?" I asked.

"Oh, I don't know. Kiss a girl, punch someone, get naked... it's all the same really."

I looked around at the scenes of excess around me. More people, workers from other companies were coming in and going crazy too. A girl lay on the bar with her t-shirt pulled up and people were doing shots from her belly button, several couples were snogging against a window, and two guys were taking slaps from each other round the face.

"What the fuck," I said, took another huge swallow of Heather's drink, then put my hand in the jug and pulled out a handful of ice. I walked up behind Joe who was still dancing with his trousers down, pulled the back of his pants down, poured in the ice, and then yanked hard upwards. Joe yelped and turned round angrily. "Oh, it's you mate!" he started laughing as he recognised me. "You utter bastard," and hugged me and we danced round the room. Too late I realised he held on to me tightly so Dylan could yank my trousers down and pour a drink down my pants too.

As the bar whirled around me, I suddenly realised that Heather was right. It was good to go crazy, to go wild and let off steam. I knew that tomorrow I would have a horrific hangover and would suffer whilst skiing round the mountain with guests all day, but that was tomorrow. Now it felt right to let go and surrender to the madness.

14

I WOKE WITH a massive grin on my face, expecting a headache but finding myself clear-headed and happy. Last night's madness had been like releasing a pressure valve; I felt great with no real trace of a hangover. I was not sure what time we had finished, but it was still twenty minutes before the alarm went off.

Heather was curled up against me, her naked skin warm and fragrant. Although she was still unconscious I could feel her snuggle in closer into me as I stretched. I put my face close to her and inhaled; she smelt of hay and summer meadows.

How had this happened again, I wondered? I liked Heather and enjoyed spending time with her, but I was not attracted to her in the same way as I was with Faye, whom I had to admit I was becoming a bit obsessed with. I had spent a good hour or two following her round in the bar the night before, but she had gone home with Claire earlier than everyone else as they had to get up to make early breakfasts for their guests.

I had stayed and drank more with Danny and Johnners at the bar, slagging off Giles. When I staggered back an hour or so later, Heather was in the lounge making tea and toast. One minute we were talking, the next we were all over each other and before we knew it were back in my loft room. She wasn't Faye, but the sex was fun.

Her eyes flicked open. "Shit," she began to say, but I leaned in close and silenced her by placing my lips on hers. I felt her stiffen against me, and start to struggle, but then all of a sudden she relaxed and started kissing me back with a passion. As my hands started stroking her back though she broke away and looked at me quizzically. "I thought we were just going to be friends?" she asked.

As if on autopilot my hands carried on exploring her body, gently cupping her breasts. "We are still friends," I murmured, and bent my head to kiss her neck.

"It's just, ahhhhh," she sighed as my mouth started biting her ear. "Look, stop a minute will you?" she pushed me off but still kept her hands tightly locked around my back.

"Sure," I said, a little surprised.

"Look, Jimmy. Let's just get one thing straight, alright?" I nodded.

"I like you and I don't want to fuck up our friendship. We have to work together and I don't want to end up either of us hating each other."

"I don't think that's going to happen," I said. "I'm not Gwat."

She shuddered. "Don't, I don't want to be reminded. I know you're not like him, but it's still not a good idea. If we keep ending up in bed with each other then it'll really make everything complicated."

I sighed. "I know. I know that you want Danny and not me but I don't mind," and strangely I realised that I really didn't mind. I couldn't blame her for wanting him; he was everything a girl could want. Besides, I was still half in love with Faye.

"Look, it's nothing to do with Danny," she said fiercely. "It's just if we keep doing this at least one of us is going to get emotionally attached, and that will not be good. But, if you want to know something," she said almost as an afterthought, "I really would like to fuck your brains out right now. Let's just make this the last time, alright?"

"Agreed," I said as my hands moved over her body, causing her to shiver and moan in response. "But," I stopped just as she was reaching hungrily for my mouth.

"What!" she said impatiently.

"What if I'm in love with you already?" I asked and managed to keep a straight face for all of about two seconds. It was worth it though to see her shocked and horrified face even for that short time.

"Bastard," she murmured when she realised I was joking and scissored her legs around me, pinning me down and with surprising strength. "Don't fall in love with anyone in Val, it'll end in heartbreak," she said just before our lips met.

As we approached the group of people waiting at the meeting point to go ski guiding, I had a sudden attack of nerves. I had felt really comfortable with the group the week before, probably because Danny had been there the first day and helped everyone get to know each other. Now I was going to have to do it all by myself with a group of strangers. I could feel my heart start to hammer in my chest, my throat go dry and my palms start to sweat underneath my gloves. Everything I learnt last week and all that Danny had told me seemed to go out of my head. "What do we say to them?" I hissed at Heather in a panic.

"What?" she looked at me quizzically, and then seeing I was nervous, smiled. "Oh, don't worry, you'll be fine. Just be yourself," she said.

I was in such a state though all I could remember was Danny telling me to be the boss.

I put my skis down, looked at everyone looking at me, and panicked. "HiGoodtoseeyouAreyouhierefortheskiguiding?" I tried to sound positive and confident just like Danny had, but I just gabbled at high speed.

"MynamesJamesandIwillbetakingtheslowergroupthisweek." Heather looked at me, laughing silently at my discomfort. I could feel myself go bright red and sweat started to soak my clothes beneath my blue ValSki jacket.

"Wewillstartbygoingonsomeeasygreenrunstotryandgetyourskilegsback." I tried to slow down but I just couldn't seem to stop. What was wrong with me!? The guests looked on, some bemused, some confused and some amused.

Heather couldn't hold the giggles in any longer and broke in. "Hi, I'm Heather. I'm the Ski Guide without verbal diarrhoea," she said laughing. "When James recovers himself, we'll get up the mountain and do some skiing!"

Fortunately, this broke the ice and the whole group started giggling along with Heather. I stood there feeling very uncomfortable for a few moments, before I joined in too.

"Sorry," I apologised. "First day nerves!"

After that it was fine. I recognised a couple from the transfer coach the day before who were quite friendly, and someone else asked me a question which I could answer. I started to relax, and within an hour or so was chatting to all the guests quite happily. We spent the day doing cruisey runs up the Solaise, and by the end of it, I felt as comfortable with this group as I had with the guests the week before.

As we walked back Heather could not stop laughing about our start to the day. "You were hilarious," she said between gasps. "I don't think I've ever seen anyone in such a state."

"I know!" I shook my head. "I don't know what happened. Thanks for rescuing me."

She looked at me, suddenly serious. "Well don't rely on it. I'm not always going to be there for you."

Part Two

The Second Week

15

THE NEXT TWO days passed quickly. In some ways, the conditions on the mountain were not as good as the week before; although it snowed at night, during the day the sky was overcast with heavy white clouds. This flattened the light, and made it difficult to see the pistes clearly. The snow, however, was still exquisite; light and fluffy beneath my skis and it sprayed up at every turn.

"How do they get it so good?" I asked Heather whilst we were waiting for the guests by a lift. "Fresh snow is usually a lot heavier than this."

"They turn the snow cannons on whenever it starts falling," Heather replied. "It binds with the larger natural flakes to make a more slippery surface, which is better on the piste. That and good grooming at night."

"What a shit job," I shuddered. I had seen the large piste-bashers, like super-sized tractors, going up and down the steep slopes, visible only by their headlights. "It must send the drivers mental, being up here at night by yourself."

Heather grinned. "Nah, they have it easy, they don't have to deal with punters. This lot are driving me mad this week, they are sooo' slow." We watched our skiers, nine in the two groups combined, slowly snake down the green run.

"Oh, they're alright," I said whilst they were still some way off. I had got to know a few of them, and was enjoying their company, even if the skiing was excruciatingly slow at times.

"Yeah, they're alright, but the snow is fabulous at the moment and we should be out doing something decent. Day off tomorrow, thank God, and we can do some proper skiing. Well done Carrie!" Heather complimented one of the guests as she managed to stop without crashing into anyone. "Much better than last time. And here is Kim and Lex too, and both in one piece. You guys go on ahead. James and I will wait for the stragglers and then meet you at the top of the lift."

Although it felt ages, the rest of the group were down in a few minutes and went up the chairlift. Heather and I took the next one and resumed our conversation.

"What does everyone do on day off then? I take it last week was kind of unusual," I said as the chair accelerated up the slope.

"Different stuff every week. On work days, everyone usually goes out with people of roughly the same ability, but on day off we usually ski as a family. We go to places that are too far or too hard to get to guiding, like the top of the Motte or down to Tignes la Brev. If the weather is good then we'll take a few drinks up and have a picnic somewhere. If it's crap then start après early, but it rarely is as mental as last week. Danny keeps threatening to take us to do some off-piste somewhere, but he says the conditions haven't been right yet. He was talking about racing tomorrow."

"Really?" Part of me really wanted to test myself against the other skiers, but part of me knew that I wasn't ready yet. I was still only rediscovering my form.

"Yes. It will be a good chance for the boys to work off some testosterone in a way that doesn't involve shagging some poor girl." I smiled. We had got on really well all week just as friends and I was getting to understand and appreciate her humour. "Oh Christ," Heather stopped and pointed. "Is that Jo caught up there?"

We were nearing the top of the chair lift, but suddenly it ground to a halt. One of the guests had caught the straps of her back pack in the safety bar, and she was now dangling helplessly in the air. I started giggling.

"Dear God, save me from fucking punters!" Heather groaned as one of the lift operators vainly tried to free her.

"Oh come on, we all did things like that when we started," I said between chuckles. "Poor girl, she's probably mortified."

Eventually, the 'lifty' managed to swing her back where he could reach up and free her straps.

"Only two more hours," Heather checked the time on her phone. "Two more hours then day off begins."

We were back at the Chamois, almost exactly two hours later. "Day off!" Heather picked up a bottle of beer and clinked it with my own. "Well, you have lasted a week. What do you think? Are you happy here? Are you glad you came?"

I smiled and nodded. "I think you know the answer to that. You've made a big difference. It would have been a lot harder without you. Thanks for everything."

"I haven't really done anything," she said, but I could tell that she appreciated my gratitude.

"No, I really mean it," I said. "You've made my week."

I thought for a moment we might kiss, but Danny came barging into the room, breaking the spell. "What's going on here then? Watch it Jimmy, three times and she's your girlfriend."

"Fuck you, Danny," Heather snarled at him in mock anger.

"Just celebrating day off." I said.

Danny sat down and stretched on the couch and reached for a beer. "Yup, day off. Hosts have got to pull another shift, but we're done for the day." But he had spoken too soon. Five minutes later, his mobile phone went off.

"What do you want?" Danny answered curtly. "I'm off duty now." I could just about make out Giles's plummy voice through the cheap handset.

"No, I cleaned it earlier; it must have been one of the guests." Danny said and then "No, I'm not coming back. I've finished for the day, it can wait until Friday." He listened for a few more moments and then said more forcefully, "No Giles, you'll have to do it." Giles obviously did not agree as the voice kept going on.

Eventually Danny exploded. "Giles, will you just fuck off!" he said, stabbed the off switch on the phone and threw it on the sofa. "For fuck's sake!" he stood up and shouted to no one in particular.

"What's up?" Heather asked.

"Fucking cockbag Giles wants me to go in for some bullshit reason," Danny was staring bitterly at the phone. "Say's the hot tub changing room is dirty and I have to go and clean it. Fuck's sake."

"What are you going to do?" I asked wondering if he was going to refuse.

Danny looked up. "Fuck it, I'll have to go in. It's my responsibility after all. I just wish it wasn't him asking."

"Do you want some help?" I asked.

"Thanks, but I'm fine. You enjoy yourself. I'll see you back here in an hour or two." He chugged back his beer and stomped off.

Heather shook her head. "Giles should watch himself. Danny is not a good person to make an enemy of."

16

"WHAT DO YOU say to the guests when you come up here?" I asked Danny as we climbed into the télé-cabine.

Danny grinned and began chanting off some facts. "The Grande Motte offers year-round skiing on the glacier. It has the second highest run in the resort at three thousand four hundred and fifty metres. From the top you can see all the way to Mont Blanc, and other peaks such as Grande Casse. The lift was built in 1956 soon after the resorts of Tignes and Val decided to join together to form the Espace Killy..."

"Give it a feckin' rest!" Johnners rolled his eyes. "We're not punters. Who gives a fuck about details like that?"

"Hey, just trying to pick up some tips," I said.

"Hey man, we're here for the pow, not for school." Dylan put on a cheesy stoner accent.

"Dylan," Heather said. "You sound like a dick. Only little rich kids here on daddy's credit card speak like that."

Everyone was tired and grumpy. We had had a few beers at the Chamois the night before, but just as I was about to be sensible and turn in, some of the hosts came back and persuaded me to go down to a bar to watch a band. I was not sure and complained all the way down the hill, but it was actually pretty good when we got there. The band belted out some rock classics, and before I knew it I was in the middle of a moshing crowd, roaring along with everybody else. Suddenly, it had gone one, I had downed several shorts, and the world was reeling about me. I stumbled back up the hill to our chalet watching the stars dance above me, trying not to throw up.

Despite being out late though, everybody was up soon after nine. I came down, bleary-eyed, to find people getting their gear on.

"Hurry up, lad," Johnners said. "We're going out soon." He tried to make his voice as jolly as possible, but his eyes were red rimmed too.

"Really? Already?" I moaned.

"Don't worry. We won't go without you." Heather said. She had gone home after one drink at the bar and looked fresh as a daisy.

"Or me!" Faye came into the room, dressed only in a t-shirt, showing off her long legs and yawned. "But I cannot possibly go without breakfast darlings. You wouldn't want me to go hungry now would you?" She turned and licked her lips at me suggestively.

Heather rolled her eyes and I turned and ran upstairs to get my kit.

It was eleven o'clock by the time we assembled at the bottom of the slopes. Almost all of the ValSki staff were there; only the older couple, Pete and Caroline, had gone elsewhere for the day. Alice, Harri and Ash looked nervous whilst Toby and Calli tried to give them tips. Dylan and Joe, although they were also new, looked more relaxed and stood with Johnners stretching forward and backward on their skis. Faye and Claire looked elegant and feminine in their fur-trimmed gear and big sunglasses, and fussed about making sure that they had enough sun cream on. Giles had on another bobble hat and tried to jolly everyone along, but everyone ignored him. Gwat was wearing a sort of camouflaged jacket and army helmet. "Military background, eee!" he kept saying between drags on a cigarette and phlegmy-sounding coughs. Danny had on his quilted gold jacket that he wore when we had gone guiding.

I hung back with Heather, suddenly nervous.

"I bet everyone is shit-hot aren't they?"

"Don't worry," she smiled at me. "They aren't as good as you."

"So, who's up for going up the Solaise and starting with some nice gentle greens then?" Giles called out trying to bring everyone together.

"We're going over to Val Claret, and up the Motte." Danny cut over him.

"Oh, right, then. Jolly good!" Giles tried not to look put out.

"We're racing today."

It took a while to get over to the area that Danny wanted to go to, but it gave me a chance to see how everyone skied. Alice, Harri and Ash were all beginners and struggled to keep up. After about twenty minutes, Toby and Calli, who were more experienced, volunteered to take them on the blue and green runs rather than the more challenging reds.

"We'll meet you at the Tignes Cuisine for lunch," Calli said. "We'd rather just have a gentle day out here." Everyone looked relieved when they slowly picked their way across the steep red slope to the easier blue.

Dylan and Joe were also new to skiing, but they were determined to keep up with everyone else. Although their technique was terrible, they had no fear and careered round the slopes, heedless of danger. Faye and Claire had obviously learnt skiing when they were young as they had a quaint, old-fashioned style, keeping their legs close together and turning sharply using their hips and knees. Giles had also had a lot of lessons too, and was surprisingly graceful on the snow. Johnners was nowhere near as refined as Giles, but what he lacked in classical training, he made up for in speed and strength. Heather was probably better than all of them though, and I reckoned that I could probably give her a good race if it came down to it.

I had seen Danny board on the first day of guiding, and had been very impressed by him then. He looked as if he had been born with his board strapped to his feet; he turned and pirouetted with such speed and grace. Gwat was also good, but completely different; he slouched on his board, lazily flicking it round and kicking out with his legs rather than using his weight to steer.

As we sat on the chair lift up to the Motte, I found myself next to Danny.

"So what do you think of everyone then?" he asked.

"Yeah, pretty good."

"But not that good!" he grinned. "So tell me Jimmy, why do you like skiing? What is it about it that you like?"

Despite his eyes being hidden behind goggles, I could feel him looking at me intently, judging me and summing me up.

"It makes me feel superhuman." I said quickly. I had thought a lot about skiing over the summer, stuck in a boring office job, dreaming of the slopes. "When you put a pair of skis on you are able to do things that only superheroes can. You can achieve speeds you can only normally reach in cars. You can fall over forty feet and land safely. You can do back flips, twists and turns. You can jump and touch the sky. And it doesn't take much, no complicated engineering, no sophisticated machines. Just two planks of wood."

Danny nodded then reached out and gripped my arm. "And what's inside, don't forget about that. It's more important than what is on your feet. Not everyone has the guts and heart to put themselves out there. When you are up on the mountain, you find out what kind of man you really are." He paused for a moment and then added quietly. "I think we are going to get along great Jimmy."

I nodded, not quite sure what to say. In that moment, it felt like I had found a true friend. The cable car creaked gently but apart from that it was completely silent.

"Now, don't get the wrong idea about race day," he said after a moment, leaning back and breaking the spell. "It's not about racing each other, about crossing a line first, about beating everyone else. We are not racing like that."

"Well how then?" I asked confused.

"Racing is about speed. Seeing how fast you can get. Seeing how far you can push yourself. See what you can do. We are not racing against each other but against ourselves, against the slope, against the snow. Against the mountain."

"So we don't try and beat each other?"

"Well maybe a little bit," he grinned. "We self-handicap, you judge yourself when you leave. Those with the least experience go first, but it is up to you when you push off. Quite often, people go in pairs and try and beat just one person down."

"You go last I bet?"

Danny smiled. "Of course. I get to try and beat everyone. Right, we are here. One more lift, and then we are at the top. Are you ready?"

I nodded.

And then we were at the top, all lined up. Johnners, Giles, Faye, Claire, Joe, Dylan, Heather,

Gwat, Danny and I, at the lip of the slope surveying the run. The sky was a deep blue, the snow a brilliant white, the mountains marched off seemingly forever and the run ahead of us was steep and inviting. I shivered in excitement; my heart was hammering in my chest and adrenalin was pumping through my body. I was almost panting with anticipation.

"I'll count you all out. We'll meet at the bottom," Danny instructed. "Ready?" He waited a moment, and then shouted, "RACE!"

For a moment, no one moved. Then Joe and Dylan pushed off. They were good for beginners, but they had only been on the mountains for a few weeks and their lack of technique showed. Their legs were too wide apart and they both took too many turns to build up speed.

When they were about halfway down, Faye and Claire went over. Within a heartbeat it seemed they were past the boys and rounding the next corner.

"Johnners, care to race?" Giles called over.

"Class feckin' war," Johnners shouted back and with a huge heave, he was speeding down, Giles only microseconds behind.

"Eeeee!" Gwat squealed, then he was over too.

"James?" Heather asked.

"After you!" Although I wanted to beat Heather, it was Danny I really wanted to race.

"Suit yourself," she said, and then she was gone, leaving just me and Danny.

"Gonna have a go at me then big-shot?"

I nodded.

"How long you gonna' give it then?" Danny shouted. "It's not just me, it's everyone else you have to beat as well."

"How long are you?" I countered.

"Let's go together then."

I nodded, and we moved to the edge. I had the advantage of skis, which were generally quicker, but he had the experience of the mountain. It would be a fair race.

"Ready? On three, two, one..."

17

AND THEN I was falling. The most delicious, exhilarating falling I could imagine. A falling that I steered, that I controlled, that I wanted.

I could feel every contour beneath me. My knees flexed unconsciously to correct the uneven surfaces, my thighs stretched to find the best grip, my weight minutely shifted to alter my line. I hunched down in a racing stance.

Skiing without checking if the guests were behind me. Skiing without worrying about the terrain ahead. Skiing without thinking about the best route down. Just mainlining down the middle of the piste, trying to hit maximum speed.

This was the skiing I had come to the mountains for. The skiing that I lived for. The feeling of being totally free. Transcending the human body we were born with, and becoming, for maybe a tiny, magical moment, a superman, an angel, a god.

Danny had said that we were only trying to race ourselves, but something inside me could not help but want to beat him and everyone else down to the bottom. I glanced round, but could not see him. He should be nearby but I could not feel him anywhere. I glanced back. He was still silhouetted on the summit, just watching. Bastard, he had tricked me into going first. He would have the glory of being the last to leave. I would just have to make sure I made it down before him.

And beat the others who had gone beforehand.

By the third bend, Joe and Dylan were in my sights. They were going as best they could, but they were too cautious, taking the bends too wide to really pick up much speed. In a flash I was past them.

I passed the cable car station to the summit, and had to slow slightly as I went past a crowd of people just starting off. Where were the others? Surely I should be catching up on them now. The piste steepened sharply, then, as it turned a corner, levelled out into a wide motorway of a run.

I caught a flash of cerise ahead; Claire, and then just beyond her, Faye, in light blue. If I pushed it, then I could take them by the next turn. My thighs were starting to burn as the lactic acid began building up, but I ignored it and carried on.

It took two more turns before I overtook them both, giving them a wide berth. Fortunately there was plenty of space on the piste. It narrowed, turned another corner, and then dropped steeply into a valley. I recognised it from the lift up with Danny; this was the last section of the run, only a minute or so before the end of the race. If I was going to beat the others, then I would have to do it soon.

I almost did not see Gwat. He was headed in a straight line down one side of the piste going unbelievably fast for a boarder. However quick he was though, he was no match for a good skier, and I was past him in a few seconds.

There was no sign of Johnners or Giles, but Heather, dressed in grey and black, was ahead. If I could catch her, then I would be happy. My thighs were really hurting now, but there was only a few hundred metres to go. I gritted my teeth and hunkered down, the wind whipping past me.

Metre by metre, I drew closer, until we were almost level. I knew that she had seen me when she suddenly cut towards me and I had to turn sharply to avoid ploughing into some other people on the piste. My thighs shrieked in pain, and I lost a few metres, but I grinned. Heather obviously wanted to beat me as much as I wanted to beat her, the gloves were now off.

The end was only fifty metres ahead when I managed to make up the distance. We were neck-

and-neck for a moment, but just before we were past the flags that marked the end of the run, there was a flash of gold, and Danny sped past, beating us both.

A hundred metres on the flat, not far from the start of the Val Claret apartments, we skidded to a stop, and ripped our helmets off. "Fuck, Yeah!" Danny shouted.

Although I was absolutely shattered, my legs in more pain than I had imagined possible, the joy and exhilaration that flooded through me was unbelievable. I knew the others were feeling it too.

Gwat pulled up a moment later. "Eeee! Race day!" He too was smiling.

"Where the fuck did you come from?!" I asked Danny. "How on earth did you get past us?"

Danny winked. "Short cut!"

"Bastard. I thought I had you."

"Where are the others?" Heather asked, massaging her knees.

"They should be here by now," Danny said and we turned to scan the slope. "There's Faye now."

But when she arrived a moment later and took helmet off, there was no wild grin covering her features. "Johnners fell," she gasped. "Giles and Claire are with him up the slope. He's badly hurt."

18

"WHAT HAPPENED?" DANNY asked swiftly, getting his mobile phone out.

"He went off piste, hit a mogul and went over." Faye answered quickly.

"How bad?" Heather asked, also going white.

"I don't know, but he was unconscious."

"Has someone called the pisteurs?" Danny asked.

"Yes, Giles called them straight away."

"Then there is nothing we can do but wait. Fucking hell. What happened exactly?"

"They were just ahead of us," Faye said, tears beginning to well up as she remembered. "Racing each other, way too close, and being fucking idiots. Giles cut Johnners up, forcing him out wide, but there were a load of punters there that Giles had not seen. Johnners had to choose between hitting them or going off the piste. He went over, but lost control when he hit a bump and went down. Danny, he was just lying there! Not moving. He could be..." she trailed off.

"Fuck. Fucking Giles." Danny stamped off a few metres, angrily cursing, and then came back a bit calmer. "There is nothing we can do but wait here. The blood wagon will bring him down. I'd better let Jen know." He dialled and then walked away to speak to Jen.

Not knowing what had happened to Johnners was excruciating. We waited for the next thirty minutes, fear and anxiety growing within us all. Heather comforted Faye as she cried, Danny paced up and down, and even Gwat was subdued. I could not believe how quickly everything had changed; one minute we were feeling on top of the world, then next it felt like it was coming crashing down on us.

Eventually, we spotted a red sled being carefully driven down behind a skidoo, Claire, Giles, and a few pisteurs dressed in black behind. They headed towards us and a waiting ambulance that had pulled up.

"He's okay!" Claire's face was ebullient as they came to a stop.

"No I'm feckin' not!" Johnners shouted out from the blood waggon. "I didn't finish the race. Giles beat me. I'll never recover."

There was an almost palpable sigh of relief from us all. If he could joke then he was going to be alright.

"I don't think he has broken anything," Giles said. "The pisteurs got him to move everything and there was no pain. He just hit his head and passed out for a few minutes. A bit of concussion is all probably."

"I'm going to miss après though," he said glumly as the pisteurs loaded him up into the ambulance. "That's the best bit of day off."

"I'll be with you," Claire said as she got in beside him.

"Well, that was a stroke of luck," Giles said after they had gone. "He could have really hurt himself up there. Now, I'm getting a bit peckish, does anyone fancy a spot of luncheon?"

"What?" Danny turned towards him, a look of anger on his face.

"Well I thought we should go and have a bit to eat, calm the nerves, that sort of thing you know..." Giles trailed off, taken aback by his ire. When Danny replied though, it was deadly quiet.

"That was your fault up there, wasn't it Giles. You forced him off the slope, didn't you? You could not bear the thought of him beating you, could you?"

"Danny, that's not fair. We were racing. He took his chances off piste, he..."

"Just fuck off Giles. Just fuck off. No one wants you here." Danny moved in close until he was just a few inches from Giles' face. "Run back off to resort," he continued. "Go and tell Jen what happened and make plans about covering for Johnners."

Giles tried to stare him down, but he could not maintain eye contact. "Right, well, er, perhaps you are right. I should get back and let Jen know," he said as he took a step back. "Well cheerio then," he added, then quickly moved off to the lifts back to Val d'Isere.

"Idiot," Danny said quietly under his breath. But a moment later, he was all smiles. "Right, who's for some lunch? Winner buys the first round, and unless I'm mistaken, that's me."

The slower group were waiting for us at Tignes Cuisine. They already knew about Johnners; Claire had rung them from the ambulance to let them know.

"Bad luck really," Toby commiserated.

"At least it was on the mountain and not in Dicks," Heather said. "At least he is no Charlie."

"Do you think he'll be back then?" I asked.

"Johnners?" Danny answered sitting down next to me with a tray of beers. "He better be. I'll have to run his chalet whilst he's down, and I can't face doing that for long."

"I'd heard you could cook," I said taking a sip of my beer.

"Oh, I can do it all. Cook, host, guide, do the hot tub. I can do maintenance better than Gwat, isn't that right, Anthony?" Gwat nodded and gave one of his eees, but he was too busy leering at one of the waitresses to take any real notice.

"And win at racing too," I added. "I thought I had you there."

"Ah well, you've got a bit to go," he smiled at me. "But you did good up there. You've got the skill, that's for sure. You've got the guts too; not many people can commit to that speed. You just need to let go of your fear, then you'll win."

"What do you mean?" I asked taking another sip. "I didn't feel afraid up there."

"You swerved at the last minute when you didn't need to. Heather pulled out towards you and you veered off, even though your speed would have taken you past her. If there were truly no fear in you, then you would have kept your line."

"Maybe," I said, unconvinced.

"When you really lose your fear, you stop making conscious choices about how you ski, where you go, what you do. When you really lose yourself, then you are not even aware of the slope, or the snow, or even the mountain. There is no difference between you. You are the mountain, you are the snow."

I did not understand what he meant, but I nodded, mesmerised by his tone of voice.

"Did you feel it James?" he asked quietly. "Did you feel that up there?"

I nodded. Even if I didn't understand, I understood.

"I could see that you did, for a moment or two at least. It is hard to feel on the pistes though. It will never happen whilst you're with guests, maybe just once or twice when we are having days like this."

"Where? Where can I feel it again?" I asked him quietly. The memory of being an angel burned in my heart like a drug. I wanted, needed to have that feeling again.

"Back country. Out there," he gestured to the mountains. "Where the pistes end and the wilderness begins. That's where you can lose your fear. That's where you can find God."

"What's that about God?" Heather came back from the serving hatch with a portion of noodles.

"Nothing H, nothing," Danny said dismissively, and lifted his pint.

19

WHEN WE GOT back to Val later that day, there was good news. Johnners had been released from the medical centre with nothing more than mild concussion and a warning to stay off alcohol for a few days. We had a few more drinks early in the evening at one of the bars near the slopes, but did not want to leave him out, so were back in the Chamois by eight for a take-out dinner.

"Doc Al said that I should take a couple of days off," Johnners said stretching out on the settee. "Think you're gonna have to pull my shift until the end of the week Danny."

"Great!" Danny smiled sarcastically reaching for a piece of pizza. "Remind me to take you racing more often."

There was no sign of Giles, however. After his confrontation with Danny, he stayed in his room.

Over the next few days I felt myself getting used to the daily routine. Get up at eight, quick breakfast and down to the slopes to meet the punters. Depending on the weather we would take them up to one of the different ski areas, with plenty of stops for drinks and food. We would bring them back down the mountain around five, have a quick drink with them in whichever bar they liked, then back home and our work for the day was done.

I began to understand the routine outside of work too. The big nights out were Sunday after transfers and Wednesday, before day off. Staff meeting was on Saturday. Monday, Tuesday and Friday were usually pretty quiet, either recovering from nights out or getting a lot of sleep in preparation for a big one the next evening. It was a hard, unrelenting schedule, but I found that I was getting used to it, and could manage the late nights and early mornings without too much trouble.

Johnners was back working by Saturday, much to Danny's, and Giles' relief. At the staff meeting that evening, Jen gave us all a long lecture about taking risks on the slopes. We all nodded, carefully keeping straight faces, but I could see that Danny was not listening and his eyes were far away.

We got up early the next morning for transfer day and humped the bags again, then went down the mountain on the coach and picked up a new set of guests. I gave my speech on the coach, and still felt nervous, but I didn't make any mistakes.

We went out that evening, and before I knew it the bar was spinning around me, and I was so drunk I could not remember my name. I didn't remember getting home, but I got up the next morning on time, met the new set of guests and took them up the mountain with no problems.

"You're really getting the hang of things," Heather said drily, as I retched over the chairlift when no one was looking.

"Thanks," I said, between gags.

The conditions on the mountain were even worse than the previous week. There were frequent snow showers and visibility deteriorated at times until it was no more than a few feet. Strangely, I found myself enjoying it as much, if not more, than the week before. At first, I was like a punter, falling over and crashing every few metres, but after a little while, I started seeing the snow through my legs and feeling the slope through my skis and I stopped tumbling so regularly.

I tried explaining it to Heather, but she just lifted her goggles and looked at me sceptically.

"Jesus, you're starting to sound like Danny. Next it'll be, 'trust your feelings; use the force'."

I laughed at her reference. Skiing in a white-out felt very much like Luke Skywalker sparring with a battle droid whilst wearing a blindfold.

My skiing was improving though. Not only was I getting more time on the slopes and rediscovering my form, but something had changed on race day. Maybe it was feeling that moment of oneness with the mountain, maybe it was letting go of fear as Danny said, or maybe it was just increased confidence from having raced everyone down, I wasn't sure.

In the brief moments when I wasn't shepherding guests, I started pulling jumps off the side of the pistes, pirouetting on my ski tips and skiing backwards down the harder runs as Danny had done. "Will you stop showing off!" Heather scolded me after I did one particularly impressive 360 off a mogul. "You will make the guests feel bad!"

But they loved seeing me doing tricks and kept complimenting me and encouraging me to do more. Weirdly though, the more enthusiastic they were, the less I liked them. Slowly, I started to get frustrated by their lack of speed and control. Day by day, almost hour by hour, I began to understand what Danny meant about how much punters irritated him.

I was waiting for the guests by the side of the Grand Pré, a wide blue run in the Bellevarde ski area, about mid-morning on the Wednesday when I heard someone calling out my name. "Jimmy! JIMMY!" I looked up and saw Danny, Gwat and Johnners pass overhead on a chairlift.

"Yo!" I called back pleased to see them. "Where are you going?" I shouted, hoping that they might come and join me and the guests.

"Back Country!" Danny called out. "Gonna find some pow. Enjoy the punters!" His voice became fainter as they drew further away from me. I saw them get off the lift and then ski to the big mountain at the side of the run.

The guests caught up with me soon after and we skied the same gentle slope for the next hour or so, but all the time I kept glancing up at the mountain. I watched the boys as they hiked along a ridge with their boards and skis on their backs.

On our third, painfully slow, descent of the green run, I saw them reach a particular ridge and then pause, obviously contemplating the off-piste on the other side. I could only imagine what kind of couloirs, powder bowls or amazing untracked snow was waiting for them. I felt sick with jealousy. When I looked back a moment later they were all gone. It was difficult to find enthusiasm to ski for the rest of the day.

Back at the staff accommodation later, Danny and Gwat were staring intently at a laptop screen. "Come and check this out, Jimmy," Danny said without looking up. "We've just downloaded from the GoPro." I hurried round to see what was on. "Eeeeee!" Gwat said as it started playing.

At first I couldn't make out much; there was a brief shot of the mountain, then some chair lift cables, but mostly it was just the white of the slopes and the sky with occasional dots of skiers. And then surprisingly, I saw myself, a little dot of light blue, below. 'Jimmy, Jimmy' someone was calling out. I heard my response and saw my forlorn waving. 'Poor punter-stuck bastard' someone said and Danny and Gwat started laughing at the monitor.

"True!" I said joining in with them. "How did you get this though? I didn't see any of you with a camera."

"Gwat has a GoPro on his helmet," Danny explained. The footage had cut to him and Johnners walking along the ridge. "Eee!" Gwat muttered as he fiddled with the computer, "this bit's boring."

The film sped up, and the two figures moved with comical speed over the snow.

"Slow down," Danny said sharply, "we're there."

The film went back to normal speed as Danny came into close focus. *'This,'* the on-screen Danny said, grandly gesturing before him, *'is the Tour du Charvet. One big powder run all the way down to Le Manchet. If we don't get caught in an avalanche!'* The camera panned round to look out over the edge. There was quite a steep drop off from the ridge, but then an enormous bowl of untracked powder, leading all the way down to the bottom of the hill. It was so strange to see so much snow without any ski lifts, huts, piste markers or any tracks. It looked empty, serene and utterly beautiful.

'Ready Gwat?' Danny asked. A faint *'eeee'* was heard and the camera angle bobbed up and down as he was nodding. *'Right. Follow me down. This,'* he said turning to the camera, *'is going to be fucking awesome.'*

He jumped his board up to the edge, stared out ahead, took a deep breath, then turned his nose down and was gone. Gwat hurried to the edge, and pointed the camera over. *'Surprise!'* Danny was only a few feet below grinning up to the camera. *'Now it's for real,'* and with a quick turn he was racing down the hill, surfing the powder, making elegant turns and leaving behind perfect tracks. A faint whooping of excitement could be heard and Gwat's accompanying *'eee'*.

"Fucking amazing!" I said.

"Just wait until you see Johnners," Danny smiled. "That's the really amazing one."

On the screen now, Johnners was edging closer to the lip. *'Feckin' 'ell, looks a bit steep.'* he said and looked worriedly at the camera. *'I'm not really sure about going over. I'm only just getting over the concussion. I don't want to hurt myself again.'*

"Eee, get on with it. Don't be a pussy." Gwat muttered in time to his on screen commentary.

Johnners looked over the edge again. *'Right, okay. Come on Johnners! You can do it!'* he said to himself, psyching himself up. *'Here we go. Aaaaaaahhhhh!'* he cried and he launched himself over the lip.

The camera bobbed up, and there was Johnners tumbling down the steep slope in an uncontrolled heap. It was almost fifty yards before he managed to stop and then he just sunk in the powder. *'Eeeeeeeee! Wanker!'* Gwat was calling out on the screen and in the lounge all three of us burst into laughter. We watched him try to get up but however much he thrashed around, he could not right himself. Occasional *'Fecks!'* could be heard until he gave up and just sat still.

Next it was Gwat's turn. The camera jumped as he went over the edge, but soon righted itself as he blasted down the mountain. A snow covered Johnners was passed, as he gracefully swerved between Danny's tracks. Strangely, Gwat was not making his usual sound; there was just his breathing and the sound of the snow swooshing beneath the board. The sensation of being there with him as he floated through the powder was almost uncanny.

I was lost for words. "Wow," I eventually managed. "That looked..." I trailed off unable to finish the sentence.

Danny turned to me his eyes sparkling. "Incredible? Yes it is. That's where the mountain really is. That's where you can really let go of yourself. That's where you can find God. Now are you coming?"

I was about to answer in the positive, but I suddenly remembered Johnners on race day. It had been chasing that feeling that had got him into trouble. Andy's warning on the way up also rang in my head; he said something about snow sending people mad and people hurting themselves pulling stunts in the back country.

I hesitated, my heart desperately wanting to say yes, but my head urging caution. "I dunno'," I said pausing. "Won't it be dangerous? Jen said we should be careful up the mountain."

Danny paused, his eyes searching out mine. "Yes James, it will be dangerous. But it will also be beautiful and exhilarating and like nothing you have ever experienced. You might hurt yourself, but you might hurt yourself out drinking in Dicks like Charlie did. Being dangerous is not a reason you shouldn't do something, it is a reason why you should learn how to master it. If all you do is try and keep yourself safe, all you will do is nothing. Now, do you wanna come tomorrow?"

I didn't reply. I knew that he already knew my answer.

20

AFTER DINNER, DANNY, Heather and I sat at the table listening intently to the weather report on the radio. *'...and after a medium snow fall tonight it will be a blue bird powder day tomorrow, sunshine all day and no wind. Almost perfect skiing conditions folks...'*

Danny turned off the radio and whistled. "Perfect conditions," he said. "I think tomorrow we'll do the Pers."

"Col or Pointe?" Heather looked at him hopefully.

"Col of course. The avalanche risk will be too high for the Point. And besides," he paused, "neither of you are good enough yet for the Point. Not yet. No offence meant."

Heather bristled, but then sighed. "Yeah, you are probably right."

"What's the Pers?" I asked intrigued.

"I'll show you on the map," Heather answered and lifted the bas relief map of the mountains off the wall and laid it on the table. "The Pers is the mountain at the end of the Le Fornet, the highest point in the ski area," she pointed to a peak on the map. "It is where the Isere Glacier starts and the Isere river begins. On the other side of it is Italy. Can you see the border here?"

"I know it," I said picturing the massive peak that dominated the Fornet Ski area. "I didn't realise that Italy was just on the other side though."

Danny nodded, "Yeah it's nearer than you think. It is possible to walk along the ridge in the summer and cross the border."

"What about in winter?" I asked.

"I don't know anyone who has attempted it. Theoretically it is possible though..." Danny trailed off gazing into space, imagining the trek.

Heather snorted. "You would need balls of steel."

"Yeah, we won't be doing that tomorrow." Danny said suddenly, snapping back into life.

"So what will we be doing then?" I asked.

"Well the top of the last drag lift ends here," Danny picked up a pen and used it to point to the end of a black line. "We traverse across the slope, then hike up to here," he moved the pen north west until it touched the lowest part of the ridge. "Where it dips down, at the bottom of the curve that's the Col. It should take about forty minutes to climb."

"And what is the difference between the Col Pers and the Pointe Pers?" I asked.

"About twenty metres in height!" Danny laughed.

"It's a bit more than that," Heather frowned. "The Pointe Pers is a couloir, here," she took Danny's pencil and pointed towards a sort of crack in the mountain, a bit further to the East. "It's probably the hardest off-piste run in the Alps. It is a narrow gully, with jagged rocks on either side. One mistake and you smash yourself on the sides. It's so steep, that it is almost impossible to turn and control your speed."

"It's not that that makes it dangerous though," Danny said a faraway look in his eye. "Because of the way it faces and the prevailing winds, it is really susceptible to avalanches."

"Have you done it yet?" I asked him.

He shook his head and grinned. "Of course! Nailed it more times than you have had sex. Just not this season yet."

Gwat came in looking smart in a new check shirt and cap pulled down low. "Wednesday night, Gwatnight! Scandi hunting! Eeeee!"

Danny shook his head. "Sorry mate, can't do."

"What!" a look of bewilderment crossed Gwat's face. "But it's Wednesday!"

"Early start tomorrow. We are going to catch first lift tomorrow and do the Col Pers. Are you in?"

"Aww man!" he sighed, the conflict of whether to go out on the pull or get fresh tracks playing across his face.

Danny laughed. "A tough call for Tony! A choice between Gwat and powder. The diabolic decisions you have to make in a ski resort."

Eventually he reached a decision. "Eeee, one drink. One drink, I'll go for one drink!"

Danny looked amused. "He always says that, and it never is," he said to me. "Odds on that one drink turns into a bellyful and some goat in his bed."

"I'll be there tomorrow, first lift. Eeee!"

"Planning tomorrow's skiing?" Giles had come into the room. He too was dressed even more smartly than Gwat, with a proper shirt and a crease in his jeans. On his portly frame though, it just looked stiff, formal and uncomfortable.

"Yes," Danny answered shortly and crossed his arms.

"Anywhere interesting?" Giles asked solicitously, trying to make an effort to be friendly.

"Up the mountain." Danny replied, refusing to look at him. "It's all interesting there."

There was an uncomfortable pause in the room. Unable to bear it, Heather broke the silence. "We are going to do some off-piste in Le Fornet."

"Oh, really?" Giles face suddenly lit up. "I've wanted to do some of the areas up there for a while. Where are you thinking of going? The Grand Vallon?"

"Err, we haven't made up our minds yet," Heather replied.

"Well you will let me know won't you? I wouldn't want to miss out on a day up there."

"I'm not sure we can let you come," Danny sat up in his chair and finally looked at Giles. "Sorry, but we have got five people already, us four and Johnners. You know that it is not advisable to have groups larger than that because of the avalanche risk."

"Oh, right," Giles said crestfallen. "I hadn't thought of that."

"Maybe you could go up with someone else?" Heather suggested.

Giles shook his head, his disappointment obvious. "No, I don't think that there is anyone with enough experience," he sighed then tried to sound positive. "Tell you what, I'll come and find you in the morning. If one of you drops out then I will take their place," he looked at everyone hopefully but was met with blank looks.

"Yeah, maybe," Danny said sarcastically after a pause.

"Well you never know. Gwat might get lucky tonight and then he won't want to come," Giles replied.

"Maybe you'll get lucky," Heather said.

Danny snorted in amusement and Giles bridled. "I'll have you know I'm going out for a dinner date tonight," he said offended.

"A date? Really?" Danny asked. "Or are you just going to the hire shop staff dinner in the hope of talking to a girl?"

Giles looked as if he had been kicked. "Danny, why are you such a shit?" he asked quietly. Danny just shrugged smiling.

"I'll see you in the morning then," Giles said after an uncomfortable moment. "If Gwat doesn't make it, then I will make up the numbers. As you said it'll be safer if there are five of us."

We muttered goodbyes as he walked out of the door and then fell into silence.

"What was all that more than five people in a group being a greater avalanche risk?" Heather asked. "That's not true, surely?"

Danny winked, "Yeah, but he doesn't know that. There is no way that he is coming with us tomorrow, he is an arse. But," he added turning to Gwat, "that means you're coming tomorrow whatever condition you are in. Even if I have to carry you there with some naked Scandi wrapped around you."

"Scandi-gwat, naked, eee!" Gwat muttered and we all laughed, forgetting about Giles.

21

AT SEVEN-THIRTY THE next morning there was no sign of Gwat in the lounge. Danny, Johnners, Heather and I were waiting with our gear on having already breakfasted.

"Where the fuck is he?" Danny looked at the clock on the wall. "He fucking knew that he had to get up."

"Can't we just leave the lazy fecker?" Johnners asked.

"No. Giles will find out and insist on coming." Danny answered tiredly. "What a fucking let down. Gwat's a fucking prick."

"Well if he doesn't come soon then we will miss first lifts," Heather said. "Come on, let's leave him and take the chance on Giles not finding out."

Danny shook his head. "Fuck it, I'll go and get him. I know what will get him up," he added darkly and walked off.

"If we've got five minutes, then I'm going to lighten the load," I said.

Heather shook her head in disgust as I walked off.

The communal bathroom was next to Gwat's room, at the other end of the chalet to me. As I walked down the corridor, I heard Danny opening up the door to Gwat's room round the corner. "Wakey, wakey, rapey Tony. Time to get up."

"Fuckoffmate," I heard Gwat groan at him.

I didn't carry on into the bathroom, but stayed quietly in the corridor. I wanted to hear how Danny was going to persuade him to come with us.

"Time to get up, soldier!" Danny said out loud. "Time to go up the mountain."

"I ain't coming. I've not had any sleep." He tried to turn over and ignore him, but Danny was not going to be put off. I heard the bed creak and a few moments later I heard Gwat 'eee'ing with pleasure. I looked through a crack in the door and saw that Danny was sitting on the bed next to Gwat and was gently massaging his neck and shoulders.

"Come on mate. I have a special treat for you later, Tony," he said soothingly using Gwat's rarely used first name. "You know Emma the blonde masseur from Mountain Massage? She is free this afternoon and she owes me a favour. I could arrange for her to come over and give you an hour's session."

"Eee, blonde massage gwat?" came the muffled reply.

"Yes, that's right. The one that you have wanted to smash for two seasons now."

"Oh, yeah," he looked up hopefully.

"And all you have to do is come up with us now for an hour. You don't have to ski anywhere; as soon as we hit Le Fornet you can come back down again. I need you there to stop Giles coming with us."

"Eee!" he thought for a moment, weighing it up. He raised himself up on his arms, then had a dizzy spell and collapsed back on the bed. "Ah, I can't mate, I'm too fuck..."

He never finished his sentence. Danny's gentle touch rubbing his shoulder suddenly turned into a vice like grip around the back of his neck, forcing his head into the pillow. He climbed over and put his knee onto his spine pushing him further into the mattress.

"Now listen to me you dirty little perverted shit." Danny hissed at him through gritted teeth. You are coming up the mountain now, drunk, hung over or fucking black and blue. Do you understand?" The change in Danny's attitude was remarkable.

Gwat started struggling and I heard him shout "Fuck off!" but the sound was muffled in the pillow and Danny held him fast.

"Fucking little animal. Pipe down now or I swear to God I will fucking destroy you!" Danny hissed in his ear. Gwat struggled for a few moments more, but whatever grip Danny had on must have been painful because he suddenly stopped moving and stayed still.

"How fucking dare you defy me, how fucking dare you? I fucking own you, you fucking goat, don't ever forget it." Danny was speaking quietly but there was a menace to his voice that made me shiver. "Do I have to fucking spell it out exactly what I can do to you if you ever cross me? Do you know what would happen if I spilt any of your dirty little secrets? Do you?!"

A sort of half whimper came out of Gwat's mouth.

"Yes, I think you do," Danny said savagely. "Now, I'm going to get up in a second. I expect you in the lounge, dressed and ready to go in less than five minutes." He leaned in close to Gwat. "Do I make myself clear? You piece of shit."

As Gwat murmured his assent I quickly backtracked down the corridor and into the bathroom, making sure that Danny didn't hear me. I was pretty disturbed about seeing such an unexpectedly vicious side to Danny and didn't want it turned on me. I waited a couple of heartbeats before flushing the toilet.

Back in the lounge, Heather and Johnners were still waiting. "Good shit?" Johnners asked.

"Charming!" Danny said smiling as he strode in through the door. "Gwat will be here in a few minutes. He is sorry for keeping us waiting." He was calm and relaxed, with no trace of the anger or violence that had so frightened both Gwat and I a few moments before. If I hadn't seen it for my own eyes, I would not have believed them to be the same person.

"How did you do it?" Heather asked.

"What do you mean?" Danny asked innocently.

"How did you get him off the naked Scandi girl in there?"

"Ha, ha!" Danny laughed. "I think he must have had a poor night gwat hunting. He was alone."

At that moment, Giles came in, also dressed up for skiing. "Thought I might get first lifts with you guys!" he said brightly. "You know, make the first tracks and all that!"

"We're waiting for Gwat," Danny said flatly.

"Are you sure he is coming?" Giles asked. "He didn't get in until about five. I know because he woke me up crashing around."

"Yes, I'm coming." Gwat came barging in through the door, pulling up his ski trousers, lurching unsteadily on his feet. He looked more drunk than hung over; his clothes were not tucked in and his hair was ruffled and straggly. Stubble covered his face and his eyes seemed to wander round independently of each other. He stank of booze.

"Are you sure you should be going?" Giles asked him.

"Powder, off-piste, back country," he muttered, but his accompanying 'eee' lacked conviction.

"Have you all got the right kit?" Giles asked me suddenly. "Have you got a pack with a bleeper shovel and probe? I'm afraid it's compulsory to have a set with you at all times. I can't let you go out otherwise."

I panicked. I didn't have any of those items but Danny came to the rescue.

"Yes," he said. "James is borrowing my spare pair. Johnners and Gwat have their own, and Heather is borrowing one from Snowberry, aren't you?"

"Umm, yes!" Heather answered surprised.

"Right, err, okay then." Giles shoulders slumped as he realised that he could not stop us going. "I will see you later. Have a good day," and he waddled out in his ski gear.

"So no Scandigwat for you last night then?" Johnners said to Gwat when he had gone.

"Eee, pulled one, but she wouldn't come home with me," his eyes lit up at the memory. "Grade A Gwat, got her phone number, eee!" he winked at me.

Heather shook her head, Johnners rolled his eyes but Danny smiled. "Tell us about it on the lifts, mate. We will have plenty of time for that." There was no trace of the Mr Hyde that he had been a few minutes before.

22

ALTHOUGH IT WAS clear blue sky outside, it was very cold. I could feel the air bite at my exposed skin. "What temperature do you reckon it is out here?" I asked as we trudged down the hill to the main road. Gwat was a few paces behind, dragging his snow board dejectedly.

Danny sniffed. "Minus ten maybe, minus twelve? My nose hairs start freezing at about minus fifteen, and we're not quite there yet."

"What do you think it will be on the top?"

"Minus twenty I expect. It may feel colder though because of the wind chill." Johnners answered this time.

"Do you think I should get another layer?" I asked a bit nervously. I really didn't want to get cold.

"No, you'll be alright," Danny looked at me smiling. "Messing about off piste is hard work. You'll keep warm don't worry. Look the bus is there, let's try and catch it." We jogged down to the road and just managed to stop it as it was pulling out.

On the bus, Danny Johnners and I sat together, with Heather in front, and Gwat sprawled out on the other side of the aisle, possibly unconscious. As we pulled away Danny swung a pack off his shoulder. "Right, listen up fella," he said to me unzipping the bag. "Have you used an avalanche kit before?"

I nodded. "Yes, I had some training a few years ago when I was just starting off."

Danny grinned. "Well, fingers crossed and touch wood," he reached over and patted Gwat's crotch, "we won't have to use it, but I'll go over it all just in case. Is that alright?"

I nodded again. "Yeah, sure. Pretend I know nothing, safer that way." I was pretty sure I knew it all, but it never hurt to be reminded how to use the kit.

"Now this," Danny said taking out a small plastic box with several straps coming off it, "is a transceiver. Mine is already strapped on under my jacket," he patted his stomach. "They send out little electronic pulses like a beacon, so if you are swept away and buried, you can be located under the snow. If I turn mine onto scan mode," he opened his jacket and twisted a dial on it, "you can hear how it works." A continuous stream of sharp little electronic beeps came out of the box. "Obviously it's very close now so the beeps are close to each other. If you move further away," he moved my box further away, "they slow down. It's pretty straightforward to find roughly where someone is buried. Now take your jacket off and I'll strap it on for you." I did as I was told and he tied the small box under my chest.

"Next is the probe," Danny undid a drawstring on a small pouch and extracted a small bundle of rods. "These are attached by an elastic string, and they snap together to form one long pole like this," he demonstrated joining the rods together until he had a slender wand of about two metres. "Once you have found the area where someone is buried, poke this in the ground until you hit something solid."

I nodded again. "I know the next bit. Then you start to dig."

Danny smiled. "Yeah, you got it!" he said, pulling out a small plastic spade with a detachable handle. "Item number three, the shovel."

"Makes a right good sledge as well!" Johnners added nodding.

"But look," Danny said seriously, "if you get caught in a big slab avalanche, even with the best kit, the chances of getting out unharmed are not great. All this," he gestured at the kit, "is an insurance that you don't want to use. The best way to survive is not to take any risks."

"Surely going off piste is going to be risky anywhere?" I asked.

"Well yes," Danny nodded, "but there are some places that will be a lot chancier than others. Today it's a risk three out of five on the European scale, but that does not mean that it will be the same everywhere. Some places it will be less and some places more."

"How do you know if an area is at high risk from avalanching then?" I asked.

"Well there are a number of factors that make it more risky," Danny sat back and crossed his legs and counted off on his fingers. "Steepness of the terrain, whether it is facing the sun or not, if there has been a big dump of snow the night before, if there have been sudden changes of temperature, if there has been a lot of wind throwing the snow around..." he leaned forward. "It takes years to know how to judge the mountains, what they are going to do, how they are going to treat you. Sometimes I think that they're alive, that they have characters or personalities. Sometimes they are generous and kind, but sometimes," he paused and carried on in a whisper, "they will play you. If you don't respect the mountain, then it will take you down."

I shivered; there was something in his tone that spooked me. I knew what he meant about the mountains being alive; sometimes it seemed to me that they loomed over the valley like sentinels, watching over us like gods. Who knew what they were thinking, whether they meant us well or not, or even if they were aware of us? Did they want us here in their untouched realm at all...?

"Ah, sharrup," Johnners laughed, breaking the silence. "Watch out for Danny, he gets poetic about the hill sometimes. There are a few simple tips to follow, and you'll be fine mate."

Danny sat back again and smiled. "Johnners has no imagination either," he said. "Tell him the rules though. It will help him respect the mountain."

Johnners pulled a face at him before turning to me. "So the basic rules are; don't ski areas where there have already been avalanches, don't ski if there are big cracks in the snow or you can hear it moving, don't ski if there are sudden temperature changes, ski one at a time, keep to the low snow areas such as the ridges or trees and keep your speed up."

"Oh, er, I think I've got that," I said, having hardly listened at all. My mind was still thinking of the mountain spirits. I looked up and saw Danny staring at me intently.

"You don't really have to know shit though," Heather leaned back from seat in front and addressed me directly. "We all do what Danny says. He knows the mountains as good as anyone in the resort and knows how to keep safe. And find the pow."

The bus pulled up by the side of the slopes. Danny winked at me as he stood up. "Yup, big 'ole powder day today. I think the mountain is going to be good to us!"

As we clattered towards the exits I tried to shake off the feeling of unease that had started to grow in my stomach. On the way up the mountain, Andy had muttered something about the mountains being haunted too. Was it true? Were there spirits? Was it haunted? Would they take us down? Or was this why Danny felt it was where he could lose his fear and get close to God?

Despite Johnners' dismissal, I could not help but feel a real sense of foreboding.

23

THE BUS HAD taken us all the way to the last stop in Le Fornet, literally the end of the valley. There were a few scattered chalets, a restaurant and the cable car building, but that was all. The sides of the valley were much closer here, making it feel more intimate and nearer to the wilderness than Val town, and if anything, more intimidating. However, the air was crisp and clear, the sky an intense blue and the sun bright overhead. It was a beautiful day. I shook my head and tried to banish the thoughts about the mountains.

Danny strode over towards the téléphérique cable car whistling, looking at his watch. "Five to nine. We've made first lift!"

"Hoo fucking rah," Gwat muttered sarcastically as he stumbled after him, pausing outside the door to retch, hawk up and spit something foul into the snow.

"Ah well Gwat, sooner up, sooner down. Look at it like that." Danny said smiling. He seemed in excellent spirits again.

"And better out than in!" Gwat stood up wiping his mouth.

The cable car was an old-fashioned gondola, capable of carrying about fifty or so people up the mountain. Only a few dedicated skiers and some of the workers in the restaurant at the top had made it for the first lift though. We filed in and stood by the window as it juddered, and then slowly started to rise, rocking and swaying.

Once we set off, Danny motioned me over to the window where he was standing, away from the others. "I meant what I said about the mountains being alive," he said quietly. The jauntiness he had exhibited outside the cable car was gone and replaced with the intensity he had shown in the bus. I nodded uncertainly.

"They fucking are you know," he stared at me unsure if I was agreeing with him or not. "I know that you can feel it too, I've seen the look in your eye." I nodded, not quite sure what he expected me to say.

"They are there, watching us, all the time. If you treat them with the respect and awe that they deserve, then they will reward you. If you don't..."

He paused, shrugged and left the sentence hanging. There was a strange light in his eyes that was at once extremely magnetic but also difficult to look at. The foreboding in my stomach was turning to dread.

"You really like it here don't you?" I asked trying to change the subject.

He smiled at me briefly. "Yes," he said simply. "It is my life, I don't know any other. I have everything that I need or want here. I'll never leave."

I turned away to look at the view. There was something fanatical about how he spoke that had really begun to scare me.

At the top of the cable car, we caught a smaller bubble lift and then skied down to a chair lift. At the top of that one, we caught a drag lift to the very top of the ski area. I had only been up there a couple of times with the guests, but it was probably my favourite place in the whole of the Espace Killy. Today, it was even more peaceful as there was no one but the lifties in sight. I felt my spirits start to rise; the enormous expanse of white under the unending blue sky was so beautiful that it banished all negative thoughts.

"Did you see all of that lovely pow' off the side?" Heather groaned as the boys clipped their boards on. "It looked amazing. I bet it will be tracked out by the time we get back."

"Don't worry," Danny said, standing up and pulling his goggles over his helmet. "Where we are going it's unbelievable. Right, you ready?" he looked round at us all and we all nodded, even Gwat, who was looking a bit perkier now. "We are headed to that ridge over there," he pointed over to a line of peaks off to our right. "Do you see where they dip in the middle? That is the Col Pers. The peak off to the right," he gestured to a large finger of rock sticking straight up, "is the Pointe. On the other side is the biggest powder bowl you will ever see. Come on, let's go." And he sped off down the run, the others quickly following. I grinned beneath my helmet and pushed off after him.

The walk to the Col was pretty hard going. Heather, Johnners and I were able to attach skins to our skis, basically a pad of little bristles that stopped the skis going backwards, and use them as snow shoes but Danny and Gwat had to take off their snowboards and walk in their boots, often sinking up to their thighs in the powder. Before we were halfway up I was exhausted, but Gwat looked like he was about to expire. His face was an ashen green colour and covered with a thin film of sweat. "Eee, eee, eee," he panted softly, every few steps.

The last section was steep. Danny pushed on ahead, climbed up the almost vertical last six feet and then hauled us and our skis up one by one. We all collapsed on the ridge, gasping for breath, Gwat was retching he was so tired. Only Danny seemed unaffected by the effort. He swung off his rucksack, pulled out four juice concentrate pouches and tossed one to each of us.

"It gets easier from here, I promise you," he said.

I opened the pouch and gratefully sucked at the sugary sweetness inside. Almost magically, I could feel it revitalising me and bringing energy back to my arms and legs. In a few moments I was able to sit up and take stock of where I was.

The ridge, or col, was a good four or five metres wide, gently sloping up to peaks on the left and right. Running down the middle of it was a low fence to mark the end of the patrolled ski area and a board with some warnings about the dangers of off-piste skiing. Danny was on the other side of this, staring silently ahead. I took one last look at the safe, secure and boring landscape of lifts, pistes and security behind us, and went to join him. As I stood by his side, I too was struck dumb.

The ridge of mountains extended in a wide arc off to the right, the peaks getting progressively higher. Snow still stubbornly clung to most of them, but at the top the rocks stood bare and harsh. An almost vertical slope dropped down from where we stood to an untouched valley of snow that descended in a gentle gradient for almost a kilometre and then dipped out of sight.

It was absolutely perfect, but it was not the view that was so arresting. It was the absolute stillness and silence that pervaded the valley, an emptiness that was almost spiritual. It was a lifeless and deadly place, but I suddenly knew what Danny meant when he said that the mountains were alive, I could feel their presence too. This was indeed a place where you could touch God. We stood together in a shared communion, awestruck.

At that moment I felt a tremendous kinship with Danny, a true understanding of what bought him back year after year. "You feel it, don't you?" he whispered, still looking straight ahead. He didn't need to explain; I knew exactly what he was feeling.

"Yes Danny, I do." I answered, also staring straight ahead and at that moment I knew that I would stay forever too.

Predictably it was Gwat who broke the spell. "Eeeeeee! Powder run! Eeeeee!" He had come up behind us and was looking out ahead too. I guessed that he had felt the intensity too and expressed it in the only way that he knew how.

"Yes Anthony!" Danny turned round smiling. "A powder run indeed. Now get your GoPro on, and let's start."

24

WE RETURNED TO Heather and Johnners who were now stood up and checking each other's gear. Heather looked up as we approached. "So Danny, which one is the Pointe Pers then?"

Danny pointed to the ridge on the other side of the bowl. "You see that big peak over there? That's the Pointe."

I looked over to where he was indicating. It was a narrow ledge, not that much higher than where we stood, but it looked perilous to get to.

"How do you get to that then?" Johnners asked.

"Climb along this ridge as far as you can, traverse across the bowl, then climb some more. You can't see the Pointe Pers couloir from here, but it makes this look like a punter's run."

"What else is over there? What's past that?" Johnners asked. "Are there any other runs?"

"No, not exactly." Danny answered with a dreamy look in his eye. "But if anything that makes it better because nobody goes there. There is another col to cross, and if you can climb up to the peak past that, then you can ski down into Italy. One day I'll do that."

Johnners snorted. "No feckin' way mate. Way too dangerous."

"We'll see," Danny said simply, and then he grinned. "But that's for another time. Today's run will be exciting enough. You ready?"

A 'Hell Yeah!' from me and Heather, an 'Eee' from Gwat but only a nod from Johnners. I realised that despite the off-piste run that he had done the day before, he was quite nervous. "Are you alright mate?" I asked him quietly as everyone else moved off to the edge.

He gulped and nodded. "Yeah, I'm fine. It's just I don't want to knock myself out again. I was putting on a brave face in front of everyone when I was in the blood waggon last week, but actually I was terrified. Going down the hill in the sled was one of the scariest things, not knowing where I was or what was wrong with me. I didn't know if I would have to go back home. Besides, I don't like the big drops and I'm terrified of getting caught in an avalanche. They showed us some videos at the beginning of the season and it freaked me right out. Drowning in a sea of snow is not how I want to go." I nodded, I could understand his fears. I too had seen some documentaries and the big avalanches looked terrifying. Unsure what to say though, I just reached out and patted his arm.

Ahead, Danny, Heather and Gwat were peering over the lip of the ridge. "You can sidestep down the steep bit if you are nervous, or you can just go for it," Danny was saying. "Gwat, do you want to go first so you can film us? Head off to the right, over to that ridge out of the avalanche fall line."

Gwat nodded and moved forward in small jumps. He didn't pause long at the edge, just a quick look round at us, a salutary 'eee' and then he was gone, bouncing effortlessly down the steep part of the slope and carving perfect turns in the powder. He came to rest a couple of hundred metres down the slope and turned round to watch us.

"Heather, you're next. Side step or jump?"

"Fuck it," she said as she stood at the edge, and then pushed herself off. I thought for a minute she was going to stack it as she missed a turn and came close to losing her balance, but the steep gradient of the slope came to her aid and she was able to right herself by using her momentum and carry on. She too came to rest a few metres from Gwat.

"Johnners?" Danny asked.

"No feckin' way!" Johnners harrumphed. "I'm side-stepping it down." He carefully edged his way down for about twenty metres before he turned his tips down the slope and sped off. His turns in the powder were perfect.

"How about you?" Danny turned to me, a look of challenge in his eye. I met his gaze full on.

"Watch me," I said with a bravery I did not feel. I took a deep breath and heaved myself off the edge.

For a moment I was weightless in the air, a magical timeless moment, a moment where once again I felt like an angel. Then my skis hit the powder and I was turning into the snow, clumsily at first on the steep section, but then with more control as the slope became gentler. I had to lean a long way back to keep my skis up, and almost immediately I felt my thighs burning in response, but it was an incredible sensation like floating across a cloud.

I was vaguely aware of a shout of elation ringing in my ears as I swept down and realised that it was coming from my own lips. Gwat, Heather and Johnners, three distant dots when I started quickly grew larger and larger as I coasted towards them, and I could hear their shouts and cheers mingling with mine. I came to rest before them still whooping and hollering whilst they stood and grinned at me. It took me a few moments to calm down and get my heartbeat back to normal.

"Ey' up," Johnners said after a few moments, "Danny's coming. Shit, what's he doing?"

I turned to look back up the slope. Danny was on the edge of the lip bouncing from end to end on his board to get some momentum before going over. "Silly fool!" Johnners muttered. "He should know better. That lip is pretty much fresh snowfall. It could give..."

I had started to say something about having a bad feeling, but at the very moment when Johnners said 'give', the section of snow that Danny was standing on just by the lip of the ridge sheared off and plunged down the slope. Danny disappeared as a cloud of snow was thrown up.

"Feckin' 'ell!"

"Oh my God!"

"Jesus!"

"Danny!"

We all cried out as the avalanche tumbled down the slope towards us. Gwat had chosen a good spot to stop, well out of the path of a potential slide so we were safe. Unlike Danny who was somewhere in its midst of the maelstrom. We watched in horror, unable to do anything to help.

But then miraculously, there he was, surfing out of the cloud of snow towards us. It looked almost as if he was being chased by a white wave. A swirling fist of ice seemed to try and reach out towards him, but he kept ahead of its deadly grasp. The storm coiled, as if it was going to try one last time to reach him, but then it collapsed in on itself, stalled and came to a rest.

Danny sped towards us. "Fucking hell!" he gasped as he came to a stop. "Fucking hell, fucking hell," he repeated again. We stood dumbstruck unable to say anything.

"Are you alright?" I eventually asked rather pointlessly.

He looked up at me. "Hang on, I'll check," he said. "Arms, check. Legs check. Head, check. Board, check." He grinned at me. "Looks like I'm all here. Yes mate. I'm alright."

"What happened?" Heather asked.

"The shelf just gave way. Fortunately it didn't cause a big slide; otherwise I would have been fucked."

I looked back up the slope. Now that the snow cloud was clearing I could see that it was probably not an avalanche at all, just a small lip of compacted snow throwing up a larger amount of the softer powder below. It looked worse than it was.

"Lucky, lucky," I said.

Danny nodded, and then looked suddenly confused and vulnerable. "I don't know how that happened. I've never slipped up like that before, never made a mistake. I can't believe that it happened. I can't believe that the mountain..." He trailed off staring disconsolately up at the slope. I realised that he was, perhaps for the first time, realising that he was not indestructible. Or perhaps realising that the mountains might not be as precious of him as he was of them.

A heartbeat later Johnners shouted "Ya feckin' nob!" and launched himself at Danny.

"Whaaa," Danny had time to shout before Johnners was on him and wrestling him over.

"Had me right fucking scared, ya bastard!" They started laughing as they both got buried in the powder. Eventually they stopped exhausted.

"Well, that was a start to the day." Danny grinned up at us, his deep thoughts about the mountain forgotten. "But do you know what best part about it is?"

We all looked at him bemused.

"We've still got all that powder ahead of us on the run down to the bridge. It's still all there. We're not going to let a little 'lanche like that put us off are we now? Come on, it's still going to be a great day."

25

THE POWDER BOWL levelled out and then dropped off to the left in gentle rolls. Danny showed no signs of the fall bothering him; he set off at a good pace and bounced through snow, pulling some neat tricks, spinning on the end of his board, equally comfortable riding switch and normal.

We took it in turns to follow him down, and pretty soon, the memory of the avalanche melted away as we too floated in the incredible powder. We jumped over little bumps, sped across small ravines and then, when we hit the tree line, slalomed through the frozen woods. The snow felt sensational beneath my skis, and I felt a huge grin plastering my face beneath my helmet.

The run finished by crossing an old stone bridge, still well above Le Fornet where we had started, and then a long *schuss* along a road back to where the bus dropped us off. When we finally stopped, I realised I was absolutely exhausted. Turning in the deep powder was an amazing experience, but very draining. I knew too that the scare up by the Col had taken more out of me than I cared to admit.

"Who's up for another run then?" Danny asked. One by one we all shook our heads.

"Really?" Danny said frowning. "The conditions are perfect. We will not get another day like it this season. I think we should go again."

"Did you not learn anything up there?" Heather said incredulously. "Sometimes you got to give it a rest Danny!"

"Yeah mate," Johnners said shaking his head. "I don't think I could take another run like that."

"Suit yourself then," Danny said after a moment. "But I'm going back up."

"You can't, not by yourself," Johnners said quickly.

"Just you fucking watch me," he said quietly.

"Danny, you..." Heather began, but she didn't get a chance to finish. Danny's mobile went off.

"Yes?" he answered, then listened intently for a few minutes. "Okay then. We're on our way back then."

"What's happened?" Gwat asked.

"Shit. Bad shit," he answered grimly.

When we got back to the Chamois, Joe was pacing round the living room like a caged lion, obviously very upset. "What's the matter mate?" Danny asked.

"It's Dylan. Fucking stupid idiot!" His south London accent had broadened in his anger. He kicked the sofa, and then carried on pacing up and down.

"Whoa fella, what's going on?" Danny moved over and held him by the shoulders.

"Dylan. He's been stealing. Jen was suspicious so she checked our room and she found a whole stash of other people's stuff. You know Toby lost those goggles a few weeks ago, well they were in there, as well as Harri's watch."

"Shit," Danny sat down. "That's bad."

"What the fuck!" Heather said angrily. "You're saying he's been stealing from us?"

"It gets worse. Jen then checked the honesty bar float. It's down about five hundred Euros. It looks like he has been at that too."

"Feckin' hell!" Johnners whistled. "Where is he now?"

"He's been in with Slasher and Giles since about ten."

"What a fucking idiot." Heather shook his head. "You worked with him and shared a room. Didn't you realise what was going on?"

Joe shook his head. "No, not at all. Oh I know he was pretty brassic, and would sweep for drinks when we were out, but I would never have thought that he would steal. I mean, he borrowed money from the bar once or twice, but he always paid it back on tip day. I just can't believe that he would steal from us. He was a mate, know what I mean?"

Danny shrugged. "You never can tell with some people. If he has been stealing then he's got what's coming to him."

We hung around in the living room, drinking tea and waiting, whilst people drifted in from skiing and were told the news. Some reacted with anger, some with confusion, and some were upset. Dylan was a popular member of staff and no one could really believe what had happened.

About five o'clock, Dylan came in with Giles, his face pale and downcast. Joe marched straight up to him.

"Mate, what the fuck have you been up to?" he demanded.

"Whoa!" Giles said, placing his hand on Joe's chest. "Let him be. We've come to pack up his stuff and then he's leaving."

"What do you mean leaving?" Joe asked angrily.

Dylan raised his head up. He looked terrible; underneath his goatee his face was white and his eyes were puffy and red. He had obviously had a hard morning.

"I didn't do it," he said simply. "I didn't do it."

"Guilty or not," Giles said stiffly, "Jen has decided to dismiss him and booked him a flight home. We've come to pack his stuff. Come on, we haven't got long. Joe, can you come with us please. We need to make sure that he takes everything of his."

"And nothing that isn't his!" Danny added when they had left the room.

Although we were exhausted, Danny, Gwat, Johnners, Heather, myself and Joe made it to the Danois that evening, and glumly sat around with a few pints.

"Do you think he did it then?" Johnners asked Joe.

"I don't know mate," Joe shook his head. "I just can't believe he would do something like that."

"The evidence is pretty strong," Danny said. "The goggles, watch and Ash's ring all hidden in his room. Not to mention all the change from the honesty bar in his bag."

"Why didn't I twig though?" Joe put his head in his hands. "I should have realised what he was up to. I knew that he had debts back home, but I never thought that he would steal."

"Maybe he's one of those, whaddya call them, klep something?" Johnners struggled for the word.

"Kleptomaniac?" I suggested.

"Yeah, that's it. They can be cunning as hell."

"Stealing, eee!" was Gwat's helpful comment.

"It's not your fault," Danny put his arm around Joe's shoulder. "He obviously had a problem. You are not responsible for him."

"I just can't forget the look he gave me when he was leaving," Joe said as if he hadn't heard Danny. "He just kept repeating, 'I didn't do it'."

I looked at Joe. His round chubby face, normally lively and animated, was ashen grey. He was really upset about the possibility of his roommate, workmate and friend stealing. Or was Dylan innocent? Something started nagging at the back of my mind but I could not put my finger on it.

"Well whatever," Danny said draining his pint. "I nearly died today and that kind of puts it in perspective. He hasn't been taken to the gendarmes, he hasn't been arrested, and he hasn't got a criminal record. He just gets to start the rest of his life a couple of months before everyone else here fucks off."

"What are you talking about?" Heather asked him.

"I get a bit fed up with these young kids coming out for a season," Danny signalled to the barman for another pint. "Five months having the time of their life here and then they go back and become lawyers or management consultants or whatever the fuck they do with their shitty lives and forget about Val and forget about us. I'm sick and tired of looking out for them and looking after them. I've only got so much sympathy in me and I'm not going to waste it on people who aren't going to hang around."

"Aww nah mate," Johnners remonstrated with him. "It's not really like that. Most of us aren't like that."

"Aren't you? Are you sure?" The waitress bought over another pint and Danny started chugging it back. "Are you going to hang around Johnners? Are you going to stay? Or are you just another of those with no soul and no commitment?" He turned to me. "What about you, Jimmy? Are you gonna be one of the important people or are you just going to abandon it all too? I haven't got time for people who can't commit."

"That's not fair Danny," Joe began. "It's not..." but Danny interrupted him.

"And you can shut the fuck up, sink bitch. When you've done a few years here then you get the right to talk back to me. Until then, pipe down." Joe crumpled like a paper bag and sat back.

Heather looked at him intently. "It's got to you, hasn't it? The avalanche today. You're frightened."

Danny tipped back his pint. "We should all be frightened, H. We should be frightened if we do take the risks and go over the back of the mountain to who knows what and we should be frightened of the life that we lead if we don't. I know which choice I will make, what will you?" He stood up swaying slightly. "Now's the time to decide, Heather. When the shit falls, what will you choose? Who will you choose? Are you with me?"

"I don't understand," she said.

"I'm leaving. I'm sick of hanging round with first-timers. Are you coming with me?" I could sense immediately what Danny was offering her. This was her chance to get with the most desirable man in Val d'Isere, a man she had wanted since she had met him. I felt sick as I realised that there was only one person she would choose.

"Don't go," I whispered, but I knew that she would not hear me.

Heather turned to look at me. I suddenly felt so miserable that I could not even meet her gaze.

And then miraculously, I felt her hand steal into mine.

"No Danny. I'm not coming."

"Suit yourself," he said, and then turned abruptly and walked away. Heather's grip tightened on my own.

We all looked at each other for a moment then Gwat got up. "I'm going," he said. "They'll always be more gwat around Danny," and he followed him out.

"What the fuck was all that about?" I asked out loud to no one in particular when they were gone. Heather shrugged and I felt her hand slip out of mine.

"That was out of order." Joe shook his head. "I can't believe he went off at me like that. It was well out of order."

Johnners drained his pint. "Heather was right, too much emotion today. I think he was just scared about the avalanche. Look, I better go with him. He shouldn't be by himself and Gwat isn't fit to look after him." He got up. "Joe, he didn't mean what he said."

"Whatever," Joe said tiredly. "I don't really give a shit." But it was obvious he did.

Back at the staff accommodation as we were climbing the stairs to go to bed, Heather put her hand on my arm. "I don't want to be alone tonight."

"Neither do I," I replied.

26

IT WAS DIFFICULT to believe that things would carry on as before but they did. The next day Heather and I got up and went ski guiding as normal and none of the guests asked about Dylan. One of them mentioned that Danny had come in to help Joe make breakfast, so they must have made up, but that was about it. We didn't really talk in the evening either; Danny was subdued and did not say anything and no one seemed to want to rake over the events of the day before.

The next day went smoothly too but again the guests did not mention Dylan and neither did we. We skied under brilliant blue skies but I could not enjoy myself. The fact that the guests did not miss Dylan really bugged me; he had worked his guts out for them and they had not even noticed he was gone. I kept professional but I knew that I would not be able to get close to them. I began to realise that Danny was right; not only was there a divide between guests and staff that could and should never really be crossed, they were also intensely irritating. Guests were becoming punters for me and nothing more.

If I was honest though, part of my bad mood was also down to Heather. After another night together, she seemed to pretend that nothing had happened again. Given her reaction last time, I decided not to raise it with her, but I felt confused and hurt by her attitude towards me. Some of the time she seemed to want me, but the rest of the time it was as if I was nothing. I just couldn't work her out.

As I left the guests in the Blue Note bar, happily knocking back beers, I realised it was staff meeting day. I had been looking forward to getting home and spending some time by myself, but that was going to be delayed. At least, I thought to myself, Jen or Giles would have to acknowledge Dylan's absence then.

Jen did, but it was pretty perfunctory. She said that 'due to certain allegations, Dylan had decided to go home,' and asked us not to discuss it with any guests. No one really believed it had been his choice, but although a few people looked uncomfortable and Joe hid his face, no one said anything. It was as if all the staff were trying to erase him from their minds and pretend that he had not been there at all. Whether he was guilty or not, I couldn't believe that everyone was so heartless.

Giles again asked us to be there at the chalets by six-thirty for transfer day, but this time even Danny could not be bothered to argue. He just muttered "whatever," and gritted his teeth.

Transfer day was long and hard but there were no problems. All the guests got on their flights home, happy, contented and completely unaware that it had been such a turbulent few days for ValSki. The next guests were all happy and excited, and although on the outside I was able to be positive, I still felt really bad about what had happened to Dylan.

I was also getting a bit unnerved about the fact that no one wanted to talk about him. It seemed wrong to pretend that nothing changed and he had never been here. Whilst Heather and Gwat were getting a second round of drinks in at the bar a bit later, I finally spoke about it to Danny.

"I can't believe that Dylan's gone," I said unable to phrase exactly what I was feeling.

Danny shrugged. "He was just another cook. There are loads of them around. He's no big loss really."

"I thought you liked him?" I asked, surprised at his attitude.

"He was too cocky; thought he knew it all and walked round the place like he owned it. Just because he knows what a fucking steak tartar is, doesn't make him King of the Fucking Castle."

"But if he didn't take any of those things then it's wrong for him to be sent home." I persisted.

"What's your problem?" Danny put his drink down and stared at me. I could feel myself wilting under his powerful gaze. "As well as all the stuff in his room, Jen found the same amount of money that was missing from the Honesty Bar in his bag. He's guilty all right. Look," he said gently and came over and put his hand on my shoulder, "we're all upset about him going. It is never very nice when someone has to go home, it makes you feel shit, but it does happen from time to time.

"It's at these moments that we have to pull together, to stand by each other, and help each other out. I've seen this before and if we don't stick together then it will start going downhill for all of us. Are you with me?"

"I suppose so," I said quietly. "I just feel bad that no one is talking about him."

"Yes, I can understand that," Danny replied. "But trust me; we have to concentrate on the people that are left. There is no point crying over the ones that don't make it."

"I'll tell you what we'll do," Heather and Gwat had come back with a tray of drinks, "let's have these drinks for Dylan, guilty or innocent, and then forget about him. We can't mourn him forever."

Heather nodded. "You are right." She picked up her glass. "To Dylan, guilty or innocent, he will be missed."

"Dylan," Danny clinked her glass solemnly. "Guilty or innocent."

"Eee," Gwat said, but clinked glasses.

I really didn't think that I would be able to forget about him with just the toast of a five-euro drink, it seemed so dismissive. Besides, there was something still bothering me about the whole affair that I still could not put my finger on.

"James," Heather prompted me quietly.

I picked up my drink. "To Dylan if guilty, and if not, then may the real culprit get fucked."

We all clinked glass and downed them, but I noticed Danny was staring at me coldly. I shivered, the memory of him leaning over Gwat in his bed in my head. Whatever I felt about Dylan going, I did not want to get on the wrong side of Danny.

"Now that's over," Danny said eventually, "let's get really fucked. Matt," he called over to the barman, "four more Jaeger bombs."

The drinks kept coming, the music was turned up, one by one the hosts trickled in and pretty soon we were getting drunk with the same abandonment as we had the week before. Transfer day frenzy had begun.

27

AFTER A WHILE we moved to the Saloon bar for jugs of cocktails and they soon started to take effect. Everybody began dancing, fighting and kissing again as if the world was about to end. Gwat got talking to a girl who pretty soon was swaying round completely out of it. Danny and Joe got into an argument with some drivers from another holiday company and had to be pulled apart. Johnners and Claire paired off and started snogging in a corner.

I saw Heather deep in conversation with a tall, handsome guy at the bar. Even though I was half expecting her to ignore me again, the pang of jealousy I felt when I saw her with another man felt like a punch in the heart.

"Who's that with Heather?" I asked Faye as she was passing on the way to the dance floor, trying not to let on that I cared.

"Henri, he's one of the French ski instructors. Not jealous are you?" she pouted at me.

"No, I'm not," I said firmly, although untruthfully.

"Good," she said cheekily. "Are you coming to dance with me then?" Her eyes, impossibly big and blue under her blonde fringe, sparkled mischievously at me.

I looked over at Heather again, talking earnestly with Henri. She hadn't even noticed me.

"Fuck yes," I said and let her grab my hand and lead me to the small dance floor. Whatever Heather did or did not do, Faye was still gorgeous and I still fancied her like mad.

We danced around like idiots to the cheesy music for a while and then she pulled me over to the bar. "So what is happening with you and Heather then?" she asked me as the barman lined up some tequila shots for us.

"Nothing," I said. "I mean, we have slept together, but decided that it was a bad idea. We have to work together and it probably wouldn't work out."

"I think she likes you, you know," Faye said.

"I don't think so!" I replied. Over the other side of the bar, I could see Heather getting ready to leave with the French guy. My stomach gave another lurch, but my heart started hammering now I was so close to Faye.

"Oh, us girls have ways of knowing these things," she said mysteriously.

"Well, it won't be happening again," I said determinedly. "Anyway, what about you and Danny? Are you going to get back together?"

She shook her head. "I know all about the dangers of having a relationship with someone you work with. I won't be having another one with anyone else. Well," she paused and raised her eyebrows at me, "not a long one anyway." My heart started thudding even harder.

"Ah, I love this one!" she cried suddenly as a new track came on. "Come on, let's dance again," and I found myself back on the dance floor. This time though, we started dancing much closer to each other. As the music started slowing down, we moved in toward each other, until our bodies were pretty much grinding against each other. Her hands linked behind my back and I felt my own start to slide down her sides until I was cupping her buttocks tightly.

She broke away suddenly. "Come on, let's go to Dicks where we can dance properly."

"What, where's that?" I asked, confused and frustrated at the end of our embrace.

"Not far," she said skipping away. "Everyone has gone already. Get your coat." It was true, hardly anyone from ValSki was left and the bar was definitely winding down.

Outside, Faye and I ran through the snow breathless, falling over, giddy and drunk. "Come on!" she was hauling me up, "We'll miss the fun." The stars above were bright, the air crisp and clear, I was drunk with a beautiful girl. I didn't want the moment to end.

Dicks turned out to be a real night club with bouncers and a queue. Fortunately, Faye knew the doorman and we were ushered to the front. "Stand up straight," she whispered as we walked past the line of people. "They won't let you in if they think you're too drunk."

Giggling, we made it through the door and then and walked into the club. It was like many others back home; thumping beats and a crush of people at the bar and on the dance floor. I saw quite a few ValSki staff dotted around, but there was no focus as there had been in the Saloon. Gwat was supporting his virtually unconscious victim in one corner, Danny was on the dance floor surrounded as always by people, Johnners was at the bar with Claire and Joe was wandering round looking lost. Heather and Henri were nowhere to be seen.

"I'm going to get a drink," Faye shouted at me over the noise. "Do you want one?"

"Yeah, just a beer," I said suddenly feeling tired and drunk. She nodded and went off to the bar whilst I looked round for somewhere to sit.

"Oh hi, fancy dancing? Plenty of fine fillies out there!" Giles was at my side, weaving and bobbing, his eyes rolling, obviously very drunk. I hadn't seen him in the Saloon but the madness seemed to have got to him too.

"No, you're all right mate," I said. I really didn't have the energy to deal with him now.

"Suit yourself," he sniffed. "I'm going for a bit of a boogie," and he jigged off like a Dad at a disco towards the crowds and his doom.

Later on, I would question what I saw. I was very drunk, and it was over in an instant, but I was no more than a few feet away when it happened.

As Giles shuffled off into the crowds, I saw Danny look over and stare at him. It was not the glance of a friend, but full of malice and anger, twisted and desperate for revenge. I stood up on my toes and watched him cut dead the girl who was trying to talk to him and head over to where Giles was trying to dance. I had no love for Giles, but I sensed something bad was about to happen, that Danny was going to do something that he might regret. A sickening feeling throbbed in my stomach. I knew I had to get over there to stop whatever was going to happen.

I tried to walk over but everyone seemed to be in the way; people were dancing all around me or walking into me. It was like trying to walk in slow motion or through treacle. It felt like I would never be able to get to Giles before Danny.

The music dropped into a thumping beat, the lights cut and a strobe light kicked in, reducing everyone to black and white ghosts, appearing and disappearing in frozen moments. "Danny!" I called out in desperation, but my voice was lost in the music.

And then I broke through a wall of people to a little clearing. Giles was dancing around with his face lifted to the ceiling, his eyes closed and his arms waving about. A sense of relief hit me, I had made it before Danny. "Giles!" I started to call out, but I was suddenly shoved in the back, tripped over my own feet and fell to the floor without finishing the word.

Out of the corner of me eye, in the flickering strobe light, I saw Danny holding Giles by the arms and kicking him violently in the knee. Giles tumbled to the floor next to me, his own eyes still closed. With a triumphant grin on his face, Danny raised a boot and bought it crashing down on

Giles's ankle. He stared at me for a moment, but before I could do or say anything he whirled around and was disappeared into the crowds.

Despite being almost unconscious with drink, Giles let out a scream of such pain and intensity that it cut completely through the music. It was a sickening noise, an inarticulate, animal wail, like no sound I had ever heard before.

Seconds later, the music stopped and the strong arms of bouncers were helping me and Giles up and off the dance floor and over to some chairs. Giles was sobbing and clutching his leg. "My ankle, my ankle," he was babbling.

"It's all right, it's all right," the bouncer was trying to console him. "The ambulance has been called. You'll be fine."

Heather came rushing over, concern etched on her face. I hadn't even seen her in the club. "Are you alright? What happened?"

"Yeah," the bouncer turned to me, "did you see what happened?"

Part of me wanted to blurt out that Danny had done it, but part of me was unsure of what I had just seen and if I should say anything. If I did, would I be believed? What would Danny do to me? I paused in an agony of indecision, but eventually muttered, "I don't know. I didn't see what happened. I tripped over and then the next thing I knew Giles was on me."

The bouncer nodded and grunted. "Accident. Happens a lot here, people slip up and hurt themselves. Are you okay?"

I stood up gingerly, stretching out and testing my arms and legs. "Yes, I think so."

"So you know this guy?"

"Yes," Heather answered. "He's the Resort Manager for ValSki."

"I know Jen," the bouncer said. "I'll call her and let her know what has happened. He'll have go down the mountain," he said gesturing at Giles who was now hunched over whimpering, "and I suspect he won't be coming back. I think you'll be looking for a new manager tomorrow."

"Thanks," Heather put her arm round me and helped me walk off to the door. Just before we left, I turned back to look at Giles. He lifted his tear-stained face, white with pain and looked straight at me. It was the last time I was to see him.

Part Three

The Next Month

28

THE NEXT DAY I was a wreck. I could barely ski, let alone guide. My mind was racing, replaying the events of the night before; Danny's face a mask of hatred and triumph, the crunch of his boot on Giles's ankle, the scream that Giles had let out and the look he had given me as we were leaving. Why had I told the bouncer that it was an accident? Why had I lied and said that I had not seen what happened? My pangs of jealousy at Heather going off with the French guy were submerged completely in the sick feelings from the violence that I had witnessed and my own complicity in it.

And what should I make of Danny? He had revealed a side of cruelty and viciousness that I just had not expected or imagined existed. No one liked Giles it was true, but he did not deserve to be attacked and a season-ending injury inflicted on him.

What could I do? Should I tell Jen or even the gendarmes? Would anyone believe me?

"What's wrong with you?" Heather hissed at me after I took the group down a wrong run for the third time. "You are all over the place!"

"I'm sorry, it's just last night, what happened...."

"Well pull yourself together," she snapped. "There is nothing that you can do about it now. You've got guests to look after! You almost took them down Face!"

I shook my head and realised that she was right. If I took the group down La Face, a steep and dangerous black run well beyond everyone's ability, there was bound to be an accident.

"Look, we'll talk about it later," she said. "Jen has called an emergency meeting at six tonight."

"Right," I said, determined to concentrate on the job at hand. I would talk it through with Heather before then and decide what to do after work.

I managed the rest of the day without making any more serious errors, but it was difficult. On the way back to the staff accommodation I told Heather what I had seen in Dicks.

"Shit!" she said. "Are you sure?" I nodded. "Damn, what a fucked-up situation. Let me think a second." She was silent for a while, concentrating.

"This is what I think," she said eventually. "Giles is a dick, he was doing a crap job and we are better off without him. It's just not worth saying anything."

"But Danny attacked him! I can't just sit back and do nothing!"

"You already did remember?" she said shaking her head. "The bouncer asked you what happened and you chickened out of telling the truth. If you change your story now then no one will believe you."

"Yes, I know. I feel really shit about that."

"Well you could tell Jen, she will know what to do." Heather offered. "But if I were you, I would just keep schtum. You don't want Danny as your enemy."

We didn't talk again all the way back to Chamois.

Jen was swift and to the point at the meeting later. "Giles will not be coming back," she said when everyone had crammed into the office and settled down. "He has a compound fracture of the talus and will have an operation this evening to insert pins and a brace. He will not be walking, let alone skiing for at least three months and may even have some permanent damage.

"He is obviously incapable now of carrying on as Resort Manager. Anthony will pack up his personal belongings and take them down to Bourg hospital tomorrow and then, at the earliest opportunity, he will go home.

"I have asked Danny if he is willing to become Resort Manager. I know that he did not want the responsibility but he has put aside his personal feelings and agreed to do this role until the end of the season. Are there any questions?"

My head immediately started whirring again. Danny was now Resort Manager! There was no way that I would be able to report him to Jen now.

Danny was lounging in the luxurious office chair, a big grin in his face, staring straight at me. He knew that I had seen him attack Giles and was challenging me to say something. I felt my throat go dry, but knew I could not just sit back and do nothing. I began to raise my hand.

"Yes, I've got something to say," Heather moved to the front of the group before I could say anything. Danny suddenly looked very uncomfortable, his eyes flicked between the two of us. I knew that he was wondering if I had told her what I had seen.

"Can we get a card and do a collection for Giles? I know that he was not everyone's best friend, but I think that we owe him that."

"Yes you're right," Jen said and Danny smiled in relief. "I'll sort that out." Before I could say anything else, she said briskly, "Thank you everyone, so, business as normal. Danny will be coming round to each of the chalets later to introduce himself to the guests. Heather, you are eating with Alice and Harri tonight, James, I want you in with Joe. I have a new chef on trial tonight and I would like your opinion on him."

"Really?" I asked surprised that Jen wanted my view on a new member of staff.

"Yes," she nodded. "You're a valued member of the team now and your opinion is important. Isn't that right Danny?"

Danny lounged back in the chair and looked up at me. I could not tell whether his grin was malevolent or friendly. "Oh yes," he said. "James is very important now."

Outside I managed to grab a word with Heather as she was walking towards Harri and Alice's chalet. "Thanks for helping, last night and today, I owe you one."

"Another one," she said smiling. "I seem to bailing you out all over the place."

I smiled too, and but then foolishly carried on. "I meant to say earlier, but it just got swept away. I just wanted to say too, that it is okay if you want to get with other guys. I'm totally cool with that, I won't get in your way."

"What are you talking about?" She stopped and looked hard at me.

"I mean I don't mind if there is anyone else you want to sleep with..." I trailed off.

"What the fuck are you talking about!" she said heatedly.

"Well you went off with that French guy," I said suddenly angry too. I was sick the way she treated me, sleeping with me one night and then pretending that I didn't exist the next day.

"He's gay, you idiot!" she snarled at me.

"Oh," I said the wind suddenly taken out of my sails. "I thought that..."

"Well you thought wrong," she began, but then she stopped as if she worked something out. "Ah, I get it," she said slowly. "This isn't about me at all is it? You tried to get with Faye last night, didn't you?"

"I, er..." I couldn't complete the sentence.

Her eyes widened. "You did, you fucking did!" She paused and then her eyes closed momentarily in pain. "James, you dickhead."

I realised then that I had made a terrible mistake. It wasn't Faye but Heather that I wanted.

"I'm sorry, I never..." I began, but again she stopped me.

"Don't," she shook her head. "I'm sorry if I haven't been the cute and cuddly girl that you wanted, but I'm not that person. Gwat virtually raped me James, do you have any idea what that does to you? I thought you might be different, but it turns out you are all the same. If you want to chase after that cock-teasing little bitch Faye, well go for it, frankly I couldn't give a shit." She spoke so softly, I could not tell if it was pain or anger in her voice. Then she turned round and walked away from me into the night.

29

THAT MOMENT WAS probably the worst of my life. I had betrayed Heather's trust and I had been too scared to say anything about Danny. I was a coward and a fool.

The pain that hit me was intense. It was as if someone had punched me repeatedly in the stomach and then stabbed me in the heart for good measure. My head started pounding and my limbs all went numb and I felt sick throughout my body.

I stared, paralysed with shame and self-loathing, at Heather's retreating form until she was gone. What should I do now? Run after her? What could I say that would not make her despise me even more? I was not even worthy of her contempt.

I just stood there and let the tears roll down my cheeks.

After what felt like hours, but was probably only minutes, I went over to Joe's chalet to help him. Maybe a mountain of washing up would help distract me from the pain. But neither that nor the bottles of red wine I drank made the slightest difference. I did not remember getting home.

The next day, Heather barely spoke to me. We talked cordially enough in front of the guests on the mountain, but as soon as we got back home, she went straight to her room. I tried knocking on her door and asking her to talk again, but there was no reply.

Johnners was passing in the corridor and motioned me out of earshot. "I'd leave it for a while if I were you," he advised. "She's pretty upset."

I nodded, and left, wondering if we would ever have a proper conversation again.

Whatever my personal feelings about Danny were, I had to admit that he made a much better Resort Manager than Giles. In the few days after the meeting he seemed to be everywhere; chatting to guests, encouraging the hosts, carrying goods up to chalets and sorting out all sorts of problems. He even found time to spend a morning ski guiding, which helped ease the tension between Heather and I, at least for the day. The guests, of course, loved having him there. He organised some free ski lessons and discounted massages for the hosts which also went down very well. Nothing seemed too much trouble for him, and his charisma and personality seemed to spread throughout the whole company, lifting everyone's spirits.

Life at the staff accommodation improved too. Danny quietly asked a few of the messier residents to get their acts together and clean the communal areas and we came home one day to a sparkling chalet. He blagged a TV, Sky box and Wii from somewhere and suddenly we had proper entertainment in the evening. Everybody started to hang round in the lounge after work, drinking and chatting or watching TV together, rather than go out to bars. It began to feel like we were a real family and not just unconnected individuals who happened to crash out drunk in the same place.

"All in a day's work," he smiled at me when I complimented him on how he was doing. "This is what the Resort Manager should be doing. I figure that if I can make your life better, you'll do a better job."

Even Jen seemed to loosen up a bit. She came to visit our staff accommodation and looked pleased when she saw how neat and clean it now was. "Looking good!" she nodded approvingly. "How was new the chef by the way?"

"Marco?" I asked. "Pretty good in my opinion, the food was tasty." If I was honest I couldn't remember anything about the meal after the staff meeting, I was too upset about Heather at the time. I could just picture in my mind the burly, black-haired chef who barely spoke he was concentrating so hard in the kitchen.

Jen nodded. "I'm going to employ him," she decided. "He can move in with Joe at the weekend. I'll get Danny to sort it out."

After that, life seemed to settle down into a rhythm. We worked, drank in our staff chalet, watched TV or played Wii. Marco moved in and proved to be a good addition to the family; funny energetic and fond of his beer like the rest of us. He was already on his third season and had many friends in common with Danny and Gwat.

After getting so close to Faye the night Giles broke his ankle, there seemed suddenly to be an inexplicable distance between us. On the surface things seemed quite normal, we chatted and hung out together in the lounge, but there was no mention of what had happened and none of the intimacy we had shared that night. I was not too disappointed to be honest as I was still very confused over what had happened with Heather and just wanted some time by myself.

Ski hosting seemed natural and very easy now. Over the next week the guests had all sorts of small problems, from stolen ski poles, to lost lift passes and twisted knees, but I was more experienced and dealt with them all quickly and efficiently. I even got a hundred-euro tip from one guest which helped renew my dwindling pile of cash.

The weather turned very cold for a few days and then started snowing for a couple more after that. This made the skiing more challenging but was actually necessary to maintain the level of snow on the pistes. I saw Danny, Johnners and Gwat occasionally out on the mountain, but I had decided to concentrate on my job rather than what everyone else was up to. After the last experience, I had had enough of off-piste and extreme skiing.

However good it got though, and however much people liked Danny being in charge, there was part of me that stayed detached. Andy's words from the drive up kept coming back to haunt me, and I made a big effort to keep some distance. Danny was more than friendly with me, but the look on his face as his foot descended onto Giles ankle and the sound of his voice as he threatened Gwat were etched in my memory.

For ten days, everything was calm. We didn't really drink and didn't go out. We had a couple of quiet beers on the next transfer day, but were home by eleven. It seemed that everyone was shocked at the sudden departure of Dylan and Giles and had calmed their drinking down.

But then it seemed that the mourning period was over, and everything kicked off again.

30

"WHERE THE FUCK AM I?"

The sounds of hysterical screaming downstairs woke me with a jolt. I jumped off my platform as quickly as I could, pulled on a hoody and made my way out onto the landing. It was seven am; the hosts would have left for their chalets but we didn't need to be out of bed just yet.

"WHERE THE FUCKING HELL AM I?"

I raced downstairs and heard doors banging behind me as Heather and Danny came barging out of their bedrooms and followed me towards the lounge. We piled through the door and then all stopped dead.

"Calm down! You are safe in a chalet." This was Gwat's voice.

My mind registered that the room was in a terrible state; benches and chairs were overturned, there was broken crockery and glass on the floor and rubbish scattered everywhere. Several of the pictures were off kilter and one, the big bas relief map of the Alps was knocked on the floor. This was all just background detail though, because our whole attention was fixed on the hysterical and almost naked girl in the middle of the room.

"WHO THE FUCK ARE YOU?" she screamed when she saw us.

She was dressed in only a sheet and a baseball cap, which hid most of her straight blond her. She was obviously in the grip of a tremendous rage or panic; what I could see of her face was screwed up and red, hot tears coursing down her cheeks. Her entire body seemed to be wracked by convulsions.

"WHAT THE FUCK HAPPENED?"

Gwat was in front of her, dressed only in a pair of pants, hopping up and down, waving his hands in the air. "Fucking calm down!" he was imploring her. The sight of his pale, naked body capering around would have been funny in other circumstances, but now it was obscene.

All of a sudden, the girl seemed to collapse in on herself, and fell to the floor sobbing uncontrollably. This jolted us all into action. Heather sprang forward and rushed to the girl and put her arms about her. Danny and I rushed towards Gwat.

"What happened?" Danny got there first.

"Fucking nut case!" Gwat spat out. "Came back with me last night and then went mental this morning. She just woke up and ran out here and started going mental, smashing the place up."

"What did you do to her?" I demanded.

"Nothing! Nothing that she didn't want me to, anyway. She just went fucking nuts."

"Jesus Gwat, you've done it this time," Danny said shaking his head. He stood still a second thinking furiously whilst Heather crouched by the girl, making soothing noises and trying to comfort her. "Okay, this is the plan. Heather, can you take her to your room and get her cleaned up? Jimmy, you go and get her clothes from Gwat's room, then get this place straightened up. Gwat, go and get dressed and try and remember her name and who she works for. We've got to get her home."

Heather looked up and nodded. "Yes Danny," she said. There was a calm authority in his voice that brooked no arguing.

"I didn't fucking do nothing!" Gwat whined as Heather led the girl out.

"Go and get dressed. NOW!" Danny raised his voice for the first time and Gwat almost jumped to obey him. I followed him out.

"I didn't fucking do nothing," he repeated to me as we went down the corridor, fortunately in a different direction to Heather and the girl.

"What's her name Gwat?" I asked.

"I dunno'," he said over his shoulder as he opened the door to his room. "Shona or summat'. Scottish gwat, works for Chalet Val."

The light was on in his room and I was able to see some female clothing on the floor. "Right," I said picking up some girl's jeans, top, socks and a hoody from the floor. "Is there anything else?"

Gwat looked over, still in just his own pants. "Yeah, a bra and knickers. Probably still in the bed." He rummaged around under the duvet. "Yes, here they are," he said handing me some ridiculously small underwear.

"Thanks. You better get dressed," I said and went out towards Heather's room.

"Heather? Can I come in?" I knocked and called out.

"Jimmy, is that you? Just leave her clothes outside. I think it's best if you don't come in."

"I understand," I said and made my way back to the lounge.

Danny was on his mobile phone. "I don't know," he was saying. "She could say anything. Look, I'll try and sort it out then give you a call back alright?" He hung up the phone.

"Fucking Hell," Danny was shaking his head. "What a fucking mess."

"Gwat says she works for Chalet Val." I said.

"Good, I know Kat, the chalet manager. Did he know her name?"

"Shona he thinks. Scottish girl."

Danny nodded. "That should be enough to identify her. I'll call her up now." He got his phone out to dial just as Heather was coming in.

"Do you not think that we should call the Police?" she said directly.

"No," he said simply, tapping buttons and looking through his address book.

"Look Danny, for fuck's sake." Heather marched over to where he was, her voice raised. "He has sexually assaulted her, possibly raped her. This isn't something that we can just ignore."

Danny put his phone down. "No he hasn't," he said forcefully. "I was with him last night in the Saloon and she left willingly with him. There are probably a dozen or more witnesses who will say the same thing. He has done nothing more than he ever does; this one is just a bit more fragile."

"Do you not get it? He's a fucking animal Danny," Heather shouted. "That girl is destroyed."

"Then you better go back and look after her. Let me deal with the problem." Danny spoke softly, but there was iron in his voice. Heather tried to stare him out, but she was no match for his steely eyes. Eventually she muttered, "Okay Danny," and left.

"Right fella," Danny said turning to me. "You better get this place cleared up ASAP. I'm gonna need Heather here with me so you will have to host both groups this morning. Is that alright with you?"

"Yes Danny," I said automatically.

"I'll go and see Gwat and try and sort this fuck-up out. I'll see you later," he said, and left the room whilst I got down on my knees and started picking up the broken glass.

31

IT DIDN'T TAKE me long to clear up the lounge. Within twenty minutes I had swept up all the broken glass, straightened the furniture, hung the pictures back on the wall and put one of the busted chairs back together. I even found time to do the washing up.

It had only just turned eight am, so I still had half an hour or so until I had to go and meet the guests and go guiding. I looked round wondering what else I could do. The girl, Shona, was probably still in with Heather, so I decided to go and see if Danny needed any more help.

As I approached Gwat's room, I heard him speaking. "Have you got any more? Don't lie to me now?" I slowed down to listen to Danny for the second time outside Gwat's door.

"You have, haven't you? For Christ sake Gwat, hand them over you idiot. What if the gendarmes find them?" I could hear movement in the room. Scared that they might come out and discover me eavesdropping, I silently moved back a few paces, then walked noisily back to the door calling: "Danny, you in there? Is there anything else I can do?"

"Hang on a sec," the door opened a moment later and Danny came out. "No I think we're alright. I called Kat, Jen's equivalent in Chalet Val and she is coming to pick up the girl."

"How is she now?" I asked.

"Heather says that she is dressed, but still in a state and not really talking. Kat will sort her out; she is good in this kind of situation."

"Is there anything else I can do?"

Danny shook his head. "No, I think we have it under control here. If you are able to do both groups today, that would be a great help."

"Sure," I said, "no problem. Anything I can do to help."

"Thanks man," Danny put his hand on my shoulder and looked directly at me with his intense brown eyes. "I appreciate it man. You've done good today, kept calm in a tough situation. I won't forget it."

I suddenly felt a lump in my throat; getting praise from Danny meant a lot. I swallowed and tried to remember that I didn't really trust him.

"No worries," I said after a pause. "Right, I better get ready."

Danny nodded. "Hopefully Heather will be out again at lunch and able to take her group, but she may be upset as well. I'll keep you posted."

I turned and went back to my room to get changed into my skiing gear with a mixture of emotions; concern about the girl, flattered by Danny's praise but also desperately curious to know what happened and what Gwat had in his room. I shrugged and tried to put it out of my mind, I could deal with it later.

As I was leaving the chalet twenty minutes later, a car painted in the orange livery of Chalet Val pulled up. An imposing looking blonde woman in her early forties, also dressed in orange, got smartly out. "Is this the ValSki staff chalet?" she asked swiftly.

"Yes, Chalet Chamois" I replied. "Are you Kat? Danny and the girl are inside."

"Thank you," she said briskly. "Who are you?"

"I'm James, one of the Ski Guides. I was one of the people who found her."

Kat looked me up and down. "Well don't let me keep you," she said after a moment. "Oh, and James," she added. "Don't talk about this to anyone, is that clear?"

"Yes Kat," I found myself responding to the authority in her voice much as I did to Jen and, indeed, Danny earlier in the day. I turned and walked quickly down the hill.

I told the guests that Heather was doing paperwork in the office that morning and that I would be leading the whole group until lunchtime. There was only six in each group so it was not too many for one guide. We cruised around the blues and greens up the Bellevarde area and at every lift stop I surreptitiously checked my phone to see if I had any messages. It was two-and-a-half long hours before one came through from Danny saying that Heather would meet me for lunch at the Toviere, one of the mountain restaurants.

By the time Heather arrived I was being eaten alive by curiosity. What had Gwat done to the girl? What was in his room? What would happen next?

"Hi guys!" Heather said brightly as she came over to us as we sat down to eat. "Sorry not to join you this morning, too much paperwork in the office!" It was a standard excuse used by guides when they were hung over and late, although we hadn't actually used it yet.

The next thirty minutes as we ate with the guests were excruciating; I was so desperate for news I could hardly eat. Finally, as we were putting our skis on, I managed to ask her quietly what had happened.

"Kat took the girl away," she said after checking there were no guests in earshot, "and Danny took Gwat to Jen. That's about all I know."

"What a fuck-up. Do you know what actually happened last night and this morning?"

Heather shook her heard. "No, Shona wouldn't talk to me although I can probably guess what happened. She would have gone home with Gwat last night when she was wasted and freaked out when she woke up with him this morning."

"Do you think he, you know..." I said not wanting to say the words. I was painfully aware that this must be bringing up some very bad memories for her.

She looked at me. "What do you think he did, held her hand? Of course he fucking did!" she snapped and then in a completely fake tone said to a guest who was approaching "Hi! Are you ready? Right, let's go!" and she pushed ahead.

I didn't get another chance to talk to Heather in the afternoon, but as we were walking back home after work, she apologised. "Look I'm sorry I snapped at you up there. It's just..."

"I know," I said. "You don't have to say anything."

"No, I do, I really do," she shook her head. "I do owe you an apology, and not just for today."

"What do you mean?" I asked.

"I've been pretty shitty with you since Giles broke his leg and you don't deserve it."

"Look Heather..." I tried to say, but she interrupted me.

"No, let me finish," she said. "I was more angry at myself really, for feeling hurt and I took it out on you. You've been nothing but kind to me, much better than most of the men I have been with. I know that you have fancied Faye since you got here and it is unfair of me to judge you."

"No, look," I said stopping here in the snow, not far from the Danois. "I don't fancy Faye, not at all really. I mean she is pretty and I did when I got here, but the more I get to know her, the less I like her. I only danced with her because I was angry at you going off with some other bloke. It's not her I want her at all."

"Really?" she turned to look at me, a questioning look in her eye.

"Really!" I said.

"So, where does that leave us now then?" she asked slowly.

"Friends or perhaps...?" I moved in closer, hoping to take her in my arms.

"Friends," she said firmly, taking a step back. "I've been through too much recently for anything else. At least for now."

"Okay," I said. "I'm happy with that. For now!" And I realised that I really was. Both of us had been through too much recently to rush into anything. "What about Gwat and the girl?" I asked suddenly, realising that I still did not know anything. "What has happened to them?"

"I don't know," she tiredly, and turned to carry on walking. "I don't know. Kat took the girl away. Jen came and took Danny and Gwat away."

"What next then?"

"Nothing. I bet nothing will happen. Gwat will get his knuckles rapped, be quiet for a couple of weeks, and then go back to his old habits. Everyone protects him, Jen and Danny, even though he is an animal."

"I suppose that they want to protect the good name of the company," I said, "and not let any scandal out."

"No, it's more than that," Heather shook her head. "It's like there is a little gang of people who have been here for a while who look out for each other. If you are 'in', then you can literally get away with murder."

"What can we do?" I asked.

"Nothing," she said bitterly. "There is nothing we can do."

32

IT SEEMED HEATHER was right. Gwat was calmly drinking a can of beer in the lounge when we returned.

"What happened?" I asked as soon as we got in.

"Fucking psycho bitch. She was fine last night but went schiz' this morning," he shook his head and took another swig of beer.

"Why was that Gwat?" Heather asked him sarcastically. "Was it because you raped her?"

"Don't you fucking start!" he shouted angrily back at her. "I've had a fucking shit day; I don't need your shit too!" He stood up and seemed almost ready to hit her but the door opened, distracting him, and Danny came in.

"Calm down will you!" he didn't raise his voice, but there was no ignoring the authority in his tone. Gwat looked like he was about to argue back for a moment but then muttered, "I'm not fucking staying round here," and marched out. Danny waited until he had gone and then said to Heather "Look H, winding Gwat up now will not help. What's done is done."

"Someone should have called the police," Heather said. "He can't just keep getting away with it."

"Actually we did," Danny said mildly to her.

"What?" Heather asked, taken aback.

"Lieutenant Colbert from the Gendarmerie came round to Jen's this morning to interview Anthony," Danny replied.

"Oh." Heather was stumped.

"Despite being advised against it, the girl, Shona, wanted to report a sexual assault. Both Jen and Kat told her that the gendarmes would dismiss it as she was so drunk and there were lots of witnesses that saw her kissing Gwat in the Saloon and leaving voluntarily with him, but she went ahead anyway. Colbert came round to interview Gwat this afternoon, and as we expected, said there is no case to answer."

"What's happened to the girl?" I asked.

"That's not really our concern, but I think Kat has taken her down the mountain to see a doctor. She was in quite a state."

"Will she come back?" Heather demanded.

"I don't know." Danny sighed and sat down. "Look, it's been a tough day for all of us. Being mardi with me won't make it any better. I know that you don't like Gwat, Heather, I know that you regret sleeping with him at the start of the season, but you can't take it out on him, it's not fair. He hasn't done anything wrong."

All of a sudden, Heather looked unsure of herself. I could see doubt and confusion in her eyes and behind them a lot of pain. Tears were suddenly coming down her cheeks. "Come here you," Danny said and held his arms open to her. After a moment's hesitation, Heather sat down next to him, crawled into his embrace and let him cradle her.

"He's a fucking bastard!" she quietly sobbed.

"Shh," Danny said soothingly and began stroking her hair. "It's alright." He looked over at me and nodded his head in the direction of the door, motioning me to go. I couldn't help but feel an intense pang of jealousy that it was him she opened up to and not me, but I still left.

I found Gwat in his room pulling his shoes on. "I need a fucking drink," he muttered. "Are you coming to Danois?" I couldn't help but notice that, with all the stress of what happened, I had not heard him let out one 'eee' all day.

"Yeah, why not?" I said. I didn't want to hang around by myself with Danny cuddling Heather.

"Thanks mate, you're a mate," he grunted. "Come on, let's go."

Twenty minutes later, we were playing pool and drinking beer. "It was fucking mental mate. She just woke up and started screaming." Gwat said.

"Really?" I asked.

"Yeah, she just grabbed a sheet and ran out. I couldn't shut her up!"

"Honestly?" I questioned him again, still not sure if I believed him.

"Honest mate, that's how it happened." He looked at me with a straight face, but I was still not convinced.

A couple of beers later, Danny and Heather came in. She walked straight up to Gwat and said directly, "I'm sorry Anthony. I didn't mean to accuse you of raping her. It was wrong of me to do that."

Now it was Gwat's turn to look confused. "What's this all about?" he asked.

"I've had a long chat to Danny," Heather continued. I think I have been letting my personal feelings about what happened between us at the beginning of the season affect my judgement." I couldn't quite believe what I was hearing; Heather had completely changed her opinion. What had Danny said to her?

"I know we don't see eye to eye on everything Gwat, but shall we just let bygones be bygones and try and be friends? There is still a long way to go before the end of the season." She stuck out her hand towards him.

Gwat looked her up and down for a moment and then tentatively shook her hand. A quiet 'eee' came out of his mouth.

Danny nodded approvingly. "I'm glad you two have made up at last," he said. "We're family and we have to look after each other."

33

THE NEXT MONTH seemed to fly by. We were well past the halfway point of the season now, and for everyone the job was becoming a lot easier. The chalet hosts finished earlier in the morning, wrapped up evening service more quickly, stayed out later each night and, if it was possible, started getting even drunker while they were out. I learnt to survive on four hours sleep a night and ski either horrifically hung over or even still drunk.

Heather and I started getting on well again, but despite getting drunk regularly together, we did not end up in bed again. Both of us were too wary of what it might mean and of being hurt again.

The weather began to change too; the cold snap of early February wore off and, by the beginning of March, we had blue skies and sun again. It was a lot warmer than the bright, clear weather of January and some of the boys started wearing shorts. Danny kept looking worriedly up at the sky, however. "If it keeps up like this," he said dourly, "we ain't gonna have any snow left by April." He was wrong though, in the second week of March the snow started coming down, and for a couple of weeks, we had fresh powder again.

People started talking about the end of the season, what they would do in the summer and if they would come back next year. For a while it became a only topic of discussion in the lounge when the chalet hosts returned from service.

"Go on the dole, mate," Gwat muttered. "I've paid my taxes and will put my feet up for the summer." He lifted his feet from the carpet and plonked them on the coffee table in the lounge.

"Gwat, off!" Danny barely even looked up his laptop screen. He was the only one sat at the table, writing a report for Jen.

"Find myself some trailer gwat back home and smash her till she's preggers, eee!"

Faye tutted in disgust and then turned to Johnners. "What about you Monkey Boy?" Claire had her head in his lap and he was idly stroking here hair. "What are you going to do?"

"Oh, I don't know," Johnners replied. "Go back to Huddersfield and coach some football probably."

"Oh no you aren't!" Claire lifted her head from his lap. "You're coming with me to find work in Hossegor, remember?"

"Oh yes, I forgot about that!" Johnners laughed. "That is if I don't dump you at the airport like Danny does to his girls. Oops, sorry Faye!" he added smirking.

"Ha, bloody ha," Danny didn't even look up from his computer and Faye looked daggers at him.

"What about you Heather?" I asked quietly.

"I'm going to Canada," Heather she said. "If I can get a visa then I will try and find work on a ranch until the winter, and then become a ski instructor in Whistler or Banff."

"Isn't that difficult? Don't you have to train for years?" I asked her.

"No, not really. It only takes a couple of weeks to get your basic BASI qualification and you are then qualified to teach kids. You're easily good enough to do that."

I turned the thought over in my mind. I hadn't thought of extending my year off. My parents expected me to go to London and get a job in the City somewhere, but I knew my heart wasn't in that any more.

"Perhaps I'll come with you," I said without thinking. Heather turned to look at me with a questioning look in her eye.

"So you are not coming back then?" Danny had closed his laptop and come over to the settee and stood above Heather frowning.

"No," she shook her head firmly. "There are other places I want to see in the world."

"Shame. I thought you were better than that," he said. "Who else is going to bail? Claire, Johnners?"

"We'll be back mate," Johnners answered and Claire nodded. "What else could we do?" she murmured.

"Eeee! Come back for more gwat!" Gwat nodded vigorously from the sofa.

"Urgh!" Claire made a face. "I think I may change my mind!"

"And what about you, James?" Danny turned his glittering eyes on me. "Are you going to come back?"

I felt the challenge in his voice, but I was also aware of Heather staring at me intently. "Umm, I don't know, Danny."

"Well think about it," he said. "You would make a great Resort Manager."

"But that's your job!" I said, secretly flattered that he thought I was good. "I couldn't do it. What are you going to do?"

"Go back to being a simple hot tub supervisor," he winked at me. "That's all I am really, just a simple hot tub guy."

"Well I am not going to make any decisions yet," I said firmly. "There is still a long way to go of the season."

"True," he said. "There is still some skiing to be done. Now look, I've got a deal to cut with you two." He looked at me and Heather.

"What?" we both asked simultaneously, intrigued.

"Well, we are not having many come guiding at the moment. How many did you have today again?"

"Three," Heather shook her head. "It's a pretty low turnout."

"Well look," he said. "I think you two should have a break from ski guiding tomorrow and come out with me. It's going to be one of the last powder days of the year; I've got something special in mind. It might change your mind about next year."

"What's that?" I said intrigued.

"What will we do about the guests?" Heather asked at the same time.

"Oh, we'll invent some excuse." Danny replied grinning. "We laminated some route suggestions a few years ago. I'll go round and drop some off tonight and tell the punters that you have some important paperwork to do or something like that. And as for where we will go..." he paused dramatically for a second. "Well I think it is about time that we attempted the Pointe Pers."

"Really?" I said excitedly. My skiing had improved beyond all recognition and I was getting seriously bored of the pistes.

"Yes," he nodded. "H, are you in?" She nodded. "Gwat, Johnners?" they both nodded. "Hmph! Don't worry about me and Faye then!" Claire harrumphed from where she was lying on the sofa.

"Sorry girls," Danny smiled. "Pros only."

"Whatever!" Faye sniffed. "Anyway, we're having a spa day. If you don't want to play with the boys," she looked at Heather, "you can come and have a pamper day with us. You too if you like," she glanced at me.

"Gwat in bikinis. Eeeee!" I could see Gwat was picturing Faye and Claire in their swimsuits.

"Sorry mate," Danny clapped him on the shoulder. "You are coming with us. You'll have to see the girls naked another time.

"Eeee," he said disappointed. I was beside myself with excitement though. I had been skiing round the pistes with guests for over a month now and I suddenly realised that I was desperate to try something more exciting.

34

IT WAS ABOUT mid-day before we managed to get up to the top of the Col Pers as we had to wait for Johnners to finish breakfast service and Danny to complete his managerial duties before we could leave. Gwat couldn't make it in the end; Jen had an errand for him to run down the mountain.

When we clambered up to the ridge, the bowl before us was very different to last time we were there. Instead of untouched white powder, there were dozens of lines zigzagging down. Hardly any part was untracked.

Heather crouched down next to me and rubbed snow in between her fingers. "It's different to last time," she said. "Much harder; it won't be as easy to ski on."

Danny knelt down beside her and inspected the snow too. "It's grainier too. The high winds have blown off the arms of the flakes."

"I don't understand," I said confused.

"Can you picture a snowflake?" I nodded. "Well all the arms, or dendrites as they are technically known, can get blown off in bad weather, leaving just the small hexagonal ice nucleus."

"What does that mean?" I asked.

"It means the snow pack is essentially composed of tiny ice ball bearings. Slippery and unstable as hell."

"Which means increased risk of avalanche," Heather added.

"Maybe," Danny replied.

"Feckin' hell. You bring us up here and then tell us the snow's crap! Shouldn't have bothered!" Johnners grumbled half in jest, half seriously.

"Relax kiddo, you are still gonna have the ride of your life." Danny grinned.

But even tracked out, the view had the same effect on me. I stood gazing at the white peaks marching off into the distance, melting into the white sky and the empty bowl of snow ahead. It was still utterly spellbinding.

"So, we are still gonna do the Pointe then?" Johnners asked, I think hoping that Danny would say no.

"Yup."

"And the risk of avalanche is acceptable?" Heather asked.

"Well, it's never great up there as you know, but I think we will be alright. Now listen up, I'm gonna explain what each of us has to do."

We all nodded a bit uncertainly. "Okay. First, hop down into the bowl using the rope over there," he pointed about twenty metres further up the ridge to where a rope dangled over the edge. "Then traverse round the bowl," he moved his finger off to the right, describing an arc round the steep ridge. "As you can see, it is really steep. If you do slip, then you will not be able to stop yourself going down. It's not dangerous, well no more than last time we were here, but you will not make the Pointe. So if that happens, just coast down like we did last time to the Pont St Charles and wait for everyone else there."

"What's that?" Johnners asked.

"The bridge, idiot!! Heather snapped at him. "Don't you know any French?"

"Nope!" Johnners said proudly. "No feckin' need!"

Heather shook her head and then turned to Danny. "If we don't make it, should we wait to see if anyone else falls?" she asked.

"Good idea," Danny said. "Wait about halfway down, by that ridge over there," he pointed to an area on the far side of the bowl. "That's well out of any avalanche fall line, and you can get there from anywhere. But that's not going to happen anyway," he looked at each of us in turn. "Lean back, keep your speed up and you'll have no problems in making it.

"Once you have got round the bowl, you stop at that point over there," his finger rested at another depression in the ridge on the far side of the bowl, about the same height as we were now. "At that point, you can edge up to the ridge. There is a rope to help you, just like the one here, but it is not easy." I looked over, and thought I could just make out the rope dangling down. The climb up to the ridge we were on was hard enough; the one on the far side looked steeper, higher and harder.

"Once we are at the top, then we unclip, put skis and boards on our backs, and climb up the ridge. That's the easiest part, but also the most dangerous. If you fall there, it's a long way down." Danny grinned, showing his teeth.

"The Pointe Pers is actually the peak, but we stop just before there. Just on the other side, you can't see it from here, there is a couloir. That is what we are aiming for."

"And is it as hard as everyone says?" Johnny asked nervously.

"Yup!" Danny said and grinned again. "Ready?"

We all nodded uncertainly. "Let's go then."

Danny walked up the ridge a little, strapped his board on, and then edged carefully up to the lip. He grasped the rope in both hands, then hopped back, inch by inch. Slowly, he went over the ridge and disappeared. For a few moments, we could not see him, but then he appeared, picking his way carefully round the bowl. He stopped about halfway round and gestured. "Okay, next one!" we heard his faint cry.

"Who's going next then?" I asked.

"Ah, feckin' 'ell," Johnners said, "I'll go," and he walked up the path to the rope. It was a slightly different procedure for him to get over the lip as he was on skis rather than a snowboard, but he managed without incident and we saw him coast along the bowl to where Danny was waiting.

"Me next." Heather stood up. "Look, James, did you really mean it when you said you might come out to Canada?"

"Yes," I answered. "I really think I would follow you there." I stood up and took my helmet off. "I think I would follow you anywhere." I realised that I meant it too. I would follow this intelligent, beautiful and quirky girl anywhere.

She watched me for a second and seemed about to say something important, but just then there was another shout from Danny, and it broke the spell. "Just don't follow me down there if I slip!" she joked.

My heart leapt inside me. She had not said anything in so many words, but I knew at that point that she had forgiven me and there was chance for us to be together. I couldn't help but grin, acknowledging the moment. "I won't. But you won't slip; you're too good for that. I'll see you at the ridge," I said, smiling.

She nodded and smiled back at me, then grabbed the rope and edged over the lip.

35

THE SMILE ON my face was wiped off a few seconds later. There was a cry from over the edge, and a moment later, Heather came into view, tumbling down the slope. With my heart in my mouth, I watched her fall.

Miraculously, her skis did not come off and, thirty metres down, where the gradient levelled off, she righted herself, put in a turn and bought herself to a stop.

"Are you alright?" I called down to her.

"FuckfuckFUCK!" she yelled, and threw her helmet on the ground.

"What's the matter? Are you hurt?" I shouted.

She put her hands on her hips and I could see her grit her teeth in frustration. "No, I'm fine. I'm just not going to make the Pointe now. I don't think I can bear Danny's and Johnners' smug faces."

"So, you are alright?" I said, still unsure.

"Yes, I'm fine! I just caught an edge and couldn't stop myself going down," she called back.

"Do you want me to come down?" I asked.

She shook her head. "Don't be silly. You go ahead and join the others. I'll wait over there until I see everyone get over the ridge."

"No worries," I nodded. I would get no thanks if I followed her down; I knew her well enough to know that she would see it as a blow to her pride. Heather put her helmet back on, flexed her legs, and then skied off to the meeting point that Danny had suggested.

Danny and Johnners were still waiting on the far side of the bowl. They would not have been able to hear the exchange between us, so I waved to them to indicate I was coming. I moved over to the rope and with my heart in my mouth, carefully edged over the lip.

It was hard on my biceps, but actually I found having the safety of the rope reassuring. Two meters down I let go and started the traverse round the bowl. The slope was so steep that looking down made my stomach churn. I was not sure that my skis would grip to the side.

But Johnners had done it and Danny had done it on his board, so I knew that it was possible. I pointed the tips of my skis fractionally downwards, and found myself skating round the bowl picking up speed. Danny's advice was good, by keeping my speed up and leaning backwards, I didn't lose too much height. Before I knew it I was next to the boys.

"Man down," Johnners said.

"What happened to her?" Danny asked.

"She slipped, but she is not hurt."

"Oh well," Danny said briskly, almost dismissively. "The next bit is easier; another traverse, and then the climb up the rope to the ridge. Jimmy, you can go first this time, Johnners, you next, and I'll go last."

I nodded, pleased to be trusted to lead the way, and then pushed off. The second half of the bowl was even steeper, and I made the mistake of looking down again. My head swam and I could feel my skis slipping, but I kept going and grasped the rope when it appeared, like a drowning man. I hung there sweating and gasping.

There was no time to rest though, as I knew that Danny and Johnners were just behind me. I heaved on the rope, jumped my skis up the slope and, inch by inch, made my way painstakingly up the three meters to the lip. When I finally hauled myself over, my arms were aching and my lungs were on fire.

From below me I could hear Johnners huffing and puffing, and then a few moments later, his head appeared. "Feck me, that's hard work," he said as he rolled over the edge, his skis up in the air. I nodded, still scarcely able to breathe.

Five minutes later, Danny came up, elegantly back rolling over the edge, hardly out of breath at all. "Easy, eh? Told you it would be alright," he grinned at us both. "Now, look over there," he pointed over the ridge. Now we were further along the ridge, the view was even more desolate, even more beautiful, even more awe-inspiring than it was from the Col Pers. I gazed, struck dumb.

"That is the Point du Gris Caval," Danny said after a few moments, indicating a peak along the same ridge. "And the big one just beyond is the Aiguelle Rousse. On the far side of that, is Italy."

"Wow!" Johnners said. "Can you get there?"

"There is a path," Danny answered, "I have walked it in the summer. But now, lost under metres of snow? You would have to be brave to attempt it."

"Or mad," I added. "Or perhaps desperate."

"And stupid!" Johnners added. He was looking pale under his tan. "Look Danny, I'm not very good with heights, I'm not sure about this. How much climbing do we have to do?"

"About a hundred meters along and about twenty meters up, I'd say," Danny answered.

"Where?"

Danny pointed along the ridge. The path snaked along, rising higher and higher. It did not look a difficult climb, but it was a steep drop on either side. The consequences of slipping and falling off were significant. "Do you think you're up to it?"

Johnners paused for a second, staring carefully at the path and then started shaking his head. "Look Danny, I don't want to be a wet blouse, but I don't think I can do that."

Danny stared at him intently as if weighing him up. "Very well, Johnners. You will have to go down the rope and ski down. If you go now, then you will catch up with Heather. She is still waiting at the meeting point."

I looked over and could still make out her dark silhouette. She was obviously watching us carefully. "Are you sure Johnners?" I asked. "I think you could do it."

"No!" Danny said coldly. "This is no place for faint hearts. Johnners has to go back, don't you?"

"Yes, I suppose so," he said glumly.

"Well off you go then," Danny said.

Johnners walked back to the rope, his shoulders slumped in defeat. We watched him lower himself over the edge without speaking.

"That was harsh, Danny," I said after we had watched him carve down to Heather.

"No," Danny's face was like granite. "This run is not for the faint-hearted. If you have even the slightest bit of doubt you endanger not just yourself but everyone else you are with. Johnners lost his nerve when he crashed on race day. He hasn't been the same since."

"Really, are you sure? I think he just needs to get his confidence back."

Danny shook his head. "He's had plenty of chances, but it's always the same. I am not sure he will ever recover from it," he said sadly. "If I'm honest, I'm not sure he ever really had it anyway. There was a moment's pause, but then he added brightly: "But you're different. You've still got yours. You've let go of your fear. You get to really experience the mountain now. Are you ready for it?" His eyes were suddenly sparkling with an intense light.

I took a deep breath. "Yes Danny, I'm ready."

"Follow me," he said, and started walking up the path.

36

AFTER THE TRAVERSE round the bowl and the jump up to the ridge, the hike up to the Pointe Pers was surprisingly straightforward. It was hard on the leg muscles, and I thought that my lungs were going to burst, but it was just a matter of putting one foot in front of the other. In what seemed no time at all, I was almost at the top.

"Welcome to my world," Danny said from above me and reached down to help me up the last few steps to the summit. He looked more peaceful and content, and yet more alive, than I had ever seen him. "Thanks," I said as he pulled me up.

If I thought the view from the last two ridges were awe-inspiring, then this one felt like the view of the Gods. We were almost at the highest point we could see, only a few isolated peaks reached above us. We really were on the roof of the world.

It was not as sheltered as the last ridge though. The wind whipped around us and Danny had to shout to make his voice audible above the howl.

"This is it," he turned to me. "This is the heart of the mountain. This is where the Iseran Glacier and then the Isere River starts. This is the start of it all." The strange glittering look was back in his eyes.

"It is..." I said, unable to complete the sentence.

"Not many people get to come up here, James," he carried on as if he had not heard me. "Not many people can make that traverse and climb, only the chosen few. You are lucky, my friend."

I nodded. "I know," I shouted back. "Thank you for taking me up here!"

Danny shook his head. "It's not me, it's the mountain. She is the one who lets people up here. She chose you, she let you in." Danny's mystical side was coming out again. "You can't let her down now," he shouted. "You can't leave. You have to come back next year."

I suddenly realised two things at once. Firstly how exposed we were up here. On one side there was nothing but a long fall onto jagged rocks. On the other was a narrow ribbon of snow through the couloir leading down to the powder bowl, two or three hundred meters below. If you mistimed or misjudged your descent, that was it. If you slipped and tumbled, there would be no chance.

Secondly, with a snap of insight and clarity, I realised how obsessed and dangerous Danny was. What Andy had said on the drive up to Val was right; the ones who stayed here season after season, year after year, were the craziest. One small slip could easily be helped by one small push and I knew Danny was more than capable of that.

"I'm coming back!" I shouted back to Danny. "I'm here for good now!"

Danny clapped me on the shoulder. "I knew you would. I knew as soon as I met you. Now, are you ready?" I nodded. "Good. This really is the run to end all runs. Can you see where we have to go?"

"Yes, I think so," I called out. "Down the couloir, into the bowl."

"That's right. Just don't hit any rocks! Ready? I'll go first and find the line. I'll shout up how to do it afterwards."

"Okay!" I shouted back.

Danny pulled his goggles down and took the board from his back. Kneeling down to protect himself from the wind, he strapped himself in. He steadied himself on the rock for a moment, looked down, and then like a skier on a downhill race, pulled himself off the edge and down into the couloir.

I jumped forward to watch his descent. He made the first two turns perfectly, but on the third, his board must have clipped a rock just under the surface, because suddenly he was tumbling down, banging off the sides, arms and legs everywhere. I watched helplessly as he fell, picking up speed, until he came to a stop at the bottom, some two hundred meters away. He lay there unmoving.

Heather and Johnners were nowhere in sight and even if they were there was no way they could have helped. I was the only person for miles around. "Danny!" I shouted, even though I knew he would not hear me. "I'm coming!"

As quick as I could I unclipped the skis from my back, balanced them on the only straight bit of rock I could find and stepped into them. My poles came next and then finally my goggles. Breathing hard, I stepped carefully up to the edge. Looking over the ridge, just before I went over, was probably the most terrifying moment of my life. The drop seemed vertical, the rocks on either side barely more than three meters apart, the snow an impossibly thin ribbon of white. It was a lethal run. There was no Danny to give me a pep talk and calm my fears, no Danny to explain the route, I would have to do it all myself. And if I made any mistakes, then it would not just be my life at risk.

I gulped, and then launched myself over the edge just as Danny had done.

For a moment I hung in the air, then my skis hit the snow. The couloir wall raced up to me so I turned sharply, but then the other side was ahead of me as well so I turned again. The snow was thin; I could hear it crunching beneath my skis and the edges failing to bite properly, but I was travelling so quickly there was no time for me to fall. A third turn, and then a fourth went by. Then I was out of the couloir and into the powder basin below.

Within a second, I was by Danny, a mixture of adrenalin and dread pumping so strongly in my stomach I thought I might throw up. He was not moving and I could not see if he was even breathing. I knelt down fearing the worst.

"Oh, God! Danny, Danny!" I lifted his goggles off his eyes but he just lay there, no colour in his face at all.

"Danny!" I called again, panic rising in my voice. "DANNY!"

And then miraculously he groaned. "Ahhh fuck!" he said opening his eyes. "What happened?"

Intense relief flooded through me, he was not dead. "Don't move," I commanded, coming to my senses. "You might be injured."

"Ah, God, my head!" he struggled for a moment, and then lay back. "What happened, where I am?"

"At the bottom of the Pointe Pers Couloir. You slipped. I think you may have hit your head."

"Ah, yes I remember now," he closed his eyes slowly.

"Does it hurt anywhere?" I asked.

"Yes, all over!" he snapped back at me, his eyes flaring open. I grinned, despite myself. If he was complaining, he must be alright. He took a few deep breaths and then said briskly, "Right, help me up. I think I'm alright."

"Are you sure?" I asked.

"Yes, I'm fucking sure." I helped him sit up and he flexed his arms. "All good so far." He reached up and removed his helmet, I could see he was grinning underneath, albeit with gritted teeth. "I'm not dead anyway, and what doesn't kill you, makes you stronger. Now for the bottom half."

I helped him stand. "Ahh, fuck," he yelled suddenly as he put weight on his legs which were still strapped into his board.

"What is it?" I said concerned. If he had broken something then we were in trouble.

"My ankle. Hang on," he flexed his knee a couple of times, grimacing. "It's not broken, just sprained. I think I can board down on it."

"Are you sure?" I asked. "Shouldn't we call mountain rescue?"

He shook his head. "Phone signal is patchy out here. Besides, I am not sure if I could take the embarrassment." He looked down the slope. "It's an easy run down to the refuge from here anyway. I could probably do it with both legs broken."

"Refuge?" I said a bit confused.

"Yeah, the Prairond hut. It's manned too, so we'll be able to rest up there. James," he said suddenly looking at me intently.

"Yes Danny?"

"You probably saved my life. Thank you."

"Don't mention it." I said uncomfortable at his praise. "Let's just get you down in one piece."

"You also did the Pointe Pers," he said quietly, ignoring what I said. "Probably the most difficult run in the Alps. I failed."

"Forget it man,"

"Oh, I won't forget that," he said even more quietly. "I won't ever be able to forget that."

37

AFTER THE TENSION of the Pointe, the ski down to the refuge was surprisingly easy. We coasted down the bowl, over a low ridge to the right, and then all the way down a gentle slope to the bottom of the valley. I led the way, but paused to let Danny catch up every few hundred meters. He was a lot slower than normal, and I could tell that he was in pain from the way he was riding, but he didn't make one word of complaint.

About halfway down the hut came into view, a cheerful wooden building, nestled into the far slope, covered in snow. I could see someone on the balcony, watching us come down.

"At least there is someone there now," Danny grunted as we stopped at the final ridge.

"You said it was manned."

"Well they open it up around this time of year, but I wasn't sure of the exact date. We're lucky."

Fifteen minutes later we were on the porch of the refuge. After unclipping myself, I helped Danny hobble over to the door. I could feel him wince with every step.

We were met at the entrance by a tall, rangy looking man, with weather beaten skin and a shock of auburn hair. "Albert," he introduced himself in a strong French accent. "I am the warden here. We are not open yet."

I explained the situation and he grunted. "You better come in then. I will have a look at his leg."

As well as running the refuge, Albert turned out to be a qualified medic. Within a few minutes he had Danny sat down in the lounge with his trouser rolled up and leg resting on a table. "You have to know first aid to be warden," he said as he pushed and pulled at Danny's leg. "Half the time people come here with injuries. Now," he said turning to Danny, "does it hurt when I do this?"

After a few more questions and some more probing, Albert sat back on the stool. "I do not think you have broken it, just sprained your ankle here," he moved Danny's foot. "But we must get you to a doctor to be sure. For now we will put it on ice; that will help the swelling." He put his hand on his chin and furrowed his brow in thought. "I have a supply run coming early tomorrow. You can stay the night, then go back with him on the sledge in the morning."

Danny nodded, and then said decisively. "I will stay here tonight, but Jimmy, you will need to go back to Val now and let everyone know what has happened. Are you happy with that?" he said turning to me.

I felt a suddenly nervous about going on by myself. "Danny, I'm not sure. I don't want to leave you up here. Besides, I haven't done the run before, I could get lost."

Danny winced as he shifted his weight. "Jimmy, you have to go. You have to let Jen and the others know that we are safe, otherwise all hell will break loose. It's an easy run, you can do it by yourself, no problem."

"I suppose so," I replied slowly, still uncertain.

"Good man!" Danny said, brushing aside my qualms.

"Have some tea first," Albert got up and went behind the bar.

"Look, when you get back, everyone will panic," Danny spoke to me in a low voice. "As soon as you get back in range, phone Jen and tell her first. She will know what to do."

I nodded. "How do I get back down?" I said realising I didn't even know the way.

"It's not difficult. Once you are out of here, the path leads down to the Malpassant Gorge. In summer, a stream runs through it, but in winter, an ice bridge forms. Albert, is the ice bridge still safe to ski?"

"Bien sûr," he called out, pouring some boiling water into a teapot and coming round the bar with a tray. "I did it myself yesterday, but you should leave soon. It is better to go early."

"Once you are through the gorge," Danny carried on, "you come out to the St Charles bridge. You will probably be able to phone Jen from there."

Twenty minutes later, Danny and Albert were waving me off. I looked back and waved just before the path ran down into the gully, but they had already gone in. I took a deep breath, and headed into the gorge.

The path was easy to follow, and under different circumstances, would have been really fun. The tracks were so well worn in the hard snow that it really was just a matter of putting your skis into them and following them down through the narrow gorge. Once you were in, there was no other way to go, a bit like a train on rails. The path wound past boulders and corners, over little hills and hummocks and occasionally past holes in the ice where running water below could be heard. In no time at all, I was shooting out of the gully and the Pont St Charles came into view. I breathed a sigh of relief; I was almost home now.

"James, hi." Jen's voice came through loud and clear, despite only having a couple of bars reception on my phone. I sat on the low bridge wall and looked down the valley towards Le Fornet.

"Don't panic Jen, but Danny has had an accident doing some off piste."

"What!" I could her take a sharp intake of breath. "What happened?"

"He sprained his ankle coming down the Pointe Pers. I've left him at the Prairond refuge. They are going to bring him back on a skidoo tomorrow."

"Shit. I'm doing some shopping Bourg at the moment, but I will head up now. Can you meet me at the office in half an hour?"

"No problem."

"Good," she said and the line clicked dead, Jen wasn't one to hang around. I sighed, I was not looking forward to the interview with her.

I got to the office five minutes early, but Jen was not there, and the door was locked. I waited for twenty minutes, but she still did not show up. When I tried calling, her phone went straight to voicemail. After another five minutes, I rang back, left a message and headed back to the Chamois. I was cold and needed to change.

It was not until I was getting in through the door to the chalet that Jen rang back.

"James, it's Jen. There has been an avalanche on the road just outside of Le Breviere. No one is coming in or out of Val."

38

"SHIT, ARE YOU alright?" I ran back out onto the balcony.

"Yes, I am fine, I just won't be able to get back tonight. Now, tell me exactly what happened to Danny."

As I spoke I looked out over the valley and down to the town. It was so calm and peaceful that it was hard to believe that Jen had almost been caught in an avalanche and, only a few hours before, Danny had almost died in fall.

When I had finished Jen paused for a moment, thinking. "It's not as bad as I thought," she said. "I know Albert, if he says Danny will be back tomorrow, then he will be. Luckily it's day off tomorrow too, so he won't really be needed anyway. Christ, if it happened at the weekend, then we'd be buggered. Anyway, once he is back, he can run things there without me for a few days."

A few days! I suddenly felt panic rise in my stomach. I hadn't seen a lot of Jen, but it was reassuring knowing she was there. Everything functioned smoothly with her behind the scenes. Would ValSki be able to run without her?

"What happened on the road? Do you think it will take long to clear up?" I asked.

"A rock slide a few cars ahead of me. Quite a lot of the mountain came down, but no one was hurt. I don't know how long it will take to clear, it won't be today or tomorrow, that's for sure."

"What would you like me to do?"

"Just tell everyone what has happened, try and keep them all calm and let everyone get on with their jobs. I will ring a few of them now."

"What are you going to do?"

"I've got some friends I can stay with in Bourg. I will be online and available by phone so it won't be that different to being in resort."

"Good luck then. I'll ring you if I need anything."

"Thanks James. You've done very well today, very well. I'm pleased with you." Despite myself, I felt myself swell with pride. Praise from Jen was rarely given and only when it was really merited.

Johnners, Heather, Gwat, Claire and Faye were waiting in the lounge when I got in.

"Where the fuck have you been?" Heather jumped up and shouted as soon as she saw me. "We've been worried sick."

"Sorry, a lot's happened."

"Where's Danny?" Johnners asked.

"Still up the mountain, up at the Refuge down from the Pointe."

"What?" "What the fuck!" What's happened?" they all called out at once.

"Look, someone pour me a cup of tea, will you?" I sat down tiredly. "I'm exhausted. If you just wait a second, I'll tell you what happened."

When someone had bought me a tea, I told them what happened up the mountain. They all sat silently, listening with open mouths.

Johnners whistled. "Wow, phew. Sounds like a close call."

"And Danny is alright?" Faye asked anxiously. I couldn't help but think about her insistence that she was over Danny. It rang false now.

"Yes, he's fine."

Just then Johnners' phone rang. "Yes Jen," he answered, and stood up to speak to her out in the corridor.

"Oh, yes, another thing," I said. "There has been a landslide on the road out of Val. Jen is stuck in Bourg. Val is cut off."

"Jesus!" "Fuck!" "Christ."

"Why didn't you call to say you were okay?" Heather asked me softly, but I could tell she was angry. "I was worried sick."

"I'm sorry, what with Danny and speaking to Jen, it just didn't cross my mind to let you know we were okay. I'm sorry."

She shook her head and said, "James, we were worried sick."

"So you've heard about Jen then? It doesn't rain when it pours, does it!" Johnners had come back in the room. "Well lad, it sounds like you did well on the mountain. Making the Pers couloir when Danny didn't is a big deal. He'll be hopping mad about that."

"Hopping, eee, that's about all he'll be doing, eee!" Gwat looked up from the table grinning inanely.

"What happened to you guys?" I asked Johnners.

"We joined the run that we did from the Col a few weeks ago. We waited at the bridge for about half an hour, but when you didn't turn up, decided to come home. Heather was up for contacting mountain rescue but I knew that you'd be alright."

"What did Jen say to you?" Faye asked Johnners.

"Oh you know the usual. Do your job, everything will be fine, call me if there are any problems, that kind of thing."

"Yeah, it will be," I said. "Danny will be back tomorrow. Everything will be fine."

"Wednesday gwat hunting tonight!" Gwat called out. I'm going to get some Scandi gwat. Eeee!"

"Pipe down you!" Johnners said in a surprisingly firm voice, and Gwat sunk back in his chair, unused to being told what to do by Johnners. "This is not the time for that kind of talk. Look, we better get ready for work soon," he turned to Claire and Faye. "I know we had planned to go out and see that band, but I don't think that I can stand going out with Danny stuck up the hill."

Claire shook her head. "I agree. I'm going to get a shower before work." She stood up and stretched. "Well done James, you were a bit of a hero today."

"No, I er..." I stumbled over my words, suddenly embarrassed.

"Take the praise lad," Johnners said. "You deserve it. You skied the best out of all of us today and you kept your head and got Danny safe. He'd have been fecked without you, so yeah; you are a bit of a hero." He stood up to leave as well, and I could feel my cheeks burning.

"I better go too. Do Danny's job for him. Hot Tub Gwat, eee!" Gwat left as well leaving Heather and I alone in the room.

I turned to find Heather staring at me intently. "I'm sorry that I was angry at you earlier. I was just so scared about you getting hurt. I spent all afternoon imagining what might have happened to you."

"It's okay, I understand," I said. "I should have rung."

"Up on the mountain, just before I fell, I wanted to say something to you."

I nodded remembering the moment.

"I didn't come to Val to fall in love; in fact it was quite the opposite. I came here to get away from all the bullshit that you get with relationships. I've been badly hurt before James, and I didn't want that to happen again. And then as soon as I got here, I ended up in bed with Gwat, and then you..." she trailed off. I sat patiently waiting to hear what she would say.

"At first I thought you were different, and I allowed myself to be vulnerable. Which is why I was so hurt when we argued..." she trailed off again.

"What Heather? What are you trying to say?"

"James, I, er..."

"What?"

"I wasn't sure on the mountain, but when you didn't appear by the bridge, I thought my heart would break. I realised that I don't want to lose you James. Can we try again? I want to be with you. Can we start again?"

I didn't answer in words, just leaned forward and kissed her. A little later, I led her back up to my little loft room, and we did not leave until morning.

39

I WAS WOKEN by the sun stealing across me. I yawned and smiled; spring was coming and it was getting light a lot earlier. It looked like another beautiful day outside.

Heather was still deep in slumber next to me, her dark hair silhouetted against the white pillow, all the lines of tension and worry relaxed from her face. I suddenly realised how beautiful she really was underneath the tattoos, jewellery and hard-arsed attitude.

Her eyes flicked open, sensing me watching her, and she smiled and yawned too. "Hello you," she smiled up at me, all traces of defensiveness gone from her.

"Hello you back," I leant down and kissed her gently, then drew back. "You are going to get breakfast in bed this morning!"

She raised herself on her elbows. "Wow, what do I deserve this for?"

I winked as I swung myself down. "Just because. Now don't move."

She lay back on the pillows and laughed. "Don't worry, I'm not going anywhere."

To my great surprise Danny was in the kitchen when I got downstairs. The coffee machine was on; there was some bacon in a pan on the stove and a bag of warm croissants on the table.

He looked up at me as I came in and smiled. "Hello, hero!"

"Danny!" I walked over and hugged him. "How the fuck did you get here so early?"

"Careful of the leg!" he said as I squeezed.

"Ah, sorry mate. But really, how on earth are you here?"

Danny was still grinning. "Magic, mate! No, simple really. The skidoo left the refuge at first light, and then I got a lift all the way here from Le Fornet with Jock from Snowberry. Picked up some supplies on the way," he shook the bag of pastries, "and thought I would make breakfast for everyone."

"How is the leg?" I asked.

"A lot better," he lifted it up to show me. "I had it iced all night and kept it raised, so the swelling has gone down. I haven't got full flexibility back, but I can put weight on it now. I'll get it x-rayed today, but I'm a quick healer. Should be okay by tomorrow and able to ski again next week, I reckon."

"Cool."

"So breakfast? I wanted to make some for you to say thank you."

"I was actually going to take some up to Heather," I said, suddenly shy.

Danny raised an eyebrow. "Something you want to tell me?"

"Erm, we kind of got back together," I said uncomfortably.

He put his hands on his hips. "Look at you, hero of the mountain and then getting the girl. It's like a fairy story!" I could not be sure if there was a hint of sarcasm in his voice or whether I was just imagining it.

"Yeah, well..."

"So you don't want my breakfast then?" There was a definite angry undertone to his voice now.

"I, er..."

Danny laughed. "I'm joking mate! Take some bacon and croissant and coffee up. I've got stuff to do."

"Oh right, thanks," I said, flustered. Danny always had the ability to make me feel foolish. "Have you heard from Jen?"

"Yeah, called her as soon as I got in range. She was already up working."

"So what is the plan?"

"Plan? Well, I think we need to reassure all the staff. We'll have a meeting this afternoon around three."

"On day off?" I said a bit disappointed. "People won't like that."

"Oh, don't worry," Danny said smiling. "Everyone will like this kind of meeting. Extraordinary staff meetings are always held in the Danois."

"Ah, alright," I said suddenly understanding. "It's that kind of meeting. I'll spread the word."

"Good. Right, let's get that breakfast ready. Can't keep the girl waiting!" he winked at me, but his eyes were cold.

Back upstairs Heather whistled when I walked in with a tray overflowing with bacon, eggs, croissant and fresh coffee. "Wow, you were busy!" she said.

"Present from Danny, he's back already," I said, handing it up to her and then climbing up afterwards.

She paused, chewing on a croissant and pulled a face. "Did you tell him that I was with you?" she asked when she had swallowed.

"Yes, why?"

"I don't trust him," she said flatly.

"What? I thought that you fancied him!" I said, teasing her.

"Well yes, I did," she shrugged her shoulders. "But, now... I don't know. After what he did to Giles, I'm surprised that you are so pally with him."

"Well," I looked down, the atmosphere of intimacy suddenly gone. "I don't really trust him either, but you have to admit he's been a good manager."

"Really? Endangering his life and ours on that idiotic off-piste run yesterday? Look, with Jen gone, he's in charge, and I'm just worried what will happen."

"Well he has asked that we all meet today at three."

She snorted. "I bet it's in a pub. It is, isn't it?" she added when she saw my face. "Let me guess, the Danois?" I nodded. "That's not going to be a meeting at all is it?"

"Maybe," I said guardedly. "Still, I think it's a good idea. He will have been in contact with Jen and can let us know any specific plans."

"Okay," she suddenly pushed the tray of food out of the way. "But that leaves almost the whole day to ourselves. I think we should do something by ourselves today."

"Like what?"

She reached over and pulled me down towards her. "Oh, I've got a few ideas," she murmured before our lips met again.

40

WE GOT TO the Danois an hour or so before everyone else intending to have a late lunch there by ourselves. Unusually, the bar was almost empty, there were only a few customers sat up in the high stools by the bar. As I went up to order our food I immediately recognised one of them.

"Andy!" I called out, genuinely delighted to see him. It had been two months since he had bought me up the mountain, and although his dark warnings had scared me, I genuinely had appreciated his advice.

"What, who..." he gazed at me blearily, and I saw that he was drunk.

"It's James. You bought me up from Geneva just after Christmas. You told me about despair remember? You warned me about Val."

"James, James, James," he mumbled, and then something clicked into place. "Ah yes, Jen's pretty boy. I remember now."

"What are you doing here anyway? I thought you hated it here."

"I do, I don't want to be here. Fucking avalanche trapped me," he brooded staring at his pint. "I was on a run up from Bourg, now I can't get back."

"Well there could be worse places," I said trying to sound positive.

He didn't reply immediately but looked me up and down slowly. "So you listened to me then? You didn't get drunk, you didn't get broken? You didn't get chlamydia? You didn't go mad?"

"No, no," I said smiling. "Quite the opposite in fact. That's my girlfriend over there," I felt a thrill as I said the word girlfriend, and pointed over to where Heather was sitting down at a table.

"Girlfriend eh?" he said bitterly, taking a swig of his pint. "Well maybe it has worked out for you after all. Maybe you will make it out alive then."

"Maybe it will be better than that. We're planning to go off to Canada at the end of the season." I felt suddenly sad for Andy. Something bad had obviously happened to him in the past, and now he was just a lonely and bitter man.

"Don't get cocky kid," he said and stood and loomed over me threateningly as if he could sense my pity. I had forgotten what a large intimidating presence he had.

"No, I er..."

"It's when you think you have got it all worked out that it all falls apart."

"Right, yes,"

"Trust me I know," he grabbed his glass and downed the rest of his drink. "No offence kid, but you don't want to see me again. I'm the fucking Grim Reaper round here. I only see people when they are broken and have to go down the hill." And with that he lurched out of the Danois.

"Who was that?" Heather asked when I rejoined her at the table after ordering our food.

"The guy who bought me up here," I replied, strangely unsettled by my conversation with Andy. "Friend of Jen's"

"He looked fucked."

"Yeah," I said slowly. "I think he is."

"Johnners, Ash, Claire and Faye, Toby and Calli, Pete and Caroline, Alice and Harri, Marco, Jimmy, Heather and Gwat." Danny counted us all off one by one. "All here. Let's make a start."

After we finished lunch, the rest of the ValSki staff began drifting in small groups and pretty soon we had colonised the whole of the back area. The hubbub slowly quietened down as Danny started speaking and everyone turned to him expectantly.

"So as you all know, there has been a landslide on the road down to Bourg and Val has been cut off. Jen was on the other side of it and so is stuck down the mountain until further notice."

"Do they know when it will be clear?" Pete asked. He was the oldest member of ValSki staff, in his mid-forties.

"The latest reports coming from the radio say a couple of days at least, but they are not sure exactly how many." Danny answered. "They have an expert coming to look at it today, so I expect they will give a schedule tomorrow. My guess is that by Saturday they will have enough cleared for transfers on Sunday."

There was a general murmuring as people digested news. "What will happen if they cannot clear it by then?" Claire asked.

"I spoke to head office about this," Danny said. "If that happens, then transfers will be delayed until Monday. Jen has sorted out deliveries of fresh meat, fruit and veg to last us until next Tuesday, and we have enough dry goods to last until the weekend after that."

"Punter's won't be happy," Johnners said glumly.

"Are you kidding?" Faye exclaimed. "It will mean a longer holiday. They will be over the moon."

"Obviously they will ask you about arrangements," Danny said, "probably at breakfast tomorrow. Just be calm and cool and let them know the facts. Listen to Radio Val, they will have the latest updates. I will try and get round every chalet at breakfast tomorrow, but I am obviously a bit slower than normal."

"Eee, Hopalong Danny!" Gwat called out to a scattered laughter.

Danny smiled. "Those that I don't get to in the morning, I will see when they get back from skiing."

"What happened to your leg anyway?" Pete asked. They did not live in the Chamois but in rooms near their own chalet. As an older married couple it was probably for the best they were away from all the shenanigans there.

"He broke it on the dance floor like Giles," Johnners called out and there was a snigger across the room.

"Very funny," Danny smiled sardonically at him. "Actually, I wanted to talk about that as well. Yesterday, as most of you know already, I had an accident off piste out past Le Fornet. What most of you may not know is that I would have probably died if it hadn't been for James."

Everyone turned to look at me. "No, I, er..." I felt my throat go dry as I struggled to find something to say.

"Jimmy is a real hero," Danny said quietly. "He saved my life. I fell fifty meters down the Pers couloir and knocked myself unconscious. If Jimmy hadn't been there to help me down to the Prairond refuge, I would probably have died of exposure up there."

"That's not true..." I tried to say, but Danny interrupted me again.

"It is true James. I would have died out there. You saved my life. I will always be in your debt."

Suddenly everyone was clapping and cheering my name. A hot flush of embarrassment spread over my face but also a great feeling of warmth in my stomach. It actually felt good to be appreciated.

When the noise had died down, Danny carried on. "He didn't panic, kept a calm head, made some sensible decisions and everything worked out. That's pretty much what we have to do here now over the next few days. So to say thank you to Jimmy, and for all the hard professional work you guys are about to do until the road clears," Danny made a sign to a waitress at the bar, "I would like to propose a toast." Suddenly trays of champagne and glasses were at the table and being passed round.

"Here's to Jimmy and keeping your head!"

"Jimmy and keeping your head!" everyone echoed and clinked glasses.

"No more notices or speeches," Danny said over the hubbub. "Now to the real point of the meeting. Cheers everyone!"

We finished the champagne, then a bowl of punch appeared. When that was gone, we moved on to the V Spot bar to play pool, and then to the Blue Note for a couple of beers. By the time that we hit Saloon I was reeling, and five minutes after Danny handed me a jug, my memories ended.

Part Four

The End of the Season

41

MY EYES FLICKED open. I was in an unfamiliar room, sitting up at the end of a bed, fully dressed. Light streamed in through a window and there were clothes strewn all about. Danny was sitting at the foot of the bed, his face creased and tired looking.

"Where am I?" I asked looking round. "Hang on, this is your room Danny. What am I doing here?"

He looked at me and asked quietly, "Why did you do it James? Why?"

"What? What have I done? And how did I get these scratches?" I looked down at my arm, they were covered in lines of red welts. "And why are you wearing my hat!" For some reason he had my favourite orange beanie on his head.

"Why, James? Why did you do it?" He ignored my questions but removed the hat and laid it carefully on the floor.

There was something in his voice, something quiet and serious that sent shivers up my spine. His eyes were fixed intently on mine. "What? What are you talking about? Look will you tell me what is going on? What am I doing here?" I asked again.

Danny just stared at me. "Why James?" he asked simply.

"What! What are you talking about? Why did I do what?" I said more loudly. There was something in his voice that was making me panic.

"Faye. Why did you kill Faye?"

If I was not sitting down, then I would have fallen. My body went cold, my heart started racing and I felt a yawning hole open up in my stomach.

"What, I don't know what you mean, I..."

"Faye's dead. You killed her," Danny said slowly.

My head started reeling.

"No, no, I didn't. I couldn't have. Last thing I remember I was in the Saloon..."

"You threw her off the bridge James." His voice was so quiet, so still, so low, that I could barely hear it.

"Oh God. Oh fuck."

"Tell me why, James. If you tell me why, I may be able to help. Was it because she turned you down? Tell me."

"Ah, I don't know. I don't remember anything!"

"Well you were very drunk in the Saloon and I tried to take you home. But as we were crossing the bridge, you saw Faye and said you wanted to wait for her. I tried to persuade you it was a bad idea, but you wouldn't listen to me. I left you there as she was coming."

"What! Why did you leave me! She was your girlfriend!"

"Ex-Girlfriend," he corrected. "And anyway, I didn't have much choice, you were very insistent. In fact you were pretty rude to me. Told me to fuck off and mind my own business and you would fuck who you liked. So I left you to it. Gwat saw you on the bridge with her a bit later, but thought you were just kissing, so he left you too."

"Oh God, I didn't, I can't remember. Faye, oh my God, I couldn't have, I only remember the Saloon..." I knew I was babbling, but I couldn't stop.

Danny reached forward and held my arm, stopping my flow. "James, can you remember why? What happened?"

I shook my head. "I can't Danny, it's just a blank. One minute I was in Saloon, and the next I was here. I didn't do it, you must believe me."

"James, look, I'm going to ask one last time. If you answer, then I may be able to help you. But I have to know what happened and why you did it."

"I don't know!" I shouted. "I don't know!"

"Then I can't help you," he shook his head sadly and stood. "I'm sorry. Faye is gone now, there is no helping her, but I would have helped you. You've proved you belong here, you saved my life. I owe you big time, but if you're not honest with me, then I will have to tell the gendarmes what I know. Now, why did you do it? What happened?"

It was too much. I started babbling again, not really aware of what I was saying. "Don't, don't! Please! Oh, God, I don't know. Perhaps I still wanted her and she refused me. Perhaps she said she still wanted you. Perhaps we struggled and she fell over. I don't know Danny, I don't know!"

Danny paused at the door. "Really? You really cannot remember?"

"No!" I hung my head.

"You know, I think I believe you." He shut the door and came back into the room.

"Thank you Danny, thank you," I could feel myself start to lose control again.

He held up his hand. "That doesn't mean that you didn't do it. I still think you did, but you were not really in charge of yourself, that much I think I believe. So what do we do now?"

"I... I... I think we should just go to the gendarmes and tell them everything," I said. "I have nothing to hide." I realised suddenly that was exactly what I wanted to do.

"Don't be an idiot, James!" Danny raised his voice. "Think about it. You have two people who saw you on the bridge with her. You have scratches up your arm. It is well known that you have made passes at her in the past and she has refused you. You made another lunge at her, she rejected you, then you struggled on the bridge and she went over. If it's not murder then it will be at least manslaughter. That's still a long stretch."

"Oh shit." My stomach did another cartwheel. Whether I did or did not throw Faye over the bridge didn't matter. I was the one who would be found guilty.

"No," Danny decided. "We won't say anything. We won't go to the gendarmes, we'll sit tight. Faye was smashed enough to have just fallen in by herself. If they come asking, we shall just say that we don't know anything."

"What about Gwat?"

"He won't say anything, if I ask him not too."

"Fuck, fuck. Faye..."

"Yes James. Faye is dead. You killed her." The enormity of what had happened was really only still beginning to dawn on me.

"Where is Heather?" I sat up, suddenly desperate to see her.

"Jimmy, I don't think that..."

"Where is she! I need to see her." I jumped up off the bed.

Danny got up too and winced as he put his weight on his strained knee. "James, I'm sorry, she went home with Gwat last night. She is in his room now still sleeping."

"Shit!" But with the news of what had happened to Faye, the significance of Heather going back with Gwat just didn't seem to matter anymore. I put my head in my hands.

Danny's phone started to ring. I heard him answer and then a moment later say, "I'll come now."

"Jimmy, Jimmy, listen to me." He was shaking me, trying to rouse me from my panic. "Look, you stay here. I'll sort it all out for you. I promise." And he limped from the room.

42

FOR THE TWENTY minutes that he was gone I was at a complete loss. I got up for a while and wandered round the room. I looked out of the window at the white sky and slopes. I lay on the bed. All the while my mind was imagining Faye falling from the bridge into the freezing water of the Isere River. What happened? Did she fall? Did I push her? I could picture us struggling on the bridge so clearly that I started to believe that maybe I had killed her.

Suddenly Danny was back in the room. He shut the door behind him and motioned me to sit down on the bed. "Listen, this is the plan," he said quietly. "Hosting is obviously cancelled, I rang all the chalets to let them know when the gendarmes called me this morning. Breakfast is off too but the hosts will have to go back and cook this evening. The gendarmes will want to speak to everyone today, but as far as I am aware, they will be treating this as an accident. Lots of people saw Faye leave the Saloon by herself, they will think that she was so drunk she fell in. I've spoken to Gwat and he will keep schtum about seeing you on the bridge with her."

"What about Heather?" I looked up suddenly. "If she was with Gwat she would have seen me too."

"Ah, yeah," Danny scratched his head. "She was pretty out of it too. I'm not sure if she will remember anything."

"I want to see her," I said. "If she went home with Gwat then she will be in a state too."

"I'm not sure that that is a good idea right now," Danny shook his head. "You are pretty emotional. I think you just need to chill out and act normally."

"If I was acting normally, then I would want to see her," I said stubbornly.

Danny blinked. "Well, whatever. She's in her room now. Come to the lounge when you are done. We are expecting Lieutenant Colbert at some point this morning."

I nodded and got up. As I passed the door, Danny put his hand on my shoulder. "It will be okay James, I promise. We have to stick together in times like this."

"Faye's dead, Danny. Nothing can be okay now," and I shouldered past him.

Heather was sitting on her bed, her eyes red from crying. She looked so anguished and vulnerable that I could not help but feel my heart tighten inside.

"Heather, I..." I began speaking, but couldn't finish.

She looked up at me. "James, oh God, I..." and then she was sobbing and we were in each other's arms.

"It happened again," she managed to croak through the tears. "I was in bed with Gwat again, I don't know what happened. I was in the Saloon one minute and then woke up in his bed again. And now Faye..." she started sobbing again.

"Shh, shh it will be fine," I said as soothingly as I could, knowing full well that it wouldn't be.

After a few moments, she pulled back. "You don't mind? About me going back with Gwat?"

"I don't think you meant to," I said truthfully. "And anyway, there is something I have to tell you. Something Danny told me..." At the back of mind, something suddenly started to nag away. Something Heather had just said about what had happened to her.

"About Faye? What James? What happened?" she looked at me deep in the eyes, sensing that I had something important to say.

"Heather! James!" Danny was calling and knocking on the door.

"Can it wait?" I called out.

"No, not really" Danny replied.

"You'd better come in," I said after looking at Heather.

"Sorry to interrupt," he said when he came in and saw us holding each other tight. "Lieutenant Colbert from the gendarmerie is in the lounge. He would like to speak to everyone."

I nodded at once relieved that I hadn't told her about Faye and then bitterly disappointed. "Come on, we'd better go," I said.

"What have you got to tell me?" she asked insistently.

I was aware of Danny staring at me intently. "Nothing. Nothing important. I'll tell you later," I said and kissed her hair.

"I look like shit!" Heather caught sight of her red eyes and tear streaked face in the mirror. "I can't go looking like this."

"It will be fine," Danny said. "Trust me, half the staff are blubbing right now."

"No," she shook her head stubbornly. "I will only be a couple of minutes. You go on ahead."

Danny inclined his head. "Don't be too long," he said to her, and then to me, "come on, let's go."

A few meters on, once we were out of immediate earshot, he turned to me and said casually, "You didn't tell her did you?"

I shook my head suddenly feeling reckless. I was sick of Danny telling me what to do. "No, but does it matter if I did?" I said belligerently.

Danny stopped and then before I knew it he had me pinned up against the wall. One hand was clamped around my throat and the other was digging painfully into my solar plexus. I struggled, but he was incredibly strong and I could hardly move.

"Listen, you fucking idiot," he hissed at me. "I'm trying to help save your fucking life. I'm going to lie to the police for you. That could get me in jail. I'm doing it because you are worth saving. Now, don't say anything to anyone. Understand?"

I nodded suddenly terrified of him. There was such anger and power in him that it seemed almost impossible to refuse him. "Good!" He held me a moment longer and then let me go. I slumped and would have fallen if he had not caught me.

"Whoa," he said, and then suddenly the angry Danny was gone and the kind, caring Danny was back again. "Look mate, it will be fine. Just don't say anything to anyone, and everything will be okay. Are you ready to go in?" He looked at me in the eyes. I nodded, not sure what else I could do. I didn't feel ready, but waiting outside seemed suspicious.

"Let's go in then," and he propelled me down the corridor to the entrance of the lounge. "Remember, nothing to anyone," he whispered at me as I opened the door and walked into the lounge.

43

I WAS WORRIED that my mixed-up emotional state was going to give something away, but I needn't have bothered. The lounge was crammed full of ValSki staff all in different states of distress. Most of the girls were red-faced from crying and the boys were white-faced and drawn. Hardly anyone was speaking, just the occasional murmur. Two police officers, in dark blue uniform, sat at the table waiting patiently with notebooks open.

The first, a young female officer with her hair tied back, kept looking round the room. She fiddled with her pen and had already scribbled down half a page of notes. The older, senior looking policeman had dark blond hair in a fringe underneath his cap. He sat impassively, scarcely moving until Danny approached. "Everyone is here?" he asked in almost accent-less English. The room fell silent when he spoke.

Danny shook his head. "One more. She will be here in a moment."

"We will wait," he said without any emotion in his voice. Thirty seconds later, Heather tried to enter unobtrusively, but everyone was watching her.

"Sorry," she mumbled an apology looking at the gendarmes. She came and stood next to me and I put my arm around her protectively.

The gendarme nodded at her and then stood up. "My name is Colbert, I am the Lieutenant in Val d'Isere. We received a call early this morning to let us know that a body had been found in the Isere River. We have reason to believe that it may be an employee of ValSki."

"Is it Faye?" Claire asked. "Is there a chance that it is someone else?"

"We must formally identify the body, but yes, we think it is Faye Buchannon."

"Oh God..." Claire began but broke down sobbing. A couple of the others started crying too.

Colbert waited a few moments for them to pull themselves together before continuing. "Unfortunately this is not unusual, it happens every other season. Is there someone who can identify the body?" Danny put his hand up. "I'll do that."

"Thank you," Colbert nodded at him. "Once we have done that then I will need to take some statements from you and everyone who was in the Saloon bar last night." He looked out at us all, perhaps trying to see if anyone had anything to hide. I felt a cold shiver run down my spine. Was it my imagination or did his gaze linger on me slightly longer than on the others? I shuddered.

"I realise this is a terrible shock to you all. I am sorry for your friend," Colbert stood.

"I'll come back after I have been to the gendarmerie," Danny said and stood as well. "I am sorry; we will have to put in a normal shift this evening, we still have to feed the guests. I know it'll be hard but they will understand if you are not on top form."

"Do they know?" Johnners asked.

"Some of them know now, but by this afternoon they all will," Danny said. "I spoke to a couple of them this morning and will visit the rest later."

"Is there any news on when the road will be open?" Joe asked. "Do we know when Jen will be back? Does she know?"

"I called her this morning. She is handling head office and calling Faye's parents, but she will probably call you all individually. As to when she can get back..." he looked over at Colbert.

"The road will be closed for at least another day," Colbert shrugged. "They hope tomorrow to clear as far as Les Brévières."

"Jen will be able to park and ski across from there," Danny said. "So fingers crossed she will be with us tomorrow afternoon."

Everyone fell silent. "Okay, we will meet you at the gendarmerie." Colbert said to Danny and he walked out of the room with the female officer.

"Gwat, will you come with me please?" Danny asked. "I don't feel like doing this by myself." And he limped out after Colbert.

After they had gone, people started to disperse. Pete and Caroline went back to their own accommodation whilst Harri and Alice crept off to their rooms muttering about phoning home. Toby and Cali made a comment about going to their chalet to get out and do something useful and Ash walked out with them. That left just Johnners, Claire, Joe, Marco, Heather and me in the lounge.

We all sat in silence, not knowing what to say. I could feel waves of guilt and fear and terror wash around in my stomach and thoughts pinged round my brain like dodgem cars. I had killed someone. I had murdered Faye. Or at the very least I had let her die. I was sat with her friends when I was responsible. What was I thinking, what was I doing, what had happened? It would not be long before the story of me meeting Faye on the bridge came out. If Danny and Gwat had seen me, there could have been a dozen or more people who saw us. What would happen to me now?

"What happened to Faye last night?" Johnners asked Claire.

"I don't know!" she wailed, on the edge of tears. "She was fine one minute, and then reeling round the next. I offered to walk back with her but Danny said that he would made sure she got home as he had to take James back. If only I had gone back with her..." and then the tears did come and she dissolved into sobs.

"It's not your fault, pet," Johnners tried to comfort her. "You weren't to know..."

"Cup of tea?" Joe asked and got up. "Do you want one?" he said looking at me. He was trying to calm the situation I knew, but it had the opposite effect. Something snapped inside of me and all the fear, confusion and guilt boiled up as anger inside me.

"No I don't want a fucking cup of tea Joe! That is not going to help."

"Calm down lad," Johnners said over Claire's shoulder. "Shouting isn't going to help."

"Nothing is going to help!" I cried. "She's dead... She's dead and I... I ..." I desperately wanted to confess, to shout out that it was me who had murdered her, who had pushed her in the river and taken away her life. There was a terrible burning pain in my heart, a feeling of guilt and dread that I could no longer bear. Not only had I killed her but by staying silent now, I was lying, deceiving and betraying my friends as well. I knew that I could not live with myself like that.

"You what?" Claire asked a strange expression on her face. Did she know already? Was the guilt written over my face?"

"I..., I..." I couldn't find the words to say, they just seemed to stick in my throat.

"James, what is it?" Heather stood up and came in close to me.

"I..., I did it..."

44

"WE ALL DID it James," Danny's strong voice called across the room, halting me in my tracks. I froze. I knew that I would never be able to confess in front of him, he just had too much power over me.

"We all did it," he repeated. "We are all responsible. We all could have saved her. We let her down, all of us. We are all responsible for her," he looked around at everyone in the room; Claire, Johnners, Marco, Joe, Heather and me, one by one meeting our eyes. "We all let her down, we let her die. We are all responsible for Faye's death. Every single one of us." The silence was broken only by Claire's quiet sobbing. Danny paused again before continuing.

"And God knows that I was more responsible than anyone. She loved me and I broke her heart. And the worst part is that I loved her too. I loved Faye more than anything. I hated seeing her with other men, I should have apologised and done all I could do to go back out with her. It was only my stupid pride that stopped me..." he trailed off and tears started to course down his cheeks. Claire came over and hugged him. "Shh," she whispered, "it's alright. It's not your fault..."

But Danny shook her off. "No, it is my fault. If I had not finished with her at the airport then none of this would have happened. That destroyed her..." Claire hugged him again but did not say anything.

I started wondering why Danny had protected me, why had he lied for me? He should hate me more than anything and want to see me punished badly.

Johnners was the first to break the silence. "Mate, I didn't realise it was like that, that you still felt that way."

Danny laughed bitterly. "Well we all have our own little secrets, don't we?" I looked up, wondering if he was talking to me.

Johnners shook his head, came up to him and started hugging him. "Mate, you should have said, you should have said."

"Well it's too late anyway. All we can do now," he pulled back from Johnners, "is look after each other. We're family here and we look after our own. There is no point in blaming ourselves or others." He was looking at each of us in the room, but it felt like his words were aimed directly at me again.

"Look, I have to go," he said after a moment. "Gwat is waiting in the car outside. I have to go to the gendarmes to identify the body. I only came back because I need to ask someone to be in the office and field any calls."

"I'll go," Johnners said. "I'm probably the most experienced here."

Danny considered. "No mate, you are going to have to be on top form this evening for the guests. It should be one of the ski guides really." He looked up at me. "James, I think. Gwat is in the car and I do not think that it is a good time for him to be with Heather, he is bound to say something inappropriate. Are you okay with that James?"

"Well, I, er..." Getting in a car with Danny and Gwat was the last thing that I wanted to do. Although the atmosphere in the Chamois was oppressive, being with Danny and Gwat would be worse.

"Good man," Danny said stopping me stalling. "I knew that I could rely on you. Now, I don't think that I will be gone long, but just try and stay positive if you can." And he led me out of the room, favouring his good leg.

As soon as we left the lounge, I could feel Danny's attitude change. Gone was the compassionate and emotional leader and back was the angry, violent and unpredictable man who had half throttled me before the meeting. He pushed passed me, turning briefly to say coldly "Hurry up. We're keeping the gendarmes waiting."

Gwat was waiting in his car outside, a battered old grey Nissan. The engine was running and he was smoking a roll up.

"You took your fuckin' time," he complained.

Danny got in the front and motioned me into the back. "Damage limitation," he said curtly.

I could not let that pass. "Look Danny..." I began hotly, but he leant over the chair and he interrupted me with such violence that I thought he might actually hit me.

"No, you look you fucking cretin. You were about to spill the beans, weren't you, don't deny it. It's a fucking good job I've got you sussed and came back to save you. Otherwise you would be on your way to the lock up right now. You're not just a murderer James, but a complete liability too. I don't know why I fucking bothered."

"Why did you then," I retorted sullenly. Even though I was petrified of him, I could not help but answer him back.

"Oh James, you still do not get it, do you. I meant what I said in the Chamois; you are one of us now, you are family and we look after each other. We can't help Faye now, but we can save you."

"You shouldn't have bothered," I muttered.

"I didn't have a choice," Danny replied quietly. "Don't you remember the Pointe Pers? It's not just me, it's the mountains. They want you back, they want you saved. That's what they were telling me when they let me fall."

"What?" I said confused.

"Oh, never mind. I don't think you understand at all," he said turning round to face forward again. I sat in the back and sulked.

"Where are we taking him then?" Gwat said as he turned the car onto the main road. "Up to the office?"

"No, I don't think he can be trusted. He better come with us."

"You're going to let him come into the police station with us? He could blab everything there," Gwat replied coughing.

"You're right," Danny brooded for a couple of seconds. "He can sit in the car and think about where his loyalties lie whilst we go and save his fucking neck."

45

"GIVE US A minute will you Anthony," Danny said to Gwat when he had pulled up outside the gendarmerie. Gwat shrugged and left us in the car.

"Now don't go anywhere," Danny turned to speak to me in back, his tone conciliatory.

"I'm surprised you don't lock me in," I scowled back at him.

"James, you have to start trusting me," he said quietly. "I'm your friend, I'm trying to save you."

"I just want you to leave me alone," I said.

"Suit yourself, but I am just trying to help." Danny shrugged, closed the door and walked to the police station, still limping from his injury up at the Pointe Pers. I sighed, glad to be away from him.

As soon as he had gone though the doors though, I wished he was back. I was scared stiff of Danny, but there was something reassuring about his presence. When he was around everything seemed a lot simpler, I just had to do what he said, even if I didn't like it.

Now I was alone, the thoughts of fear and guilt came crashing back.

I had killed Faye. I was a murderer. I had pushed an innocent girl off a bridge into an icy stream and her death.

I had deceived my friends, letting them think that it was an accident when really the guilty culprit was standing next to them, pretending to be one of them.

I was letting Danny and Gwat lie to the Police for me, risking their own reputations, all to try and save my own sorry life.

And all because I was too frightened of the gendarmes and going to prison.

No, I realised suddenly, I wasn't frightened of the gendarmes. I wasn't even frightened of going to prison. It had to be better than the feeling of guilt and pain that I was carrying now.

I was frightened of Danny.

I was frightened of standing up for myself.

I was a coward and that knowledge made me hate myself even more.

"FUCK IT!" I shouted, and before I knew it I had opened the door and was running up the street. I had no idea where I was going or what I was doing, I just couldn't bear sitting in the car any more.

The feeling of doing something physical felt good. I could ignore the whirling thoughts in my head and the churning emotions in my stomach and concentrate on the sensations of my feet hitting the compacted snow, the cold air hitting my lungs and the slow build-up of lactic acid in my limbs.

I realised after a few moments that I was headed out of town up towards Le Fornet, where Danny had taken us up to the Pointe Pers. It was only two days before but it felt a lifetime ago. I accelerated, an intense energy filling my body.

But by the time I reached the Fornet gondola two kilometres outside of Val d'Isere, this energy was gone. I hunched over trying to catch my breath. A bus stopped and disgorged a group of skiers and boarders, carrying their gear and chatting happily about the snow as they passed around me.

I straightened up. The mountains were towering above me, dark, forbidding and unforgiving in the morning light.

Danny had said that the mountains wanted me here. The mountains had saved me. They were responsible.

"FUCK YOU!" I cried suddenly. "FUCK YOU ALL!"

The skiers turned to stare at me. "FUCK YOU!" I shouted again staring up at the sides of the valley. "FUCK YOU!" I shouted one last time before I collapsed on the floor.

I was vaguely aware of someone calling my name, of hands helping me up and then I passed out.

I came to with warm air blowing on my face. I was in a car, no a van seat and the fan was turned onto maximum. Somehow it felt familiar.

"Back with us then?" It was Andy's voice. I was in the van that had bought me to Val d'Isere.

I turned, and sure enough he was sitting in the driver's seat next to me, sober this time.

"What happened?" I asked slowly.

"I think you better tell me," he answered. "I picked you off the floor and drove out of the way. I didn't think that it was a good idea to leave you with a load of Frenchies after you told them all to go fuck themselves."

"Thanks," I said and then stopped. I didn't know what else to say.

"Look, I'm sorry about yesterday. I was drunk and out of order."

I shook my head. "It doesn't matter now," I said sadly.

"So, what happened then?" he asked quietly.

"I, er..." I couldn't finish.

Andy shook his head and then laughed suddenly. "See I told you that I was bad luck, I am the fucking Grim Reaper. Running about and collapsing up at Le Fornet? Sounds like you have got the Val disease good and proper."

He had obviously not heard about Faye, but it was good to hear laughter and be around someone who was not involved.

"Yeah," I agreed smiling darkly to myself. "You could say that. I've found despair alright."

"So, what went wrong?" he asked again. "Yesterday it was all peaches and cream. Come on, you can tell me. Is it the girl? Have you done something bad?"

I realised that I desperately wanted to tell him what had happened and to ask his advice, but I knew also that I couldn't just come out with the truth.

"Yes," I nodded slowly. "Both those things. I have done something I really regret. Something I do not think I can fix."

"Really?" Andy seemed amused. "You think you can't fix it? Well in my long experience, there are few situations that cannot be resolved. I am sure you can do something."

"No," I shook my head. "This time I don't think I can."

He snorted. "Of course you can, you just don't realise what it is yet."

46

ANDY DROVE ME back into town and dropped me at the office. I couldn't bear going back to the Chamois to face everyone just yet and as Gwat's car was no longer outside the police station, I knew that Danny would probably be at the chalets. I didn't really want to see him either, but I knew that I would have to face him at some point. The chance meeting with Andy had helped me calm down though, and I felt better able to deal with him now.

Sure enough Danny was in the office on the phone. "No problem," he was saying, "I'll make sure everyone knows. I think most of them will be alright, it's just Claire and the girls that may not cope." He motioned me to come in and sit down whilst he continued. "I'm about to go round and speak to the guests, but I'll give you a call later." He paused listening to the reply, then said goodbye and hung up.

"That was Jen," he said. "If any of the hosts can't cope tonight, then she has authorised me to send the guests off to a restaurant for dinner. We've cancelled ski guiding for the week as well, to give you and Heather a chance to recover too." He was calm and professional sounding, which was a relief. I thought that I might find the angry Danny and I was not sure I was able to cope with him.

"Thanks," I said. "I don't think that I could face guiding now. Do you think that the hosts will be alright?"

"Yeah, probably better for them to have something to do," he said tiredly. "Probably better than us."

"What happened at the police station?" I asked quietly.

"I saw the body, it was Faye alright. We then gave a statement each."

"And?" I asked my heart thumping.

Danny looked at me sardonically. "Oh, don't worry, you're in the clear. They don't suspect any foul play. They think it was just another tragic case of a drunken English seasonnaire not paying enough respect to the environment. They may come and take some more statements, but I don't think they'll bother to be honest."

I sat down heavily on one of the chairs, not quite sure how to take the news.

"What happened to you anyway?" he said after a few moments.

"I, er, went for a walk," I said, not really wanting to talk about Andy.

"Fair play, I guess you needed some space." He gazed out of the window before continuing. "Look, I'm sorry if I was intense with you earlier. I realise that I may have come across a bit strong, but I was just desperate to try and salvage something out of this shit storm. Part of me wondered if you would go and do something stupid, but I guess at some point that I have to trust you, don't I? I mean, you have to trust me, don't you?"

"Yes Danny, I suppose I do," I said a heavy feeling in my heart.

"So we all cool then?" he held out his hand. "You're not going to do anything stupid again are you?"

I hated myself for doing it, but I shook my head and took his hand.

"I have to go round the chalets now," he said quietly standing up. "This needn't be the end of everything," he paused. "Just be patient, ride it out, things will get better again. The magic will come back I promise."

But I knew deep down that it never would.

I was not sure how I got through the rest of the day without cracking up. I sat in the office, waiting for the phone to ring, or Danny to come back, or the gendarmes to come round and arrest me, but nothing happened. Eventually I started to get bored, so I surfed the news on the Internet, made a cup of tea and then paced up and down. After an hour or two, Gwat stuck his head in the door to tell me he was going back to the Chamois, but that was it.

I tried with all my might to remember what happened. I replayed every moment from the night before, from the drinks in the Danois, to Danny's speech, to the drinks in the Saloon, but it all ended when Danny handed me the jug. I just could not remember anything after that.

In the absence of any clear memories, I began to imagine the scene. I pictured myself on the bridge with Faye, saw myself lunging at her, saw her trying to fight me off, saw her trip and tumble over the railings... until I wasn't sure if it was imagined or real.

My emotions fluctuated wildly. One moment I felt elated that I was not going to go to prison, the next I was overcome with remorse and anger at myself for trying to cover up my crime. Next I hated Danny with every fibre of me being, the next I was overwhelmed by gratitude for what he was doing for me. I felt sick and then pumped and then shivering cold and then burning hot.

There was still something at the back of my head nagging me. Something just wasn't right, I just couldn't work it out. Something about what happened...

But the worse thing was the confusion, not knowing what to do, or if indeed I could do anything. Was it as Danny said I just had to ride it out, be patient and things would get better, or was it Andy said, should I do something to make it right? I paced up and down, the thoughts and questions going round and round in my head.

Around three, Danny came back in. "That's it, all done. We can go home now."

We walked up to the Chamois in silence and as soon as we got in through the door I went straight to my room where I carried on my pacing. I could not bear to see any of the staff, let alone talk to them. I might have been able to keep myself together in front of the hosts, but I would never be able to keep the truth from Heather.

With a guilty start, I realised that I had not thought about her all day. I had been so sunk in my own misery and torment that I had not even thought about what she must be going through.

She had been as good as raped by Gwat and I had spent the day with him, relying on him to save me. My levels of self-loathing reached a new low. I wanted desperately to see her, to hold her, for her to tell me that everything would be alright, but I knew that I didn't deserve to touch her or even be with her. She deserved better than me.

But Heather had other ideas. An hour or so later, when the hosts had left for evening service there was a knock at my door. "James," she called. "James, can I come in."

I stood staring at the door, part of me wanting to throw it open and welcome her in, but a stronger, better part of me not wanting her anywhere near me. I could not let her be tainted by my actions, my guilt. I loved her too much for that.

"James, I know you're in there. Let me in."

"Go away," I whispered.

"James, I have to speak to you. Let me in."

"Go away. I don't want to see you," I said, every word like a dagger in my heart.

"James, please!"

"Go away!" I said louder. "I've got nothing to say to you!"

"James! I need you..."

There was something I could say, something that would keep her away from me, but I knew that it would break her heart. Could I do it, could I hurt her, even to save her? Andy said that there was always something you could do to make a situation better. Was this it? I paused, then gritted my teeth. It was better to destroy any affection she had for me now rather than have her love a murderer.

"You slept with Gwat, Heather. You betrayed me, you betrayed us. You went back with him and you fucked him. Go away. Leave me alone. I never want to speak to you again."

I heard a sharp intake of breath, then an animal like cry escaped from her lips, a cry of anguish and pain and then anger.

"FUCK YOU JAMES!" she shouted. "FUCK YOU!" And then she was gone.

47

AS SOON AS she was gone, I began to question my decision. How could I have been so cruel? How could I hurt her so much when I loved her? Was breaking Heather's heart the right thing to do? Even if it was in order to save her from loving a killer?

I collapsed on my bed, thoughts and emotions once again whirling round my head threatening to overwhelm me. Guilt, remorse, anger, pain, and, above all, confusion. How could this all have happened? I still could not comprehend how quickly everything had changed; only twenty four hours before I had been a hero, I had saved Danny, I had won back Heather and I was the toast of ValSki. Now I had killed Faye, I had lied to my friends, I had let Danny lie to the gendarmes for me and I had broken Heather's heart.

How had it all happened? Where had it all gone wrong? What should I do?

I lay back on the bed, praying for sleep to come and take away the pain and confusion, but it didn't come. I looked up out of the skylight, at the stars and the mountains outside and waited. But sleep still did not come.

What had happened? Where had it all gone wrong? What should I do?

Something at of the back of my head, some little part of me was still nagging. Something wasn't right, I knew it. But I just couldn't work it out.

But despite this, in my heart of hearts, deep down, I knew what I had to do. In the cold stillness of the night, after the hosts had come back, after the chalet had gone quiet, in the empty, still, dead night, I made my decision. Andy was right, there was something I could do to make it better.

And then I slept.

I waited until Danny, Gwat and the hosts had left for the chalets in the morning before I left my room. I stole quietly down to the lounge, picked up the phone and dialled a number. "Johnners, it's James. Can you get up here without Danny knowing? Bring the others if you can."

An hour or so later, Johnners came into the lounge with Claire, Joe and Marco. "Is Danny with you?" I asked quickly.

"No, I left him dealing with some guests in the chalets. Look, what's this about?" he asked.

"Claire, can you go and get Heather for me," I said ignoring his question. "She needs to hear this as well, but I don't think she will come if I ask."

"I should think not after what you said to her yesterday," she brushed past me and out of the room.

"We've all been under a lot of strain mate, but you've got some cheek saying that to Heather last night," Johnners said.

I stiffened. "I didn't realise our private conversations were up for everyone to comment on," I said quietly. "Anyway, it doesn't matter now anyway."

"What?" Johnners asked. "What is it?" he said coming closer.

I waited until Claire had come back into the room, leading a pale but composed Heather in the room before answering him. She didn't even look at me but sat next to Claire, her eyes on the floor.

"Sit down everyone, I've got something to say that you all need to hear. I tried to say it yesterday, but Danny interrupted me." I paused. This was the moment. This was the moment that there was no going back from. It felt like I was on the edge of a cliff, a deep yawning chasm lay before me. I didn't know what was at the bottom, but it was the only way forward. Did I have the courage to jump off?

I took a deep breath.

"I did it. I killed Faye."

"What!" Johnners jumped up.

"I did it. It was me. I pushed her off the bridge." I said calmly.

Everyone started shouting, "What!" "Fuck!" "No!" "Jesus!"

Johnners came over me, eyes flashing in anger. "I think you better start talking!" he grabbed my shoulders.

"I'm trying," I shook myself free. "I don't know what happened, I can't remember. Danny tried to take me home, but he said I saw Faye on the bridge and wouldn't come. Gwat saw us there too."

Joe suddenly got up. "Shit. I saw you with you her on the bridge as I was getting a burger. It looked like you were both out of it, she was swaying drunk and you were limping along trying to carry her. But by the time I got to the bridge you had gone, I thought you had gone home together. Fuck, I've only just remembered!"

Everyone was staring with open-mouthed shock. Then Claire got up and slapped me round the face. "You fucking, fucking..." she burst out into hysterical sobs. Johnners, turned and put his arms round her.

Heather looked up at me. "What happened on the bridge James? Did you try it on with her? Did you push her off? Or was it an accident?"

"I don't know," I said honestly. "I can't remember."

"You fucking arsehole James," she said quietly then walked out of the room.

"Why didn't Danny say anything?" Joe suddenly asked. "He knew, but he didn't say anything. Why?"

"He was trying to save me," I replied. "He said that giving me to the police wouldn't bring Faye back and that it was just a drunken accident. There was no point me going to prison for it."

"Fuck, fuck fuck." Johnners said shaking his head still holding Claire.

"You killed Faye, you killed Faye," she kept repeating.

"I know," I said, "believe me I know. Danny wanted me to pretend that nothing had happened, but I realise that whatever he says, I cannot do that."

"So what now then?" Joe asked.

"Now?" I said quietly. "Now you take me to the gendarmes, I have to tell them. Johnners, you stay with the girls, they'll need you. Joe, Marco can you come with me? I don't think I can do it by myself."

48

JOE AND MARCO walked on either side of me down the hill, a march of the condemned man to the scaffold. Now I had confessed and Danny was not around, I felt clear and knew for certain that I had to go and face the music.

For some reason I was intensely aware of the snow on the trees, the blue sky above and the mountains encircling the valley. Val d'Isere was as pretty as a postcard, but it could not dispel the darkness I felt within.

As I walked, a hundred different memories of the places we passed jumped up into my mind. Gwat begging a girl to go up the hill with him one night, Johnners throwing up by the poubelles another, Heather and me skiing down to the road one morning when we were late, buying bread and pate in the Spar by the petrol station with Joe. I swallowed, tears in my eyes, I knew that it would be a long time before I saw any of these places again.

The gendarmerie was at the far end of town, on the way to Le Fornet. It took about ten minutes for a bus with space for us to turn up and then a further ten minutes for it to wind its way through a crowded town centre. Joe and Marco didn't speak and I didn't try and talk. There was nothing really to say.

I paused in front of the police station where twenty four hours earlier I had sat in a car whilst Danny and Gwat lied for me. I wished bitterly that I had had the courage to go in then.

"Are you sure mate?" Joe asked, probably more kindly than I deserved.

"Yes, I'm sure," I said and walked in, the other following behind.

I marched straight up to the counter and the officer on duty. He was balding and fat-faced, but dressed smartly. "My name is James Knight," I said clearly. "I would like to make a statement to Lieutenant Colbert about the body found in the river."

All the police in Val were supposed to be bilingual, but he looked at me for so long that I wondered if he actually spoke English. Eventually though, he pointed a pencil at a bench and said gruffly "Wait there please." and then he went through a door behind the counter.

I turned to Joe and Marco. "You can leave me now. Thanks for taking me here."

Joe seemed about to say something, but then he just nodded and turned to go. Marco looked at me a moment longer, then they both walked out of the room together. I had never felt more alone.

I sat on a small row of plastic seats by the door with my back against the wall. Where was Colbert? Now I was here I was desperate to get the process started. My mind started playing back the events of the last forty eight hours again. The nagging feeling at the back of my head was stronger than ever. Why could I not remember anything at all? I banged my head in frustration.

The last memory that I had was Danny handing me a drink in the Saloon. Claire had said Danny would get Faye home. Then I was lying on his bed and he was sat at the foot, wearing my beanie. He had left me when I said I wanted to wait for Faye on the bridge. Joe had seen me limping along with her. Gwat had seen us on the bridge whilst he was taking an unconscious Heather home to have a go on her. What had happened? Why had Danny let me alone with Faye on the bridge? Why had I argued with her? Why had I pushed her into the stream? Something wasn't right, I was so close to working it out, but I just could not see it.

Then the feelings of guilt hit me again and threatened to interrupt my reasoning. I had killed Faye. I had killed. I was a murderer. I was going to go to prison. I had visions of my family crying as I was led away, my mother refusing to speak to me, my father turning away. My future loomed like a hole and I felt myself sucked in, the questions and feelings whirling round making me nauseous as I tumbled down into the depths of despair. Andy was right, this place was truly named.

But as I hit rock bottom, as I felt the misery and self-loathing overwhelm me again, the nagging voice at the back of my head started shouting louder than ever. Something wasn't right, something didn't make sense. Despite all the evidence, something was wrong. I didn't feel like a killer and I had no feelings towards Faye any more. If I had killed her, surely I would remember. At least something. But I remembered nothing.

But there were witnesses who saw me with her; I had a motive and an opportunity. The facts started running through my head again.

Losing consciousness after a drink in Saloon.

Joe seeing me limping with Faye.

Danny at the foot of my bed with my beanie on.

Gwat carrying Heather home unconscious.

Then, all of a sudden, it clicked. I knew what had happened. Faye had been killed. But it was not me who had done it.

I jumped up. "Please tell Inspector Colbert to come to the ValSki staff accommodation," I shouted to the bemused looking fat gendarme who had returned to the desk. "Tell him I know what happened to Faye Buchannon." And then I ran out of the door.

A bus was just indicating to pull away from the stop as I came out of the gendarmerie, blinking in the bright light. I could see Marco and Joe silhouetted in the window as I ran to it, but it pulled away before I could flag it down. I stamped my feet in frustration and began jogging away from the gendarmerie for the second time in twenty four hours. This time though it was towards the Chamois.

Twenty minutes later, out of breath, I was back at the staff chalet. Once inside, I took a deep breath, and paused before the door to the lounge. If I was wrong, then I would undoubtedly be guilty of murder. If I was right then I did not know what would happen. I opened the door wide and walked in.

Claire was still sitting red-faced on the couch, wrapped in a blanket, Heather next to her, staring into space. Johnners was pacing up and down. Joe and Marco had obviously got there only moments before me as they were sat down and removing their footwear.

"What the feck are you doing here!" Johnners stopped mid pace. Everyone turned to look at me.

"I didn't kill Faye," I said calmly. "But I know who did."

"What do you mean?" Heather said.

"Faye was murdered. But not by me."

"You better start talking lad," Johnners said grimly taking a step towards me.

I took a deep breath. "Claire, did you say that Faye was alright one minute and then really drunk the next?"

"Yes," she said, her eyes distant remembering. "We were in the Saloon talking and then she suddenly slumped against a wall. Why?"

"Heather, what about you?" I turned to her.

She turned her head listlessly to me. "I don't remember. I just don't remember."

"Well the same thing happened to me as well. I was fine one minute and the next I woke up in Danny's bed."

"What's so strange about that? People get drunk in the Saloon all the time!" Johnners was clenching his fists looking at me angrily. He wanted someone to blame and I was the obvious person.

"Not like that," I shook my head. "We all know what it feels like to get drunk. I've never had a black-out like that before."

"I have," Heather suddenly seemed to come too. "Last time Gwat had sex with me. I was in the Saloon one minute and the next thing I knew he was..."

"It's alright," I said and came to stand next to her. She looked up at me with pain in her eyes.

"What are you saying?" Johnners asked.

"Can you remember who bought the drinks last night?" I asked quietly.

"Gwat," Heather whispered. "Gwat bought the drinks."

"Not ours," Claire shook her head forcefully. "Danny bought drinks for Faye and me."

"Danny bought my drink too. But I don't think it was just drink."

"Oh my God," Claire put her hand to her mouth. "Do you think that...?"

"Johnners, what happened to me in the Saloon?"

He thought for a second. "You were swaying around and Danny said that he would take you back. I thought it a bit odd, but Heather was already wrapped around Gwat at that point. What were you thinking?" he looked at Heather.

Heather shook her head. "I don't remember."

"Well you were all over him. I thought you were actually going to..."

I swallowed, hating the thought and interrupted him. "Joe," I said swinging round to look at Joe behind me. "When you saw me last night with Faye, you said I was limping."

He nodded. "She looked well out of it, swaying around. You were helping her, but you were definitely limping."

I walked towards him. "No limp. Now can you remember what I was wearing?"

"Yes," he nodded. "The clothes that you are wearing now, with that stupid orange beanie you wear."

"The hat that Danny was wearing yesterday morning when I woke up." I said slowly. "This is what happened. Gwat buys drugs over the Internet to cure any diseases he picks up, that is common knowledge. I think he has been using other drugs to get girls back here to have sex with them, including the girl from Chalet Val. Danny took them off him a few weeks ago and used them last night on us. He took me home, put my clothes on, then took Faye down to the river and threw her in. He's the murderer."

49

THERE WAS A moment's stunned silence then everyone started shouting. "Fucking hell!" "That explains it!" "Fucking Christ!"

"Quiet!" Johnners bellowed and held his hand up until everyone was quiet. "There is no proof of this at all," he said to me. "You've got no proof, but there are three witnesses that saw you with Faye on the bridge last night. At the moment it is just your word against his."

Heather got up and walked over to me. "I believe you James," she said quietly and looked into my eyes. The strength that this gave me was unbelievable.

"I've known Danny for three years," Johnners said. "I can't believe that he would do something like this."

"Oh, you can and you know he did," I said grimly. "He is capable of evil and you know it. He broke Giles' leg to get him sent home. He planted money on Dylan and got him sent home too. Danny is capable of anything."

"What!" several people called out.

"I didn't say anything at the time, but I saw him stamp on Giles leg and break it."

"What about Dylan?" Joe asked.

"I think that Danny planted the money on him. Remember he identified all the things that were found in your room like Ash's bracelet and Harri's watch without being told about them."

"Giles I can understand," Joe shook his head, "he was a cock. But why Dylan?"

"Dylan made a pass at Faye early in the season," I said. "Danny was jealous and besides, didn't like the way Dylan thought he knew everything."

"But why? Why would he kill Faye and try and frame you?" Heather asked.

"I can answer that one," Claire said. "Faye wouldn't get back with him. None of you knew but Danny pestered her loads of times, but she couldn't forgive him for breaking her heart last season. Oh, she loved him alright, she just didn't trust him."

"But why frame James?" Joe asked.

"Jealousy, he is jealous of James," Heather said bitterly. "Jealous that he could get with Faye and jealous that he didn't. Jealous of what a good skier he is. Jealous because James would not suck up to him like everyone else does. I bet saving his life up on the glacier made him sick."

"Whatever," Claire said suddenly. "We still need proof."

"Like what?" Johnners asked. "How can you prove any of these things?"

"I saw him stamp on Giles!" I said. "I saw it..."

Johnners shook his head. "It's still your word against his. If you really saw it happening, why didn't you say anything at the time?"

"I don't know I ..."

"He told me," Heather said defensively. "I know that it happened."

"We still need proof." Johnners said obstinately. "I still can't believe that he did this."

"It's simple," Joe stood up. "We search his room. If we find any more drugs then we know that it's him."

Johnners thought for a moment. "Alright," he conceded. "We'll do that."

We all got up and followed Johnners out to Danny's room. He put his hand on the doorknob and then paused. "I can't believe we're doing this. Danny is a friend, there is no way that he would..."

"I'm afraid," Claire said quietly. "What will he do when he finds out that we..."

"Out of the way," Joe pushed past him. "You know that he is guilty, you're just afraid to admit it. Well I am not afraid of him, I have never trusted him." Suddenly, the door was open and we were all in his room where I had woken up the day before. It seemed like a lifetime ago.

"So what are we looking for?" Heather asked. "What do date rape drugs look like?"

"Roofies," Marco said. He had quietly followed us in. "They're called roofies, short for rohypnol. Usually they're oval and green, but the older ones are just white circles with a cross on."

"How do you know that?" Heather asked him suspiciously.

"Chef mate," he grinned. "I've tried most drugs!"

"Come on, let's see what we can find," and I went in and started picking up the clothes on the floor and checking the pockets. After a moment, everybody else crammed into the room and started searching.

Ten minutes later, after Danny's room had been turned upside down, there was no sign of anything.

"It's no good," Johnners said. "There's nothing here, if there ever was."

"Shit!" I stood with my hands on hips. "I was certain that we would find something."

"What about Gwat's room?" Heather suggested.

I shook my head. "Danny took them off him a few weeks ago, after that Chalet Val girl was here. I don't know what he was going to do with them."

"Perhaps he used them all up?" Heather asked.

I shook my head. "No, Gwat had a stash of them. Now where would he put them...?"

"What are you doing?" Danny was framed in the doorway. He was looking at us without any emotion.

"Oh, er, Danny, hi," Johnners stood up and started to stutter. "We were just..."

"Looking for drugs Danny," I said quietly. "I know that you did it. You killed Faye. You wore my clothes, but it was you who did it. People saw your limp, you were wearing my hat. It all adds up. We know it was you, we just have to find the drugs now to prove it."

Danny stared at us without saying anything.

"Why!" Heather asked him. "Why did you do it? Was it jealousy? Were you jealous of James turning down Faye? Jealous because he saved your life on the mountain?"

"Fools. You just don't get it, do you?" He snarled at us and his face transformed from being calm and impassive to a hate-filled mask. We all took an involuntary step back.

"Jealous! Don't make me laugh. Faye deserved to die. She could have stayed, forever, but she told me that this was going to be her last season. And as for you James..." he paused looking at me. "You could have stayed. You're good enough. The mountains accepted you. I was trying to save you. I was going to let you stay."

"Let him stay!?" Johnners took a step forward. "What about everyone else! What about me, what about Claire?"

"You!" Danny frowned. "You're afraid of the mountain. You won't jump, you won't take chances. You're not meant to be here, I don't know why you have stayed so long. The mountain doesn't want you here at all."

It was at that moment I realised that Danny was mad. Completely and utterly mad.

"Danny, I..." I started to move towards him, but he jumped back, slammed the door behind him and there was the unmistakable sound of a key turning in the lock. "I'm sorry, all of you," he called out through the door.

"Danny! Open the door!" Johnners moved forward and started hammering on it. "Open the door."

"I'm sorry!" he said again and then he was gone.

"Feckin' hell!" Johnners punched the door in frustration.

"Well at least we all know it was him now," Heather said. "I think that was pretty much a confession."

"Shit, fat lot of good that is going to do us now. Or Faye."

"What do we do now?" Joe asked.

"Nothing much we can do really," Marco was at the door testing it. "It's a knackered old chalet but the doors are pretty solid."

"Window?" Claire asked.

Joe jumped up to the small high window and pulled himself up to look out. "I wouldn't risk it," he said dropping down. It's a difficult climb to the roof and a steep drop if you slip. Someone will come along in a bit and open the door. There is nothing that he can do now."

I wished he had been right.

Ten minutes later there was a thump against the door, as if something solid was thrown against it. A few seconds later, there was another.

"Danny, Danny what are you doing!" Johnners leapt up and started hammering on the door again. There was no reply, but a couple of more thumps.

"Danny, what's going on?"

"I'm sorry everyone," we heard him call out, his voice strangely muffled, as if he had something in his mouth. "I didn't want it to end like this, but you have left me no choice." There was a splashing noise against the door and then when he spoke a couple of moments later his voice was clear. "I don't have any choice. Goodbye everyone, I love you all."

There was scratching sound and then a sudden *whumph*. Smoke started coiling in underneath the door and there was the unmistakable smell of petrol.

"Feckin' hell, he's set us on fire," Johnners shouted. "Back everyone!"

50

THERE WAS PANDEMONIUM in the room as everyone started shouting. Smoke was coming under the door thick and fast and we could hear the wood crackling outside.

"He must have got the logs and petrol from the fire place. Feckin' hell!" Johnners shouted.

"This place is a fucking firetrap!" Joe said. "It'll go up in moments!"

"Open the window," Heather shouted. "It's the only way out."

We all looked up at the small window, high up in the wall.

"We'll never get out through that," Marco objected. "I'll never fit. Perhaps I can barge the door down?"

"No chance mate," Johnners said.

"But we're three stories up!" Claire objected. "We can't jump from here."

"We are going to have to," Johnners said grimly. "There is no other way. Come on." He dragged the bed over to the wall, then stood up on the end and stuck his head out through the aperture. A few seconds later he was back in.

"Right, it's a damn steep drop from here, straight onto stones, but as Joe said there is a ledge just off to the left where you can climb onto the roof. If you can get onto that, then I think there is an easy jump down into snow on the other side. Joe, you go first," he said. "You've done some climbing. You can help everyone through."

Joe nodded and then stepped up on to the bed and wriggled his way out through the window. "I'm safe," we heard him shout out. "Send the next one out."

"Claire, that's you." Johnners helped her up to the window, and then she was through. Heather and then Marco followed, leaving just me and Johnners. The smoke was thick in the room now and we could hear the roar of the flames as it took hold of the rest of the chalet.

"Right pickle we are in lad, eh?" Johnners smiled at me.

"Tell you what, first pint's on me when we get out," I said.

"You're on. Now, out you go."

"Will you be alright to get out by yourself?" I asked.

"Aye. Now go on." He boosted me up and I poked my head though the window.

The first thing I noticed was the drop. Ten meters or more onto a solid row of rocks. I swallowed and my head started to swim.

"Over here, Jimmy." I turned my head. A metre or so off to my left, I could see Joe's outstretched hand.

"Once your body is out, get your leg over the edge. There is foot hold just below, and you should be able to get over here. The drop on the other side is soft snow, it's easy. Don't look down mate, that's my advice."

I swallowed hard and pushed my body through as much as I could. Just as I got my body out, I swayed and almost lost my balance. "Whoa! Easy!" Joe called out. "Now have you got the foot hold?"

I nodded. "Yes," I called out. "You ready?"

"Hurry up!" I could hear Johnners below me, an edge of panic in his voice.

"Here I come!" and with my foot on a small ledge beneath the window, I swung myself round. Joe's hands were suddenly underneath me and hauling me up onto the flat roof. I lay panting unable to move. "Johnners!" I could hear Joe shouting. "Your turn."

There were some scrabbling noises, and then I heard Johnners say "I can't Joe, I can't do it!"

"Come on Johnners. You can do it. Just get your foot on the ledge."

I remembered what Danny said about Johnners losing his nerve and that he had told me himself that he was nervous about heights. There was no way he would be able to swing round the building. Why had I not remembered a few minutes before so I could have helped him out of the window?

I peered over the edge. Johnners had one leg over the sill, but was frozen, unable to move, his face white with fear. Behind him, through the window, smoke was starting to come out. The flames could not be far behind.

"Johnners!" I called out to him desperately.

"Jimmy, I can't do it!" he looked at me with a terror stricken expression.

"Shit, shit!" Joe pulled me back out of sight of Johnners. "The fire is going to be under here any minute," he hissed at me. "The roof could go. We've got to get off!"

"We can't leave Johnners!" I said aghast.

"If we stay here any longer, we could be trapped as well."

"Fuck. Fuck." I said knowing there was only one thing I could do. "Right, I'm going back to help him," I said. "Hold me!"

"What!" Joe said, "You can't..." but I had already levered my body over the edge and was scrabbling round for the foothold underneath the sill. "Hold my hand!" I called up to Joe.

"Fucking idiot!" he snarled, but he knelt down and grabbed my hand. "Put your leg a bit further to the left," he called. "Up a bit, a bit more..." and then I felt the small ledge beneath my feet and I was able to swing my body round back to the window ledge where Johnners was sat straddling the sill.

"What are you doing!" he said, as I pulled myself up beside him.

"Getting you out, you bloody fool! Now, get your leg over here." I reached over and placed his leg on the ledge below. Behind me I could hear the crackle of flames and feel the heat start to burn against my leg. "Hold onto the edge here and swing yourself round. Joe is waiting there for you..."

But as his leg was reaching round, it slipped. I was holding him by the waist, and his weight suddenly pulled down on me and jerked me off balance. "Johnners!" I cried as I felt both of us start to topple off the side of the building.

Somewhere above me I heard Joe screaming, and then we were both falling. And for the second time in less than forty eight hours, I then remembered nothing.

51

"JIMMY, JIMMY!" I could hear Heather's voice. I opened my eyes and saw her face creased in concern and worry.

"No need to shout!" I said wryly. "Ow!" I tried to move my head and suddenly felt a splitting pain.

"Stay still, you idiot!" she said. "The ambulance is on its way. They will be able to check you out."

I sank back on the floor and then remembering what happened sat up quickly, this time ignoring the pain. "How long have I been out? Johnners, is he..."

"Will you be still!" she said exasperated and pushed me back down. "Only a couple of minutes. Johnners has a broken ankle, I think, but he is conscious. Everyone else is fine."

I closed my eyes in relief for a moment, but then opened them up again and looked up at her. "Heather, look I need to say something to you about last night. I didn't mean what I said, about you and Gwat. I was just trying to..."

"Yeah, I get it. I do. We'll sort it out later. Although I don't know where we'll do it..."

"The Chamois!" I said sitting up again. "How is it!"

"Well now you're up, look for yourself."

I turned my head, wincing a little, but the pain was already receding. I was sat by the side of the road, Joe, Marco and Claire were standing nearby, with Johnners grimacing on the floor. They were all staring at the chalet, blazing away about thirty meters from us. "Shit..." I trailed off.

"Exactly," Heather said grimly.

Joe saw me sitting up and came over. "I've called the fire brigade and ambulance. They will be here any minute."

"Is there anyone else in there?" I said panicking.

Joe shook his head. "I have rung round all the staff. Ash, Toby and Cali were at their chalets and Harri and Alice had gone for a walk. It is only Danny and Gwat that are unaccounted for."

"Thank God."

"Here come the cavalry," Heather said, looking up as several vehicles started racing up the hill.

"It is going to be a long day," I sighed. "Help me up. We have got a lot of talking to do."

We had to wait before we could tell our story to the authorities as they had their hands full with the fire. First the fire brigade arrived in a small truck and, after a quick conversation about how many people there might be inside, the firemen immediately started spreading round the building and taking out firefighting equipment from the van. Two more vehicles appeared in quick succession disgorging more firemen and gear.

Next the medics arrived. I was pronounced fit but they fussed round Johnners for ten minutes before strapping him into a stretcher and then loading him into the ambulance. Claire got in next to him, holding his hand.

"Just like race day," I said to him as he passed.

"Deja feckin' vu! Who would have thought it!"

"Except you really have broken your leg this time," Heather said.

"I know," Johnners grimaced. "It could be worse. Jimmy, Jimmy, are you there?" he tried to turn, but the strapping was holding him down.

"Yes mate," I came round the stretcher so he could see me.

"Looks like I owe you one as well mate. If you hadn't come back for me..." He trailed off.

"I'm sorry, we have to go," one of the medics pulled me away.

We watched the ambulance go slowly down the hill, standing in a little huddle, blankets given to us by the medics round our shoulders.

The gendarmes were there a few minutes later, but they had their work cut out holding back the onlookers crowding on the road. Within ten minutes dozens of people from nearby chalets had come out to watch. Half an hour later there must have been hundreds of people from all over Val d'Isere witnessing the Chamois burn down.

Heather, Marco, Joe and I were asked to wait by one of the cars until they had the blaze under control. It took longer than they expected and it was almost dark by the time Inspector Colbert came over with one of the firemen.

"What happened? Do you know how it started?" he asked.

I nodded. "Deliberately. We are all witnesses."

"By whom?" he said seriously.

"Danny," I said pulling Heather in close. "Danny DeMarco. He locked us in a room and started the fire with petrol. We also believe that he murdered Faye Buchannon."

"Danny!" Colbert said in amazement. "But why..."

"It was Danny," I said firmly. "He got away. He could murder again."

"Right," Colbert said decisively. "I think I better take you in to make a formal statement."

"What about Danny? He might escape." I said.

Colbert shook his head. "The road from here is cut off remember. He will not be able to leave Val d'Isere."

"Let me through, let me through," there was a commotion and then Jen was through the crowds, heading towards us in her ski gear. I had forgotten completely about her coming back today. She had obviously just skied over from Brévières. "Jesus Christ. Will someone tell me is happening? Where is Danny?"

"Jen will need to go us as well," Heather said. "She has to hear what happened."

Colbert took us to a small, featureless interview room in the gendarmerie to make a statement. He sat with Jen and another gendarme, wide-eyed whilst I retold the events that had led up to the fire.

"I just can't believe it," Jen shook her head as I finished. "I can't believe that Danny would..."

"He did," I said firmly. "All of those things. He is a murderer."

"I will put a warrant out for his arrest," Colbert said calmly. "He will not get far. If he tries to use the road the police blocks will get him. If he tries to use any of the lifts, then he can be tracked by his pass."

"He won't use the lifts. He is too clever for that," I said.

"Danny..." Jen was still staring into space.

"Jen," I said gently. "The chalet is still alight. The staff are going to need you to sort things out."

"Yes, yes of course," she suddenly snapped back into the efficient capable Jen we needed. "I must get back. Can one of your drivers take us up?"

Colbert nodded. "I will take you myself. I need to see how the fire is getting on. Now, is there somewhere the staff can stay tonight?"

"Chalet Val," Jen answered after a moments thought. "The Eagles Nest is free this week. I'm sure Kat will let the staff stay there."

"Good," he nodded. "Right, let's go."

52

BY THE TIME that we got back to the chalet, the firemen seemed to have the blaze under control. I could not see any flames but smoke was still rising from the blackened shell of the building. The front was almost completely gone, exposing the rooms inside and the roof was just a crumbling skin. Flakes of black soot floated in the air mixed with a light snow that was falling gently. In another situation, it would have looked beautiful.

As soon as she got out of the police car, Jen was like a whirlwind. She flew round the edge of the chalet, speaking with firemen and police officers, talking rapidly into her phone and giving orders to the remaining staff or other people she knew. Kat from Chalet Val was there with a whole crew of her own staff to help as well. There seemed to be order emerging from the chaos.

Heather came and put her arms round me. "Is it over now?" she asked in a low whisper.

I shook my head. "No, not yet. Not until they catch him."

"What happened at the police station?" Joe had seen us and came over too.

"Not much," I said and filled him in on what had happened. "Where do you think he's gone?"

"Christ knows, but he will be around somewhere. He's not likely to give himself up."

Jen came barrelling over, Alice and Harri in her wake. "I need your help, please," she said directly. "We are not going to be able to serve dinner tonight so the guests will have to go out. I have spoken to the Canyon restaurant and they will serve a basic menu and charge it to ValSki. I need one of you to go round to the chalets and one of you to remain in the office as a point of contact."

"Yes, of course," Joe said. "I'll do the guests, Jimmy, will you do the office? We can swap round after an hour if you need to."

I nodded. "Have you heard from Johnners? Is he alright?"

"No word yet, I'm afraid," she turned to go. "I will be back in the office by nine pm. I've confirmed with Kat, we can have the Eagles nest tonight. Heather, can you take the other staff up there?"

Just then there was a commotion from the chalet. The firemen were bringing out a body on a stretcher.

"Oh God," Heather put her hand to her mouth.

"It's Anthony," Jen said flatly. "It's Anthony, it has to be. God help us."

I turned away as the body was put into an ambulance.

Several hours later all the Val staff were sat up in the lounge of the Eagles Nest, a beautiful if slightly dated chalet at the top of the town. Jen had put a ban on alcohol, so we sat round, huddled in blankets, drinking tea.

Two calls came in quick succession.

The first was from Claire. She and Johnners had been choppered down to Bourg-St-Maurice hospital. He had fractured his ankle in three places and would need an operation in the morning but he was in good spirits. "I feel guilty about not being with you," she said, but I assured her that down the mountain was the best place for her.

The second was from a tearful Jen confirming that the body was indeed Anthony.

"I hated him, but I would not wish that on anyone," Heather said sadly. "He did'nt deserve to be burnt alive. No one does."

"Where is he? Where the fuck is he?" Joe was pacing up and down.

No one needed to ask who he was talking about, but no one could answer the question.

Whatever state we were in, there were still guests that needed looking after the next morning. We were four hosts, a maintenance man and a manager down, so both Heather and I had to go in and help the other hosts. Even Jen did a spell washing up.

After we finished, we gathered in the office to hear the latest news. Jen was looking tired and drawn.

"Head office have decided that we will close for the rest of the season," she said flatly when we were all there. "We cannot continue to operate nor would it be right to. They are going to try and find alternatives for the holiday makers that have already booked."

"Do they know when the road is going to open and we can get these guests home?" Heather asked.

"They are working on it. Today, maybe this afternoon or tomorrow at the latest," she replied.

"What about Danny?" I asked. "Has there been any news from him?"

"No," Jen shook her head. "Colbert called this morning and said they are still looking for him. Obviously he cannot get down the road and the

STVI have blocked his lift pass. If he tries to get on the slopes, then the lifties will detain him. It won't be long before he is caught."

I wasn't so sure. Danny had already proved himself to be ruthless but he was cunning as well. He also knew the resort as well as anyone. I couldn't see him letting himself be caught so easily.

"What about us?" Harri asked. "Do we have to stay?"

Jen shook her head. "Providing that the gendarmes don't need you, you can go with the guests. There is still a lot of work to done though and I would appreciate it if anyone can stay a bit longer. I will need all the help I can get." She paused, looking up at us hopefully.

"I'll stay," I said on impulse. "I want to see this through."

I felt Heather's hand creep into mine. "Me too," she said quietly.

"I'm in," Joe said. "I'm not going to leave now. Not until we get the bastard.".

"I'm not going either," Marco smiled. "Not when it is getting interesting."

One by one, all the other hosts said they would stay. Jen looked almost ready to cry. "Thanks," she said softly. "It means a lot to me."

Just then her phone rang. She looked at the number and answered quickly. "Yes?" she asked, then nodded a few times. "Thanks, please keep me informed," and she hung up.

"That was Colbert. They've caught him at the La Daille Funi. He's on his way to arrest Danny now."

53

THERE WAS A moment's silence and then everyone started talking at once. There were a couple of cheers, questions shouted out to Jen and, from some, just a big sigh of relief.

I stared at the floor. Something did not feel right. It was too easy. Surely Danny would make it harder than that. I walked out of the office into the yard.

"What is it?" Heather had followed me out, sensing my unease.

"I don't know," I paused. "Something isn't right. He wouldn't have gone there. He would have known that they would catch him if he used the lifts."

"Where else would he go? What else could he do?" Heather asked.

I thought hard. What would Danny do? He knew the net was closing in on him. Where would he go? I stared at the distant mountains trying to put myself in his shoes.

Suddenly I knew exactly where he was and what he was going to do. I looked at my watch and worked out the timings. If I hurried, I might just make it.

"I have to get my ski stuff. I know where he is."

Ten minutes later we were on a bus to Le Fornet. "This is madness!" Heather said. "Why can't we just let the gendarmes know where he is?"

"Not enough time," I said grimly. "Even if they believed me, they are going to be ages down in La Daille. Unless we can say for sure that we have seen him, they will not come."

"Jimmy, don't try and be a hero. He's a killer."

I sighed. "I don't intend to try and stop him personally," I said. "As soon as we see him then we'll call the gendarmes and get them to come. Do you have your phone on you?" she nodded. "When we spot him, we'll call Jen. She can call Colbert. He'll listen to her."

Heather thought for a moment and then nodded. "Okay, if you promise. But where do you think he is?" she asked.

"Climbing the Pointe Pers," I said. "He means to go over the ridge and into Italy."

Heather gasped. "But that's suicide! The ground is warming up and at this time of year the chances of a slab avalanche is crazy high. Especially after the dump last night. Any wrong move and he will bring half the mountain down."

"What has he got to lose?" I asked. "He knows that there is no way out of Val. What better way for him to escape? Besides, you know what a mystic he is about the mountain. He'll take his chances there."

"Maybe," she shrugged. "I still think he is hiding out somewhere in town."

"Well, we'll see," I said. "Come on, let's get up there."

The téléphérique gondola and then the bubble up to the glacier seemed to take forever. "Come on, come on," I found it difficult to contain my impatience, but Heather managed to sit quietly.

At the top of the glacier, a chalk board displayed the conditions for today. The risk of avalanche was four out of five, and in big lettering 'Hors Piste Tres Dangerouse!' The wind was whipping around us with small flecks of ice stinging our cheeks. "Just the T-Bar to go," Heather called out over the noise. I nodded, and clipped in to my skis.

Finally we were at the bottom off the ascent to the Col Pers. "If he came this way, then we should be able to see him at the top. Are you ready?" I asked Heather. She nodded. "James, I..."

"What?" I turned round.

"I love you. I don't want to lose you." Her eyes were full of tears.

I leant down to kiss her. "Don't worry. It'll be fine."

Compared to the excruciatingly slow pace of the bubble, the ascent to the Col seemed to take no time at all. Within a few minutes we were hauling ourselves over the edge and onto the ridge. Despite the adrenalin pumping round our systems, we still lay there panting for a few moments before we could get up.

The wind had erased any tracks that might have been there. I looked out at the empty white bowl ahead in disappointment. There was no one to be seen.

"There!" Heather shouted and pointed at the far side. "Up on the ridge, to the Pointe Pers. Can you see?"

I scanned where she was indicating. Sure enough, after a couple of seconds, I could make out a faint dot moving over the rocks on the far side of the bowl. "It's him, it has to be him!" I said. "Quick, call Jen."

"Shit!" Heather cried out in frustration a few seconds later. "No signal!"

"Fuck."

"We are going to have to go back down and call the gendarmes. There is nothing else we can do." Heather said, getting ready to climb back down to the pistes.

"You do that," I said. "I am going to go after him."

"James, no, don't be an idiot!"

"I have to," I said. "If I don't try and stop him, he'll escape."

"Then I'm coming with you!" she said obstinately.

I shook my head. "No Heather. One of us needs to make that phone call. It has to be you."

"James!" she implored me. "You can't!"

"I have to. I have to try. I owe the others that." I said grimly.

"I won't leave you. I won't let you!" she shouted tears her eyes.

I held her for a second. "Look, you know it makes sense. We have to hurry, he's getting away."

"Shit, shit!" She was frantic with indecision.

"It'll be alright," I held her shoulders. "I'll keep my distance. I'm only going to follow him."

Eventually she nodded. "Okay, just make sure you do."

"I will," I nodded, and moved off to the lip of the bowl before she changed her mind.

54

THE TRAVERSE ROUND the bowl to the Pointe Pers was as tricky as before but now there was the added danger of avalanches. I moved as quickly as possible round the rim, following in the tracks that had already been made. It felt very unstable, as if the whole pack might go at any minute. The rope on the other side was a welcome sight.

Once I had hauled myself up, I took my skis off and began the climb up to the Pointe. A set of snowboard boot tracks made it obvious which way Danny had gone. He must have had about thirty minutes' start on me. He would be past the Pointe and the couloir where he had fallen down and be on his way to the next ridge. What was it called, the Point Caval or Rouge something? I struggled, but I could not remember.

It would be difficult to catch up but that was not really my idea. I just wanted to keep him in sight until the gendarmes arrived. As I puffed up the hill, I tried to calculate how long it might take before they got here. Heather would have made the call to Jen by now, and she would have called Colbert. If they were in La Daille, then it would take a good twenty minutes to get Le Fornet, and then another thirty minutes to get up to the top of the glacier. What about if they called some of the lifties or the ski patrol? They would be able to get here a lot quicker, maybe in about another twenty to thirty minutes.

I was so intent on working these numbers out that I wasn't paying enough attention to what was ahead of me. The summit of the Pointe Pers was only a few meters away when I sensed a movement behind me, then felt a massive blow to the back of my helmet. I felt myself go down on to my knees, and then there was as second hit to my side of my head and I passed out.

I came to sitting against a rock with my head throbbing. My helmet and goggles had been removed and I had to squint so I wasn't blinded by the bright light. I tried to move, and realised that my hands were trapped behind my back. I panicked and started to struggle.

"Don't bother," Danny's voice came from somewhere behind me. "You're tied securely. You won't be able to escape."

"What are you going to do?" I said slowly and sitting back against the rock. Fear slowly started to spread through me.

"Well now, that depends," Danny said, walking into view and squatting opposite me. He lifted up his goggles. "I will probably have to kill you, but we'll see."

"The others will be here soon," I said. "They're already on their way."

"I don't think so," he leant back and smiled. "I have just climbed up to the viewpoint to check. There's no one on the ridge. We're alone."

"Where did you go? They gendarmes thought they had you down La Daille." I said stalling for time. If I could keep him talking long enough then maybe something would turn up.

"Idiots!" he snorted contemptuously. "That was simple. I sold my pass to a student in the queue at the lift pass office this morning."

"And where did you stay last night?" Behind my back, I tried to move my hands. They moved a fraction of an inch.

"There are lots of places to hide out if you know Val. Boot rooms left unlocked and heated garages that are left open. It wasn't difficult to find somewhere for a few hours."

"Why Danny? Why did you do it?" I subtly pulled my wrists apart and the rope moved a little bit more. Perhaps I could wriggle one hand free.

"Why what? Kill Gwat?" he grinned at me. "He deserved to die; he was a serial rapist, you know that. It wasn't just that Chalet Val girl, there were loads of others. He's been doing it for years now. I'm surprised you're even asking."

"He was one of your best friends!" I shook my head, the movement disguising my attempt to move my hands. The chord cut into the exposed skin between my gloves and jacket. What had he used, a boot lace?

"Really? Do you think so?" Danny watched me with a trace of a smile playing about his lips. "He didn't love the mountains, he just liked it here because he could chase girls. He was a waste of space, a lazy-arse maintenance monkey. Really, I did everyone a favour."

"What about Faye?" I asked. If I could move my hands a little bit more, then I might be able to slip one of them of them out of the loop.

"Ah yes, Faye. That was," he paused, "regrettable. I didn't really mean to... I just wanted to teach her a lesson. She was getting way too cocky..."

"You mean she wouldn't sleep with you anymore?" I felt the cord give a little but I could feel a stubborn knot still holding my hands together. My heart skipped a beat. One more big pull and they might come loose, but there was no way to tell.

"Well partly that," the smile on his face faded. "But it was more that she was going to leave. I offered her everything here, but she still turned me down."

"Is that why you framed me Danny? Was it because you thought she might prefer me to you?" I was sure that it would only take a moment to free myself now, but I would not be able to do it with him watching, that would be too obvious. I would have to distract him somehow.

"No it wasn't because of Faye. Even if she wouldn't go with me, I think we both know she would never go with you."

"Why then Danny, why did you frame me?"

"You let me down, Jimmy." Danny had stopped smiling and was now talking slowly and softly. "You could have been one of us and stayed up in the mountains. I offered you the chance, but you turned it down. You saw all of this," he gestured at the mountains around us, "and you were still going to leave."

"I said I would stay Danny," I said raising my voice.

"You were lying," he said flatly. "Don't deny it. You were going to skip out at the first opportunity. That is so disrespectful to the mountains, I couldn't let it pass."

"You are fucking mad Danny. Crazy. 'Disrespectful to the mountains' my fucking arse. They're fucking mountains!" I was shouting at him now. If I could distract him by making him angry then perhaps I could get myself free.

He laughed again and I realised that it would not work, he wasn't going to rise to the bait. "You don't have to say it out loud James, but I know you feel it too. Look around you, at the beauty, the peace and the serenity. This is worth fighting for, worth living for."

I shrugged, moving my hands again. "Maybe. Anyway, what are you going to do now? They'll catch you."

"Don't bet on it," Danny smiled. "Once I get over the border into Italy, it will be easy to disappear. There are all sorts of transports over to Africa that will turn a blind eye for the right price. Once I am there, well who knows... ?" he trailed off.

"But what about the mountains Danny? How will you be able to leave the mountains? You'll never be able to come back. You'll be betraying them." My ears picked out a low drone. Was it possible that a helicopter was on its way? A moment of hope sparked in my chest. Danny had not heard it.

"Be quiet!" he suddenly flared up in anger. "You don't know what you're talking about. You know nothing about the mountains."

"You talk all that shit about the mountains being alive, but it is just shit, Danny. It's all just make-believe in your head. Did they tell you to murder Faye? Did the mountains tell you to kill Gwat? Did they?" I carried on desperately trying to provoke him so he woul not notice the sound. It was almost certainly a helicopter.

"Shut up!" he shouted and stood up. "Right, I have had enough of this. I think it's time..."

Suddenly the sound of the helicopter could not be ignored. "What's that? It's..." he turned round to see a big red chopper rising up from below the mountain. "Shit, you..."

I took the moment to wrench my arms apart as far as they could go, but my hand would not slip through. Desperately I tried to stagger to my knees.

"No!" Danny had turned round and had seen me trying to rise. "No, this isn't supposed to happen!" He started towards me with his hands outstretched. I did the only thing that I could think of and dived towards him, trying to overbalance him.

This was the last thing that he expected. My shoulder connected with his waist and my momentum pushed him backwards.

For a moment he fought on the edge, trying to regain his balance, his arms windmilling crazily. Then then he was gone, tumbling over the edge of the Pointe Pers and down the couloir where he had fallen a few days before.

I flopped over to the edge to see him tumbling down the slope, strangely silent. In the soft snow he would not be harmed and would be able to be picked up. But with a huge cracking sound the entire wall of the couloir gave way in a huge slab avalanche. Millions of tons of snow started sliding down towards Danny, and my last sight of him was the snow catching up with him and washing him away.

55

IT TOOK A long time to come down from the mountain. The chopper pulled up sharply when the avalanche fell then circled round for about twenty minutes, waiting for the snow cloud to subside. Eventually the pilot must have decided that it was too risky to try and drop a man, because it headed back down the valley. I staggered up to the view point and waited, too shocked to do much more.

Ten minutes later a pair of mountain rescue guides came over the Col, round the bowl and then up the ridge to where I was sitting. After I had given my name and explained what happened they decided to try and find Danny. One carefully climbed down the couloir, belayed on a rope by the other. When he got to the avalanche, he switched on his bleeper, and began combing the area, but there was no answering signal. Danny had either not bought his kit or not turned it on.

Over the next hour more mountain guides arrived and climbed down to the avalanche. They poked at the ground with their poles at regular intervals, whilst I sat at the top watching, but with no result.

Eventually one climbed back up and said that he had been requested by the gendarmes to bring me down. Part of me didn't want to leave the mountain and have to face the real world, but part of me could not wait to leave.

We climbed back to the ridge, and then skied down the bowl. At the lip I turned to look back up the slope. Dozens of guides were now over the avalanche area but I knew the chances of finding Danny alive now were tiny. I turned and followed the guide down to the Pont St Charles, not even noticing the wonderful off-piste skiing.

Heather was waiting for me by the Fornet Téléphérique cabin. She ran up, hugged and kissed me, and then started shouting, almost incoherent with anger. I smiled and took the telling off. I knew it was just emotion coming to the surface and that I probably deserved it.

Behind her, Colbert was waiting with Jen. After holding Heather a second time, I straightened up and walked over to them. "Let's get this over with then," I said and walked off to the waiting police car.

It took almost four days before Colbert and the gendarmes were satisfied with the statements from me and all the other ValSki staff. Four long, crazy, painful days.

They wanted to know every detail of what had occurred up on the mountain, back in the Chamois, at the Saloon and when Danny hurt himself. I spoke about when Giles was hurt and when we found the Chalet Val girl with Gwat. I talked about Dylan and I talked about Faye. I talked until I was hoarse, and until my head hurt. And then I talked some more.

When we were not cloistered in the small interview rooms in the gendarmerie, we stayed up at the Eagles Nest, talking late into the night in the lounge, trying to understand and come to terms with what had happened.

We talked a lot about Danny and Gwat. We pooled our memories and searched for clues about their actions and behaviours. Why had they done what they had done, why had they acted that way?

On one level, Gwat was easy to understand; he was a serial, predatory, sex offender. What was much harder to accept though, was the issues this raised. We tolerated his casual sexism and laughed at his flippant misogyny but deep down, we had all known that he was a monster. None of us did anything about him and we let our friendship with him blind ourselves to his behaviour. By saying and doing nothing, we had enabled him to sexually assault and possibly rape several girls. This was very difficult to first admit, accept and then come to terms with.

Danny was much harder to understand. Everyone was stunned that he had been guilty of so many crimes over such a long period. We came to the conclusion that none of us really knew him at all. He had lied, stolen, assaulted, murdered and attempted to burn all of us to death. No one could understand why.

Although I had known Danny for a shorter period than anyone, I felt that I understood him better. I had been with him up on the mountain, I had shared a moment of communion with him as we gazed out on the emptiness, I had felt the presence and spirit of the mountains in my heart as he had. Maybe, if I had spent as long as he had up there, then I would be as mad as he was and commit some of the evil that he had. There was no chance of that happening now.

We all reacted in different ways at different times; anger, frustration, incomprehension, sadness and grief; storms of different emotions and moods swept across us all like the winter weather that could rage outside.

There was also plain physical, mental and emotional exhaustion. Several months of hard, unrelenting work, excessive drinking and then the events of the last week meant that we spent a lot of time simply sleeping; when we were not kept awake by bad dreams that was.

I noticed that Toby and Calli argued a lot. They had been together a long time, but what had happened really strained their relationship, to the point where I was not sure it would survive. At different times each one expressed doubts whether they would stay together.

Alice and Harri cried a lot. Ash barely got out of bed, and when he did he scarcely said anything. We did not see Pete and Caroline again. Jen informed us on the second day that they had packed their car and left the resort without leaving any contact details.

Marco distracted himself in the kitchen, turning out an endless supply of cakes, soups and stews that none of us could stomach eating. Joe tried to be nonchalant and brave about what had happened, but I could tell he was badly shaken. He barely slept and spent hours pacing around the lounge and going out on the balcony for cigarettes.

Jen was probably the hardest hit of all. Whilst she had something to do, she was fine, but on the second day, a company director and several staff from the main office came out and took over. Without the responsibility of running the company, she was nervous and vulnerable and as human as the rest of us.

For the first two days, Heather would not let me out of her sight. She insisted on being with me in the interview rooms, and then back in the chalet she stayed firmly by my side. I was not sure if this was to make sure that nothing happened to me, or that nothing happened to her. At nights we clung to each other and took turns comforting each other when we cried.

On the third evening, just when things were becoming intolerable in the chalet, there was a loud 'Feckin' hell' and Johnners shuffled in on crutches. "This place is feckin' nice," he exclaimed cheerfully. "If I'd known that we were going to end up here, I would have burnt down the Chamois months ago." His presence made an immediate change to the morbid atmosphere, and for the first time in ages, I could feel a smile, however brief, cross my lips. "Good to see you man," I hugged him.

Claire followed behind, carefully watching to make sure he did not slip or fall. She looked as if she had lost a lot of weight, but there was something different about her, an inner calm and strength. She told Heather and me later that Johnners had proposed to her after he came round from the operation. "He asked me just before he went into surgery," she said. "I thought he was joking, but when he came round he remembered everything he had said." She rung her hands and looked at the floor. "It's all I have ever wanted really. A man like him, a decent, honest, kind man. They are hard to find, especially up here." We hugged them both, and even opened a bottle of champagne, although none of us could stomach more than a couple of sips.

The rest of Val d'Isere rallied round and helped us where they could. Chalet Val staff came in their free time and cleaned and bought more food to add to the piles that Marco made. Other ski companies made a collection of clothes for us as virtually nothing was salvageable from the Chamois. The shops sent up pastries for us and even some of the bars sent up wine and beer for us to drink. Not that anyone really had an appetite for alcohol.

The guests went the day after the avalanche and then, bit by bit, arrangements were made for us to go home too. Alice, Harri and Ash went on the third day, Toby and Calli on the fourth. Later that evening, Jen announced that the gendarmes were happy for all of us to go too. Joe gamely said that he would be happy to stay and help close down, but Jen shook her head. "No, I have booked flights for you all. The consul has signed letters of release for you so there is no problem about passports. It's time for you to leave."

I was unsurprised that it was Andy who appeared in a big minibus the next morning to take us to the airport. I had always imagined that one way or the other that it would be him that took me down the mountain. In front of everyone else, he was as taciturn as he had been on the way up to the resort, but when we had a moment alone as we were packing the van, he turned to me and said, "Well done kid. You did it. I didn't think you would."

"Did what?" I asked. I remembered the moment in the Van at Le Fornet when he said that there was always something you could do. I wondered briefly if he had known all along then about what had happened to Faye.

"Survived. When I drove you up here, I really didn't think you would."

Val was still white and beautiful as we pulled away. What was it Andy had called it, a frozen never-never wonderland, a magical Shangri-La where nothing bad ever happened? I laughed silently and humourlessly to myself. It was a fantasy dream world, it was true, but a dark, twisted, nightmare place.

As we drove out of the tunnels down the mountain, the beautiful white snowy vistas faded and became muddy grey and brown fields. We were leaving the mountains but the memories of what had happened would never leave us, the wounds and scars would be with us forever.

I looked over the people in the van; Marco had stayed in Val, but Joe, Johnners and Claire were with Heather and I. Friends, workmates, house mates. Andy was right, but wrong at the same time. I had survived, but only because of the people around me. Without them, I would not have survived at all.

I felt Heather's hand creep into mine. I looked down at her tired drawn face and her eyes closed as she rested her head against my shoulder. Perhaps, even in d'Ispere, there was hope.

Authors Note

The characters and the events in this book are completely fictional, and bear no relation to anyone, living or dead.

The setting however, is very much alive and kicking. I have tried to keep my descriptions of Val d'Isere and the Espace Killy ski area accurate, but I have taken some liberties with my descriptions of the off-piste area around Le Fornet.

The Pointe Pers is not usually reached from the Col Pers, but by hiking across a ridge from the top of the T-bar. In fact, it is actually quite difficult to get to the Pointe that way, as there is an outcrop rather than a bowl at the top of the Col. I have also exaggerated the difficulty of the couloir down from the Pointe for obvious dramatic purposes.

Although there is no real path, it is theoretically possible to cross over to Italy from the Pointe Pers, but in Winter, it is impossible.

If you would like to see photos of the real Val d'Isere and some of the locations used in the book (especially the bars!), there is a gallery on facebook.com/Dispere . You can even post some of your own!

Acknowledgements

First and foremost, I have to thank the following: Mikey, James, Dave, Chapman, Jade, Emma, Josh, Ryan, Jane and Emily. You know why this is and you know how you helped me. I hope that I have not let you down. One day I will make good on that promise Mikey.

Thank you to everyone else in Ratton who for two seasons put up with a strange bloke scribbling upstairs. You will understand now that I had things on my mind other than boozing and boarding.

Chris Radford of Henry's Avalanche Talk was kind enough to spend a couple of hours and a couple of beers with me discussing the finer points of avalanches. They are amazing phenomena and I urge anyone in Val d'Isere to drop into one of their talks (www.henrysavalanchetalk.com/).

Thanks to Alex Allen and James Bishton for help with some of the technical details about skiing in Val. As a not particularly accomplished boarder my knowledge of the skiing is minimal.

Thank you to Dane McIsaac for proofing the final manuscript. I hope I spelt your name right!

Thank you also to Sean Bell for reading, proofing, correcting and editing the manuscript so many times. Your encouragement really helped give me the confidence to publish d'Ispere.

A heartfelt thanks to Jennifer, who not only put up with me during the painful process of editing, but helped talk me down when I got lost in the stormy make believe world of this story.

And finally, thank you to Val d'Isere. You breathed new life into me when I was lost and broken. You gave me the reason and inspiration to try something new with my life. You almost destroyed my liver and gave me gout. You will always be part of me.

About the Author

Benedict has led several lives; IT engineer, Secondary School Teacher and Chef to name but three. He grew up in the south of England, but has travelled extensively. He divides his time between Asia, the Alps and Brighton.

To find out about his other books, including the 'A Last Chance Powerdrive' quartet about riding a motorbike over the Indian Himalayas, please visit BenedictBeaumont.com.

Printed in Great Britain
by Amazon